Dream of Fire

Dream
of
Fire

Nicholas C. Prata

Arx Publishing
Bristol PA

Arx Publishing
Bristol, Pennsylvania

Dream of Fire
© 2001 Nicholas C. Prata
All Rights Reserved

First Edition

ISBN 1-889758-28-0

Library of Congress Cataloging-in-Publication Data

Prata, Nicholas C.
    Dream of Fire / Nicholas C. Prata.—1st ed.
      p.   cm.
    ISBN 1-889758-27-2 (cloth)
    ISBN 1-889758-28-0 (paperback)
    I. Title

PS3566.R267 D74 2001
813'.54—dc21

                           2001023001

This book is dedicated to my friend,
John Principe.

erebos *Ikar* stood alone on the northernmost cliff of Pangaea's only continent, gazing down at a boiling ocean. Incoming icebergs hissed in the steaming water and gave thunderous voice as they cracked asunder. The giant, black-clad warrior paid scant attention. He was too busy contemplating his own, internal fractures.

Cracked the length of my soul, he mused. *Can feel it leaking out when I walk. Surprised I've any left to lose.*

Kerebos eyed the nearest iceberg, saw the vapor rising heavenwards. *Where are you going?* he thought. *There's no escape up there.*

Seagulls piped piteously as dawn's gray fingers inched across the sky. Kerebos liked the little birds. They sounded as miserable as he felt.

"Land and I'll end your suffering," he muttered.

A gust of wind frosted the *ikar's* cropped black hair. He squinted dark eyes and a frown settled on his scarred face. An ethnic *Chaconne* from a warm inland region, he despised the cold.

The earth trembled between his feet and a tongue of magma spewed from the side of the cliff into the sea, igniting the oil which had seeped up from the broken depths. Kerebos reached for the distant flames as they spread across the surface, but another gust struck him, lifting the cape from his broad shoulders. Droplets froze on his black armor.

Merciless hell! he thought, shielding his face with a huge gauntlet. He half turned toward the Legion's distant campfires. *I spend my life freezing. Except in my dreams...*

1

Kerebos wrestled a sudden desire to throw sword and armor into the ocean.

I could leave these desert lands, he reasoned. *Leave these men I hate. I need never wear iron again.*

He trembled at the thought and pulled a stiff, green *kraal* leaf from a cape pocket. He munched the drug, sighing as it strengthened him.

Don't dream the impossible, son, his father had often warned. *Even the possible rarely comes true.*

Kerebos rubbed his eyes. He had loved his father dearly, and every night since killing him, Kerebos had dreamed of fire.

Every night.

The *ikar* heard a slow, stealthy tread behind him but did not turn. "Good morning, Triskeles," he greeted the First *Elhar* without enthusiasm.

"Good morning, lord," came the *Boru's* barbarically accented *Chaconni*.

Triskeles sidled up to his commander and placed a booted foot on the edge of the world. "Some wonder of Wyrd, eh?" he asked.

Triskeles, a rawboned giant, doffed his black helmet and a blond topknot spilled onto his cuirass—men of the First *Elhar* traditionally wore knots. His thin, purpling lips curled into a mirthless smile as he inched a stone off the precipice and watched it splash below.

"A wonder, eh, lord?" he repeated.

Kerebos knew he had to answer or the *elhar* would just go on repeating himself. *How I loathe him*, he thought, but replied: "It is."

Triskeles chuckled to himself, cooed really, but did not reveal the source of his amusement. He often did that, which Kerebos particularly hated about him.

"Wyrd schicksal macht aus allem nichts," Triskeles hummed a proverb in his native tongue.

Kerebos translated: *Fate makes nothing of everything.* He studied the *elhar*, dubbed "Triskeles" because his great speed made it seem he possessed "three legs". Triskeles returned the stare with the icy blue eyes so common among his people.

There was that strange look in Triskeles' eyes again, Kerebos noted, but it had never been quite this overt. What was it?

Adoration? Kerebos shifted uncomfortably and turned back to the sea. He shuddered with disgust at the thought of Triskeles watching him, wondering if he could afford to heave the *Boru* into the growling water. He came within a hair's breadth of the attempt, but concluded he would need Triskeles in the coming battle.

"It is refreshing, though, isn't it?" Triskeles chuckled as he moved closer. They stood nearly shoulder to shoulder.

Kerebos eased a spiked gauntlet onto his sword.

"What?" he snapped.

Triskeles nodded at the water. "The destruction." Just then a titanic berg cracked a booming report. "See!" he chortled, pointing.

"Why don't you swim out there?" Kerebos suggested.

Triskeles shrugged and pulled his private *kraal* cache. He placed three leaves into his mouth, a potent amount.

"That's quite a lot," Kerebos noted.

Triskeles shuddered as the drug worked on him, his breaths came in gasps. His eyes fluttered and he dropped the *kraal* purse.

Idiot, Kerebos thought.

Triskeles soon mastered himself. He bent to retrieve the drug and asked: "Do you know I've taken over guarding your tent?"

Kerebos felt a cold finger play his spine. His eyes narrowed. "Oh?"

"Yes, lord. Personally."

Kerebos felt ill; he knew how pathetic he sounded in his sleep. "Why?" he demanded.

Triskeles appeared troubled. It took a moment for him to answer. "I fret about the legion, sometimes." he managed at last. "Is that so wrong?" He appeared so inconsolable Kerebos feared the *elhar* might embrace him!

Kerebos played it all off with a laugh. "No," he said. "If you didn't worry about the brotherhood you'd be of no use. Let's get to work."

Triskeles posed like a stroked dog; he leaned close enough to share his fetid breath. "I want to be of use, Lord," he said. "The legion is the only home I've ever really wanted."

"Good," Kerebos grunted and stepped away.

"Fate placed me in its hands, and…" Triskeles trailed off.

How I hate this game, Kerebos thought. "And?"

"I fear I'm losing it," Triskeles replied.

"Explain yourself."

"Well," Triskeles began, "you must agree we've witnessed many wondrous strange things this tribute year. Even the very earth breaks and sinks."

"So?" Kerebos said. "We see odd things every tribute year."

"Yes, but every tribe we've crossed seems more afraid of the future than of us. I can't help but think that wrong." Triskeles mulled the implications. "They all speak of The End."

"The end of the world!" Kerebos scoffed. "Stories to frighten children!" His mood festered. He was bored of the conversation and very much sick of Triskeles. "Fate make nothing of everything, eh, Triskeles? *I* am the end of the world!" he insisted with vehemence. "They must fear *me*!"

Triskeles grinned, reassured. "Yes, lord."

"And as for this dross," Kerebos waved toward the water, "it's not real." He pulled his black sword and held it between them. "*This* is real. Blooded swords are all the end Pangaea needs or deserves!" Triskeles beamed, exposing sharp canine teeth. "I understand, my lord. I can weather anything while among my brothers."

Kerebos sneered. "That's manly of you."

"Thank you. But one thing troubles me still."

"What?"

"Every night I've stood outside your quarters, I've heard you cry out in fear."

Kerebos' ears burned with embarrassment; he quite forgot the cold. "What did I say?" he demanded through clenched teeth.

Triskeles showed a palm in bewilderment. "Mostly babble, but I heard the word 'lama' clear enough," he replied. "I'm no *Chaconni* scholar, but doesn't that mean 'daddy' or some such thing?"

Kerebos stiffened then snarled into action. He struck the *elhar's* face with a fistful of spiked knuckles. Triskeles cried out, staggered and crashed onto the hard ground.

"Bastard!" Kerebos roared. "Don't ever again lurk outside my tent! I should kill you!"

Triskeles lay sprawled out, groaning.

Kerebos brandished his sword, Mistaaka. "Next time I'll strike with this!" he threatened.

Blood streamed from Triskeles' wound, painting his white skin. The holes in his cheek were large enough to admit his tongue. He pinched the largest gash closed. "Understood, my lord," he gargled.

Kerebos sheathed Mistaaka. "I require no night guard. No one," he said.

"But we're the First *Elhar!*" Triskeles protested; that unit had been the *ikari* bodyguard since ancient times.

"Shut up!"

Triskeles sat silent a moment. "As you wish, *ikar,*" he said finally.

Kerebos nodded, satisfied. He felt better after hurting Triskeles. He always felt better after hurting people. Pain was the only thing that took his mind off his dreams. He produced a needle from his cape and tossed it at Triskeles.

"Sew your wounds," he ordered. "And start your men on drills. I want the *elhari* in my tent as soon as possible. We'll catch and finish the *Stalenzka* rabble this very afternoon."

"Yes, lord," Triskeles gurgled.

Kerebos marched down the slope toward camp. He reached the perimeter and a pilum-bearing guard saluted, fist over heart.

"Lord *Ikar!*" the man cried.

Kerebos strode past as he picked pale skin off his gauntlet.

Back on the cliff Triskeles stitched himself, and though the new wounds pained him greatly, he savored them and silently prayed Kerebos might someday strike again.

*   *   *

Kerebos entered his austere tent, unhitched his swordbelt and dropped onto the oily bearskin that served as his bed. He pulled a skull from beneath his pillow and dug a leather pouch from the trophy's mouth.

"Good morning, Diakonos," he said, dumping a few claylike chunks onto his chest. He tossed one into his mouth. The drug worked quickly; the tent walls tilted and spun. This was *Ikaros Heretos, kraal* in its most potent form and manufactured for Kerebos

5

alone. Kerebos' private stash, it was fitting that it was stored in the skull of a king.

King Diakonos, a *Chaconne* monarch who had overestimated his power, had died grovelling at Kerebos' feet. A weeping Diakonos had begged for life even as the *ikar* nailed Mistaaka through his head.

Kerebos studied the hole in the back of the skull.

Fool, he thought, slipping away. *You should have paid like the rest…*

Kerebos reflected upon the legion's humble origins.

Once the brotherhood had been but a single legion in the Imperial *Chaconni* Army, and an undersized auxiliary, to boot. That was before General Desia took over. That commander of vision, fresh from the intrigue of Korenthis, well knew the kingdom's instability and had gone renegade after crafting the unit into one of the crown's best. He moved his men to a sparsely populated region, killed or enslaved the citizens he found, and recruited the meanest, toughest fighters available. Bloodletters and bad men swelled the ranks. Soon Desia could afford to be most selective in the recruiting process. Strict standards of size and strength were set and maintained.

The legion flourished as the empire withered through the fierce Ducal Wars; Desia was already a separate power by the time of the Second Republic. The Republic vacillated between buying off and hiring the *landesknectos*, and only Desia's utter disdain of politics kept him from seizing absolute power. The Second Republic faded into the Third and the *Chaconni* entered a tailspin that persisted until the days of Lasctakos *Ikar*, Kerebos' predecessor. Only then had the revitalized "Old Kingdom" managed to both expel the *Boru* from two lost provinces, and set its house in order. Even still, the *Chaconni* would never reclaim the heights possessed before Desia's day, and they remembered still that *landesknecta* renegades squatted on royal land.

There can be but one master, Kerebos thought, lobbing the skull into the corner.

Lights and colors danced and mingled before his eyes; his extremities tingled. He barely heard the sounds of the waking camp or smelled the grains which fried for breakfast.

Eyes wide, Kerebos dreamed.

Desia strolled into the tent and stood before him.

Kerebos recognized him from a crypt sculpture. "My lord!" he cried.

Desia, clad in archaic chain mail which hung to his knees, stared in reply.

Kerebos nodded. "I hate them, too."

Then kill them! Kill them all! The whole damned world! Desia commanded.

Kerebos shook his head, which felt twice its normal size. "I don't have enough men."

Desia glared down at him.

Murder the world! Desia insisted. *It can be done!*

Kerebos pictured rivers of blood and himself drowning in them. The vision was intoxicating. He could make Pangaea suffer for his sins, then erase himself. There would be nothing and no one to bear witness to his crimes.

"How?" he whispered. "I've barely sixteen hundred swords."

More legions, came the reply.

Kerebos bolted upright. Desia was gone.

"More legions? That's against the Scriptus!" he gasped. "How shall I have more that the 'perfect' number?"

I give you the authority, Kerebos heard.

The tent again flapped open and a short man in a cloth tunic entered. His head wobbled on a shattered neck, the neck young Kerebos had snapped with his bare hands.

"Father!" Kerebos screamed, scuttling backward over the bear skin. His father smiled and reached out as his palms burst into white flames.

Kerebos screamed again.

"Lama!"

His father loosed a wheezing laugh and knelt to embrace him.

Triskeles and Kaiaphos *Elhar* crashed into the tent.

"Ikar!" they shouted in unison.

Kerebos woke with a moan, groping for his sword.

"My lord, what ails you?" Kaiaphos demanded, pulling his own sword and glancing suspiciously around. His face, a hideous mass of scars, was flush with excitement.

Triskeles helped Kerebos to his feet; the *ikar* was in no state to refuse the aid. Triskeles handed over a wine skin.

"Another dream, my lord?" he whispered.

Kerebos could only nod as the other four *elhari* filed into the tent, weapons drawn.

Erebas, a black from the eastern coast, asked: "Was there an intruder? I wouldn't put it past the *Stalenzka* to try murder in your quarters."

Syranos of the Least *Elhar*, a boy of barely twenty, scoffed. "There's not enough of those shovel wielders to take one of my men, much less the *ikar*!"

Kerebos hung his head in exhaustion. He dropped the wine, which ebbed onto the ground.

"Desia," he whispered and steadied himself against the center pole.

"What?" they asked.

"He spoke to me. The Lawgiver was here."

The *elhari* took the news in stride, steeped as they were in the quasi-religious *landesknecta* tradition.

"What did he say, lord?" Triskeles asked solemnly.

Kerebos noticed the wounds on the elhar's face. The Boru had done a neat job, but had used far more stitches than necessary. Kerebos waved off the questioning.

"Start the men on drills," he said.

"I've done that, lord."

"Then wait outside. I'll call when I'm ready."

"Yes, lord."

Triskeles and Kyros, a slant-eyed *Hsia* from one of the ferocious plains tribes, herded the younger *elhari* from the tent.

Alone, Kerebos collected his thoughts. *Of course, More legions! How many could I raise, Two? Ten? Why haven't I realized this before?*

He sheathed Mistaaka and started for the exit, but stopped to grab Diakonos' skull. This he held at arm's length and crushed with a single punch. The bone crumbled into a dozen pieces. Kerebos kicked the *heretos* as it hit the ground.

No more of that, he decided. A gust of wind hit the tent and sand pelted Kerebos' from behind. *How'd that get in here?*

A quick investigation revealed two burn holes in the wall. They were still smoking.

Kerebos swallowed hard on a dry throat.

Moments later Kerebos led the *elhari* through a forest of tents to a quiet spot near the supply wagons. He bade the men sit, then did likewise. Triskeles planted himself on the *ikar's* right.

The clouds had passed and the pale sun had risen.

Kerebos read concerned expressions and felt like kicking himself. How could he spook his men so near to a fight?

"Comrades." he started, "I believe we'll all be happy to lay this long road behind us."

They grunted.

"There's one more battle, though," Kerebos continued. "Then a short rest before we start our greatest mission."

Puzzled faces. Kyros asked: "What 'mission', lord?"

Kerebos eyed the *Hsia* who, as "keeper of the Scriptus", served as the legion's chief priest and watchdog of Desian orthodoxy. The Scriptus, upon which were inscribed the legion's commandments, was used to brand new recruits. The ceremony was the legionaries' last initiation rite, the death of many, and Kyros' greatest joy.

Kerebos glowered. "May I continue?"

Kyros nodded slowly. "Forgive me, lord."

"In any case," Kerebos went on, "Desia came to me today and proposed a new testament."

Kyros licked his lips; Kerebos knew the *Hsia* was preparing a sermon.

Syranos interjected. "What does The Giver say, Lord Ikar?"

"He orders we grasp the reins of the entire world," Kerebos replied casually as though discussing the weather. "We are to wrestle them from impotent grasps."

Kyros shot to his feet.

"A *power separate ye shall be.*" he quoted. "*And never more.*"

Kerebos held his temper. Kyros would hang himself if given the time.

"I didn't ask you to speak, and won't allow your tone," Kerebos said calmly.

Kyros pointed a brown finger.

"You are disrespectful!" he cried. "Shall I get the brand and read it to you? We are not to be a country or an empire—we are the brotherhood! Desia rejected the Old Kingdom's values! '*Bodies grow old*

9

and die, minds grow old with the body,' he said. We must stay as we are."

"Maybe the brand will fit up your ass?" Triskeles said.

Kyros was too far gone to hear him. "Kerebos!" he began in a loud voice.

"Sit down fool!" the *ikar* screamed. "You think I don't know what the brand says? I was guarding it when you were still playing with wooden swords! It doesn't say anything about owning slaves, either, but we do! Times change, Kyros, look around," he said in a more conciliatory tone. "A quarter of the nations we've visited have tried to thwart our levy. They've lost proper respect."

"And they died for it!" Kyros shouted.

"You'd better sit," Triskeles warned his peer. Syranos and Erebas nodded.

That's enough rope, Kerebos thought, rising to his feet. He smiled at Kyros, saying, "They may not be the only ones to die. Who is your lord?"

Kyros's hand trembled on his hilt. He was sweating.

"Who is *ikar*, you or I?" Kerebos asked and grasped Mistaaka.

"I am more an *ikar* than you," Kyros said in a husky voice. "You are a heretic who would destroy that which Desia created."

Kerebos gave Triskeles a quick glance and saw the *Boru's* malevolent smile.

"Kill him, my lord!" Syranos shouted.

Kerebos remained calm for a dozen heartbeats, until he knew Kyros was about to strike, then shook his head. "That isn't necessary, lad."

Kyros relaxed ever-so-slightly.

Kerebos reacted with the lightning speed which had made him the terror of many terrifying men. He drew his sword, and sliced at Kyros' head in one smooth motion. The sharp blade caught the *elhar* beneath his right eye, and screeched out the left side of his skull, trailing a spray of blood.

Nothing happened for a moment then the top half of Kyros' head slid towards the ground. Kyros, still pointing an accusatory finger, crumpled into a heap. Blood-splattered brains slopped onto the hard dirt.

Kerebos viewed the corpse with a professional's eye. *Not bad*, he

10

thought. *Even these vultures never saw anything like that!*

The *elhari* wore expressions of approval, though Syranos appeared unusually pensive.

"Not that I'm complaining, lord," he said, "but I thought it wasn't necessary for him to die?"

Kerebos wiped Mistaaka on Krystos' hair. "It wasn't," he allowed, "but it was desirable. Syranos, my lad, who is *ikar?*"

"You, my lord!"

The other officers nodded vigorously, impressed anew with Kerebos' swordsmanship. The thirty-nine year old *ikar*, second oldest in history, was still too tough to be gainsaid. None of them would challenge him during the autumnal "winnowing" rite.

"You answer well," Kerebos said. "I give you the Second *Elhar*. Replace yourself with your most capable *cohar.*"

Syranos jumped to attention and saluted. "My lord!"

Kerebos scowled. "I trust your Scriptus interpretations aren't superior to mine?"

"I can't even read *Chaconni*, much less that ancient stuff," Syranos promised.

"Good." Kerebos nodded at the corpse. "Now chop him into pieces for the birds. He doesn't deserve a proper burial."

Syranos quickly obliged.

"The rest of you get ready to march. Triskeles, leave the wagons behind with a Power Guard."

"Yes, *ikar.*"

Syranos was hacking his former comrade into bloody chunks when Erebas approached Kerebos. The black looked sheepish.

"What?" Kerebos demanded.

"My lord, may I have Kyros' sword? He won her from me at dice last year and I've missed her."

Kerebos shrugged. "Very well. He no longer needs it." He looked suddenly somber. "Wherever he is."

Chapter 2

The parchment read: *To be sure, this Kerebos of the murderous Legion is unworthy, as are all. God, infinite and perfect, works in our flawed universe, and when He moves through that medium, He must, obviously, use defective tools. What better way for Him to demonstrate grace than through the most evil among us? Of course, being used in God's plan in no way assures salvation, you must accept the gift. But remember, even the Dark One, self-cursed and eternally damned, has a place in God's great design.*

Antiphon al-Caliph, a priest in the Order of the White Flame, shook his head. He dropped the scroll onto his desk and allowed it to roll.

"Oh, indeed!" he snorted, unconvinced by Grand Master Dokein's thesis. "At least you didn't award Kerebos the keys to heaven."

Antiphon's dark eyes smouldered as he stared at the *magnannon* candle on his desk; the metal wick, an innovation from the Order's early days, burned white.

Why did the Magisterum buy Dokein's arguments? he asked himself. *Bloody Kerebos, God's herald of the last days? Kerebos the child slayer? Kerebos the rapist as the Lord's prophet?*

The priest slammed small fists onto the wooden desk. His swarthy face twisted in revulsion.

"It cannot be! How can that honor be awarded him?" he asked the empty room.

Antiphon recalled his earliest memory of the Black Legion. Lasctakos *Ikar*, Kerebos' predecessor and mentor, had murdered all the adults of his desert tribe; only Dokein's benevolence had saved the children. The fledgling Grand Master had drained the Order's coffers and ransomed the children at a dear price. But that was when the *Aharoni*, who had "tended the flame" in Kwan Aharon for two thousand years, were still under the *Chaconni* King's protection. They could afford such mercies in Dokein's youth. Today, they counted their daily bread a mercy. The dispossessed *Aharoni* that continually flooded the city had greatly depleted the Order's revenues.

Antiphon remembered 11:17-19 from the apocryphal book of Nestu: *God will once again show his compassion and patience by choosing the most wicked of serpents as Pangaea's last prophet. Mark it well, the very guard of hell shall be beaten into a drawbridge over which the faithful will march into the kingdom.*

That particular scripture was being touted by eschatological Masters, and was increasingly linked to Kerebos. Antiphon was disturbed by the association, as were many of his brethren.

"Well, there is certainly no more evil man on the planet," he sighed and adjusted his woolen chlamys. *But Nestu isn't even canonical,* he thought. *Anyway, why believe Pangaea is dying?*

Antiphon thought hard on that one. He recalled stories told by those who had crossed God's Anvil—the great desert in the continent's center. Shepherds and nomads had relayed frightful tales of nature gone mad, of giant, toothy lizards and cataclysmic earthquakes. Some whispered of worse things.

Last week terrified tribesmen had reported tales of demonic apparitions, winged specters that had raided tents and dragged screaming victims into the night. Antiphon was skeptical, but the Grand Master took it as a sign. Dokein was so convinced the stories were portents he was sending Antiphon to rendezvous with the Black Legion. Antiphon was to learn Kerebos' disposition first hand and, if possible, was to bring him to Kwan Aharon.

"I don't know what Kerebos has on his mind, but it seems we ought to oblige God and send an emissary," Dokein had said. "You shall be that man."

"My reward for faithful service, Grand Master?" Antiphon grumbled. "Aren't you fond of me?"

"You are as a son to me, Ani," Dokein answered. "But I feel this is the right course. I must send you."

"Me? I'm nobody!" Antiphon had argued. "I'm not equal to the task!"

Dokein had studied Antiphon's face, weighing his capabilities.

"No, you're wrong," Dokein concluded with conviction. "You shall be enough." Here he smiled, his white teeth contrasting sharply with his tanned face. "Though God knows your theology is muddled, and your

13

heart suspect…if I correctly gauge the glances you give my daughter."

"She has grown beautiful, Master," Antiphon allowed. "But my designs are honorable. I've never resolved myself to a widower's life."

Antiphon's beloved, Khloe, had died birthing their only child, Yeshua, over a decade earlier.

Dokein nodded solemnly. "After your return you'll have my permission to woo Selah, though I fear you're not her type. Too bookish, I'd wager."

Antiphon ignored the warning. He knew Selah well enough.

"Don't judge too harshly her lovely willfulness," he replied. "She is still young. Besides, I enjoy a challenge."

"Like the one I've handed you? You didn't seem so eager."

Antiphon grew sullen. "I think she loves me," he said.

Dokein simultaneously shook his head and tugged his shaggy beard. "You children hear but cannot think," he sighed. "In any case, if all goes well, you may pursue her. Who knows? Maybe you'll be able to tame her. I have failed."

A knock on the door pulled Antiphon from the reverie. He turned to see Montanus, the only *Chaconne* in the Order, peeking into the tiny chamber. Antiphon smelled the spindly priest's unwashed body.

Montanus did not quite sneer. "The Grand Master is ready for you," he said. "If you aren't too busy in your criticisms to grant him time."

Montanus, widely disliked for his sharp tongue, had openly questioned both Antiphon's intellect and his ability to handle Kerebos. In addition, he made no secret of the fact that he considered himself Selah's best prospect, though she had derisively dubbed him "the scarecrow".

Antiphon glared at Montanus' pock-marked face, which looked even dirtier than usual.

"Thank you, *brother*," he snapped. "It must please you to be favored with such important errands."

Montanus scowled and slammed the door. Antiphon smirked at the priest's easy ire but the expression quickly faded. He looked at the scroll and shook his head.

"Kerebos," he sighed.

*   *   *

"Come, Ani, sing for me." Dokein persisted from behind his great desk, which was littered with tomes; the Grand Master was a voracious reader.

14

Antiphon blenched at the hated nickname, it sounded too feminine.

"I've a sore throat, Master," he lied, rubbing his Adam's apple as evidence.

"Don't give me that."

"But you promised I wouldn't have to sing again after leading the Council chorales last month," Antiphon complained. "I did the canticle, too."

"You used to be a common cantor," Dokein pointed out. "You may be again."

"Defrock me, then. Who would be your scribe? Who else can read that scrawl of yours?"

"All right!" Dokein's eyes blazed suddenly. "Don't sing! Maybe I'll die before you return and you'd never need chirp again, you ungrateful desert brat."

It was then Antiphon knew he had lost. No one could assign guilt like Dokein.

"But it's embarrassing," he said.

Dokein waved a gnarled hand in dismissal, saying:

"I just told you that you didn't have to."

"But—"

"No, no, don't worry about making me happy, I probably *will* die before you return. Our medicine isn't what it was in the old days." Dokein half turned away.

"I'll die first," Antiphon prophesied softly. He gazed out the stained glass doors behind the Grand Master and into the courtyard beyond.

Dokein looked grave. "You're probably right," he admitted. "Why not give me something to remember you by?"

"Oh, good God!" Antiphon cried, raising palms in defeat. "You win. What do you want to hear?"

Dokein beamed in triumph. "Oh, anything. I'm not particular."

Antiphon rose to cantor's position, placing both hands on his breast.

"If anyone sees this…" he warned, but Dokein's eyes had already glazed over into music appreciation mode.

Antiphon took a deep breath and eased into *Pray For Me, Mother of God*. After his throat loosened up he gave the Grand Master a rare treat and switched from modern to early Aharoni. His pitch and timbre were perfect; his fine tenor had lost nothing during years of relative inactivity. He ended the classic hymn with a few lines of his own, on-the-spot invention.

15

"Faith, he says, and pray,
God moves in odd ways.
To survive the day,
All must go my way.
I must bear the burden,
To survive the words he says."

Not very good, but to the point, Antiphon thought.

If Dokein sensed the reproach he gave no sign. He stared into the courtyard where birds began to sing.

"Well, are you satisfied?" Antiphon asked.

Dokein nodded. "Thank you. I'm sorry."

"Don't be silly, it's a trifle."

"I mean about sending you to that devil, Kerebos."

Antiphon stared at the floor. He had managed to forget about his mission for a moment.

"Neither the scriptures nor my dreams inform me what to do about the *ikar*," Dokein went on. "I'm blundering in the dark, my son. I fear that there are no right choices."

"I'll return shortly, Master," Antiphon promised. "If not, wait for me in the Kingdom."

"Oh, yes," Dokein scoffed. "God always has room for failures like myself."

Antiphon was troubled. The remarks were quite unlike the old man. "You've been a splendid Grand Master," Antiphon said in all sincerity.

"Yes, of course." Dokein slapped the desk. "Anyway, what's done is done! Find him, Ani. That's all I can tell you to do. Hopefully God will direct you from there."

"If you believe that, I will."

Dokein stood. His flowing white robe and long beard lent him majesty. He looked every inch God's earthly vicar, lacking only one of his benign smiles, which he soon supplied.

"Come," he said and laid a wrinkled hand on Antiphon's shoulder. "Let us enjoy a last meal together, then you must say your goodbyes. I want you to be on the trail tonight."

He would look so much better without that beard, Selah thought, watching Antiphon pace the breadth of her chamber. She studied his lean body. Not exactly her type. She liked them brawny. *But he must*

16

have done something right to have kept Khloe happy. Anyway, he makes me laugh.

"So you understand, lady, I'm to leave tonight," Antiphon concluded.

"I'm sure you'll return soon enough," Selah said cheerfully. She swept long black tresses from her elfin face and bound them with a perfumed scarf. "It can't be as bad as you think."

"But Dokein is sending me to the Black Legion," Antiphon said miserably. "They'll probably flay me."

Selah's amber eyes displayed practiced sympathy. "I'm sure father's thought of all this." An impish smile curved her full lips. "Did you tell him you've been visiting me?"

"No," Antiphon answered quietly. "But he knows."

Selah's robe creased open as she slid from the silk divan, exposing considerable cleavage. She laid a cheek on his chest.

"I'm sure he forgives you, Ani," she said. "Aren't your intentions honorable?"

Antiphon pulled a hand through her hair, stopping an inch above her narrow waist. "I want you to marry me," he replied. "I've been too long alone, and next to you, all women seem lifeless."

Selah pulled away. *Marriage!* she thought, stunned. *I only thought he wanted me!* She smiled and retreated to her couch. "Ani, you're too sweet. What kind of wife would I make?"

Antiphon also smiled.

"Properly trained, a perfect one." He seemed prepared to elaborate but said, "I have to go."

"Don't you even want to kiss me?" Selah purred.

Antiphon chuckled drily. "It's been so long since I've kissed a woman, I've quite forgotten how."

Selah stood. "Try to remember."

Antiphon needed no further prodding. He crossed the room with two quick strides, grabbed her and planted a rough open-mouthed kiss.

Selah was pleasantly surprised. *Not bad at all*, she thought as he released her.

Antiphon held her at arm's length. "I'm sorry. I had no right."

Selah leaned forward for another one. "Don't fret," she whispered. "I like it like that."

"I must be going," Antiphon replied. "I have to see Yeshua."

He left without a backward glance.

17

Selah followed at a distance and watched him descend the long stairway into the gynaeceum's atrium.

Not bad at all, she mused, pursing agreeably sore lips. *Who ever would have expected it? He might even be of some use if he wasn't so serious about priesting...*

Shekkinah, the rotund House Mother, ignored Antiphon as he left the building. She glared at Selah, who gave a patronizing smile and returned to her room. Selah sat before a mirror and stared at herself. Maybe Antiphon did deserve to be one of her suitors, but why worry now? He was leaving and there were plenty of other men in the meantime.

Selah applied her most lurid lip embellishment, snickering as she imagined Dokein's reaction. She admired her reflection. The image that smiled back at her was one neither her father nor Antiphon would have recognized.

Antiphon, Yeshua and Dokein reached Kwan Aharon's outermost gate.

"Are you taking a sword, father?" the raven-haired lad asked. He was firmly convinced his sire was undertaking a military expedition. "All roads outside the city are dangerous, my friend Juntha says."

"He must be a well-traveled eleven year old," Antiphon laughed and led his donkey past two mercenary pikemen in mail shirts.

Yeshua pointed towards the desert. "What's that light?"

Antiphon looked into the Anvil; a ghostly orange-pink glowed on the horizon.

"That's only the sunset, Yeshua," Dokein replied, though he knew it was not. Only a week before he had sent men to investigate, but none had returned and no more were dispatched. The "ghost light" was yet another thing to worry about.

The boy placed fists on his hips. "It doesn't look like any sunset I ever saw."

"There are many things for you yet to see," Antiphon said and stroked his son's head. "Keep the scriptures in your heart and pray I come back to see them with you."

"I will," Yeshua promised, and buried his face into his father's chest. "But I still wish you had a sword."

Antiphon pulled a whittling knife from the donkey's pack. "I've this," he joked.

18

Yeshua eyed the dubious weapon. "Too small."

Antiphon and Dokein locked gazes.

"Don't worry, I'll take care of him," the Grand Master said. "I'm already watching two hundred and sixteen priests, one more charge won't matter."

"Thank you," Antiphon answered. He quickly embraced the old man. "Keep me in your prayers."

"As always," Dokein assured him. "Godspeed and return for our final, great victory."

"I hope you're right about this, Master," Antiphon said just over the rising wind.

"I am," Dokein replied. "And if I'm not, I'll sing for you!"

"No thank you," Antiphon forced a laugh; Dokein had a terrible voice. Antiphon turned to his son, who was watching the desert lights. "Come here, you!"

Yeshua ran to his father, who bent to kiss him.

"Hurry back!" Yeshua said. "And don't let anyone abuse you!"

"Sound advice," Antiphon nodded, trying not to cry.

"Come, Yeshua," Dokein called. "It's time to shut the gates." "Take care of the Grand Master now, 'Shua," Antiphon told his son.

"He'll be fine," the boy promised.

Dokein handed the donkey's reins to the younger priest. "It's time to set you on your ass."

"I hate riding these things," Antiphon grumbled then climbed atop the animal. He looked toward the endless dunes. "My death is out there," he said in ancient *Aharoni*.

"I hope not," the Grand Master replied. "Priest of the one true God," he lifted his voice, "Tender of the White Flame, do your duty."

"I hear and obey God's will," Antiphon finished the liturgy.

"Watch out for snakes, father," Yeshua yelled.

"I will. Farewell!"

The priest urged the donkey forward and was soon lost to sight. Dokein stood long outside the stone wall with a hand on Yeshua's shoulder.

My God, he thought, shivering in the desert cold. *What have I done?*

Chapter 3

Kerebos mounted the grassy rise, followed by twenty-five tough veterans from the First *Elhar*. He gazed across the plain toward the approaching *Stalenzka*. He could not guess why the tribesmen had chosen to confront him, but it mattered not; he would kill them all.

The *Stalenzka* had refused the legion its biennial tribute of weapons and armor and, more importantly, had killed six of Kerebos' messengers. They must be made an example.

They think they've grown strong? he thought, contemplating the tortures he would use. *I'll show them power. They'll see why their fathers have served us without complaint for a thousand years.*

At that moment a small mounted party broke off from the *Stalenzka* host and galloped toward the legion. One horsemen bore a white flag.

"Good, good!" Kerebos grunted, his breath hanging in the air. He slapped a topknotted bodyguard on the back and said: "See that, boy? They seek to barter. They're beaten already."

"They shall pay for their insolence, my lord."

"They shall."

Kerebos donned his crested, black helmet and adjusted the eye slits. "Call the *elhari*," he told the bodyguard, who immediately signalled to an unarmored runner.

Again Kerebos wondered why the steelmakers had not taken their chances in the Anvil. Certainly they did not hope to strike a truce?

The *elhari* soon arrived. Together with their commander they made an impressive sight against the rising sun.

Triskeles screwed spikes into fistguard. "My lord, the men are completely rested after today's chase. They could each strangle a shark and drink its blood."

"Satyrnos," Kerebos hailed his Fourth *Elhar*, so named for his enslavement to fleshly pleasures. "I want you to absorb their cavalry assault. Shield wall and spears."

Satyrnos, a dusky *Razkul* with the widest shoulders in the legion, spat at the approaching horsemen. The *landesknectos* never used horses, considering cavalry an unmanly, shameful practice. They also shunned archery, though Kerebos had privately mulled hiring auxiliaries since an enemy had inflicted some casualties with mounted archers.

If I can unwed the men from the notion of a single legion, there's no reason why I can't change other traditions, he mused. *How intelligence would be improved by a few horses!*

Kerebos knew it would be tough to trick a winning army out of habit and tradition. Some heads would have to roll, surely, and the innovations would have to be immediately successful.

But I already have the Elhari; it can be done, he thought. "Satyrnos, send a runner down," he ordered.

"As you wish, *ikar*," Satyrnos replied, and summoned a loin-clothed messenger. The unarmed man, a probationary *landesknecta*, made off at a brisk pace.

"Pathetic!" young Syranos spat. "How can they shoot arrows and call themselves warriors? Any weakling can shoot a bow. There is no honor in this. Nothing is decided by this."

Kerebos laughed to himself. He had been quite a marksman as a youth, able to hit a rat at fifty paces.

"My lord?" Syranos asked.

"Don't worry," Kerebos replied. "They can't puncture our armor unless very close, and they don't have enough horses to hit and run."

"Fear is one thing I don't have, my lord."

They watched the messenger make his way back from the *Stalenzka*.

Kerebos' fingers worked in anticipation. No matter what the steelmakers offered, he would not accept. He wanted to kill.

Syranos leaned close. "My lord, please tell me..."

"Desia!" Kerebos erupted. "Aren't you ever silent, boy?"

"I'm sorry."

"What?"

"It's nothing, lord," Syranos said, sounding chastened.

"Oh, just ask me!" Kerebos snapped.

"I hear you chose your own name when you joined the legion," Syranos replied. "Triskeles says you are the only one who has ever pick his own *chiampuglia*."

A legionary's *chiampuglia* or "war name" was usually given by a superior upon initiation. The name, always in archaic *Chaconni*, was meant to reflect the man's personality or accomplishments.

"Triskeles talks when he should not," Kerebos muttered. "It might someday be the death of him."

"You commanded me to ask, lord," Syranos defended himself.

"I was originally dubbed, Patricides," Kerebos began, barely to be heard, "and I didn't like it. I asked my *sestar*, Boros, if he'd rename me, and he said he would if I could best him. So I killed him. The *cohar*, Lasctakos, whom I eventually killed for the *ikar's* ring," here he winced, "thought the situation unbearably funny, and laughed that a raw boy had slain a *sestar*. He said I was either destined to be *ikar*, or I kept the keys to hell in my pocket."

Syranos' brows knit into the befuddled expression he wore so often. "Can't both be true?" he asked.

Kerebos nodded and laid a hand on Mistaaka's hilt. He caressed the plain, gold *ikar's* ingot which circled the pommel.

"Rather than putting me to death for killing my *sestar*, Lasctakos allowed me to pick my own name," he said. "From then on I lived under his eyes. I made *elhar* before I reached my eighteenth birthday."

"But shouldn't you have been killed for attacking an officer outside the Winnowing?"

Kerebos shrugged. "I guess Lasctakos saved me for a higher purpose—*ikari* sometimes interpret the Scriptus their own way. That's something Kyros should have remembered." Kerebos' smiled. "You'll someday learn, Syranos, that often the authorities we esteem don't honor us in return."

Triskeles, who lurked behind, grunted. "He gives you fatherly advice. Don't forget it."

"I won't!" Syranos replied, then looked to Kerebos, who had stepped away. "By the way, lord, what does your name mean? I'm not so good with the olden speech."

"It is from the ancient myths," Triskeles answered for the *ikar.* "Kerebos was the three-headed dog charged with the gates of hell."

A myth I hope to fulfill, Kerebos thought. *I want to send everybody there.* Though he was a materialist and a believer in Desian Uniformity, which held that the mind and body were one without a soul, Kerebos found the thought of hell a reassuring fantasy. He liked the notion of people getting their just punishments, kinslayers first and foremost.

Oh, father, forgive me! he thought for the millionth time.

Kerebos relived in slow motion the blow he had leveled at his sire, and heard yet again the sickening crunch of vertebrae. He recalled how his father has died looking into the eyes of a son he loved above all else. Kerebos decided that if Triskeles were correct about the end of the world, it could not happen soon enough.

"All must die," Kerebos said.

"Hear, hear!" the *elhari* agreed, assuming he meant the *Stalenzka.*

The runner arrived and saluted. "My lord! They beg to be allowed their old contract. They say they have killed the chief and council that led them here, and wish only for peace."

So they're leaderless now? Kerebos thought. *So much the better.* He looked past the outriders to the bulk of the *Stalenzka.* "All must die," he repeated. "Tell them that. I will not even take slaves. Their name shall be nothing more than a memory. There are other smiths in the world."

"Very good, lord *ikar.*"

The messenger saluted once more and turned to go, but Kerebos grabbed him and growled: "I'll answer them myself."

Kerebos waved the *Stalenzka* closer, then picked a rock off the earth. When the riders were close enough, he heaved the stone, striking the nearest horse. The mount screamed and reared, throwing its master. The horseman landed on his head and lay still.

The legion roared approbation as the other riders raced away.

Kerebos watched the retreat for a moment then said, "Let's go."

The *elhari* jumped to their duties as nearby legionaries broke into a battle song. Kerebos smelled *kraal* as leaves were pulled and broken.

Those steelwizards have no hope, he thought and drew his sword, a

Stalenzka product. *They'll dine on their own work.*

"You, Janus!" he called the bodyguard commander, a *cohar* nearly seven feet tall. "Keep your unit tight. We'll be moving fast."

"Yes, lord," Janus replied and offered some *kraal.*

"No. There's nowhere to hide from the fire," Kerebos said.

"Yes, *ikar,*" the bodyguard nodded in perfect misunderstanding.

Satyrnos' *elhar* had reached the bottom of the slope and reformed, standing shoulder to shoulder and three men deep. In addition to their regular menu of swords, daggers and greatshields, each man bore two black spears.

The First and Second *Elhari* set up as prongs on Satyrnos' left and right flanks, repectively. In the distance Kerebos could make out approaching cavalry. The report of hooves was like muted thunder.

"It is good to fight again, my lord," Janus said and took another *kraal* leaf. "Don't you think?"

Kerebos called over a half dozen runners and grasped the nearest by the arm, saying, "Tell Triskeles to pull back a little."

The runner left without comment.

The *Stalenka* gained speed; soon they were close enough to allow a good estimation of their numbers.

About a thousand of them, Kerebos silently reckoned. *Their infantry will be ten times that, at least. Fair enough. I'll wait and see how the initial wave is repelled before committing the reserves.*

The horse charge was now a hundred paces from the motionless *landesknectos;* the noise was deafening. The steelmakers waved swords and leveled pikes at the enemy. Satyrnos' *elhar* had pilum hoisted and pointed at the incoming tide like a company of lightning-wielding gods. The mounted host held its course.

Kerebos did not breathe until the first rain of pilum struck the cavalry. A hundred horses went down in the volley. Equine screams cracked the cold air. Men cried out in agony as they were crushed by their rolling mounts or trampled beneath hooves.

Kerebos sensed from the way the *Stalenzka* line softened that this stage of the battle was won. The tribesmen were either undisciplined, demoralized, or both.

The slowing cavalry pressed clumsily forward and the Brotherhood retreated onto the gentle slope and dug in. The

Stalenzka reached the shieldwall piecemeal and the legionaries buried spears into the horses' bellies.

More screams. The scent of blood wafted through the air.

With half the horsemen engaged, the First and Fourth sprung their trap. Hundreds of legionaries fell on the *Stalenzka* flanks. The ground grew slick with blood. Kerebos' superbly trained giants made short work of the crowded, disorganized tribesmen, whose very numbers worked against them.

Kerebos smiled through his sweat as the black tide engulfed the robed rabble, killing men and beasts. The massacre was completed efficiently. Kerebos sent runners to the *elhari*, identified by their dyed helmet crests, and watched with satisfaction as the officers swiftly executed his orders.

Satyrnos' men dispatched the wounded *Stalenzka* as the First and Second *Elhari* moved on a short distance and fused into a phalanx. Kerebos ordered two more *Elhari* down onto the plain and pulled Satyrnos back into reserve.

A perspiring runner arrived. "My lord!" he cried, "Satyrnos lost only three men, and begs for some real work!"

Kerebos opened his visor and calmly shook his head. "No. Send him my compliments but, tell him to stay put—he has done enough."

The messenger lowered his eyes. "My lord, the *elhar* seeks prisoners for entertainment."

Ah, so that's what is on his mind, Kerebos thought. "Only if he tortures them to death when through," he said.

"Yes, lord!" the runner replied and darted off.

"You!" Kerebos called another. "Tell Erebas that after we grapple the first wave, he is to flank the *Stalenzka* for their women and children. They won't be too far behind."

"Yes, Lord!"

With Satyrnos in reserve, and Erebas as spoiler, Kerebos committed the rest of his men. Moving with startling quickness and perfect form, the remaining formation marched toward the steelmakers. Satyrnos' men cheered as the fresh troops stormed past and joined the right flank.

Battle cries filled the air as the two hosts collided. The First barely slowed as it drove a deep wedge into the *Stalenzka*. Triskeles pushed the perfect depth and stopped. The *landesknectos* refused the line and went to work.

It was slaughter.

Desperate as they were, and despite vast numerical superiority, the tribesmen were cut down almost as fast as the *landesknectos* could lower their swords. Bodies were dismembered where they stood, heads lopped off or clove to the teeth. The *Stalenzka* were thrown back on all fronts and so bunched up their dead could not fall to earth.

Damn!, Kerebos thought, startled, *I'd better get down there before this thing is over!* He barked some orders to a trio of nearby runners then turned to his bodyguards, shouting:

"Let's go!"

Kerebos waded into battle, wedging between the First and Second.

Syranos came tramping over. "Kerebos *Ikar!*" he cried, skewering a *Stalenzka* and lifting the smaller man off the ground. Syranos laughed like mad as the enemy wriggled overhead, bleeding his life onto him. The entire *elhar* chanted "*Ikar!*" along with their young officer; the cry spread throughout the legion. Up on the hill Satyrnos' men pounded swords on shields.

Syranos threw the shrieking *Stalenzka* back into the fray then drove his twelve inch shield spike through another's forehead. The spike squeaked into the skull like a nail through hard wood.

Adrenalized, Kerebos barely thought as he slew his first two men. The third he caught in the crotch with an upstroke which severed both mail and pelvis. He wrestled his sword from the convulsing wretch, thinking, *Death is the only thing that makes life worth living!*

He whirled just in time to catch a sword on his greatshield. The bearded tribesman, eyes wide, struck again before Kerebos clove him between neck and shoulder. Hot blood sprayed the *ikar's* face as he wrenched the sword free.

An arrow bounced unheeded off Kerebos' breast as he grabbed a stumbling tribesman from behind and shoved Mistaaka through his neck. The *Stalenzka* made an inhuman bubbling noise as the blade leaped from his throat. The *ikar* lost his sword as the man fell, but punched another warrior in the back with his spiked fist; the spine gave like a rotten stick.

"Some hunting we're having, eh lord?" Janus cried, handing him Mistaaka.

Kerebos nodded and bulled back into the fray.

A tribesmen immediately lunged at him, but the *ikar* sidestepped and chopped downward with all the strength of his mighty arm. He had to pull Mistaaka from the victim's mouth.

It was then that Erebas' *elhar* attacked the enemy rear. The *Stalenzka* were thrown into pandemonium. Soon they had had enough. Many threw down their swords and begged for mercy, but these were hewed even as they knelt. The others fought with renewed vigor when it became apparent that surrender was impossible. It made little difference. The circle of resistance shrank by the second.

A wild-eyed tribesman, dagger in each hand, charged Kerebos, who remained stoically in place.

"God curse you!" the tribesman cried and thrust both blades.

"Yes," Kerebos replied, taking the blows across the shield and crushing the man's insole with a booted foot. Bones snapped and the attacker fell with a groan. Kerebos dispatched him with a slash to the head.

Syranos nudged Kerebos and pointed out a runner who was being escorted into the battle by three of Satyrnos' men. Kerebos pulled out of the battle.

"What is it, boy?" he asked the messenger.

"My lord, Satyrnos *Elhar* bids me tell you that Erebas found only a few women and children."

"Where are the rest?"

"He does not know. Erebas says they claimed that monsters from the Anvil had killed them."

Kerebos pondered this news. What could have scared the *Stalenzka* more than facing him? "Did Erebas kill the women and children?" he asked.

"Yes."

More lives trickled away behind Kerebos. *Curse it*, he thought. *I must know.*

He pulled a flare from his belt, struck it with his sword and threw it over the battlefield. The legionaries disengaged at once. and fell back into a defensive formation. They stood, weapons poised, for the next command.

Kerebos was swamped by runners.

"Tell the *elhari* to disarm and bind the enemy," he said. "I want to interrogate them."

The battlefield was silent but for the gasps of the dying and the buzzing of the huge, hairy insects. Triskeles limped to Kerebos' side.

"What is it, lord?" he asked and removed his helmet. "Why spare them?"

Kerebos related Erebas' tale.

"Strange," Triskeles admitted and relieved a passing legionary of a wineskin. "But I fear there aren't a hundred left to examine."

"They are enough," Kerebos said. "Have the baggage train brought up. We'll camp here tonight."

"Yes, lord."

"And get all the arms and armor from the dead," Kerebos said.

"Of course, lord."

Kerebos slowly made the top of the incline. His energy had ebbed and he was feeling fagged. He looked out over the battlefield, ignoring the stench which blew up the hill.

Time to clean up, he thought.

It was not long before the legion's oxcarts rolled onto the scene. Tents were erected even as a dry moat was dug around the camp. Guards were posted, wounds dressed and slaves set to repairing armor. Cold night was approaching before Kerebos took food.

After the evening meal, Kerebos slid into his black robe and witnessed the burial rites of twenty-two *landesknectos* who had been killed in action. Afterwards he made his way to his tent and undressed. He cleansed some superficial wounds before crawling beneath his bearskin blanket. Though exhausted, sleep eluded him. When he closed his eyes all he could see was himself standing atop the world, directing Pangaea's last battle. A skin of wine eventually helped him drop off.

That night, Kerebos dreamed of fire. Never had his nightmares been so intense. The flames first appeared on the lance of a mounted *Aharoni* champion, but the knight soon disappeared, leaving him alone with the flames. The white fire spread over the *ikar's* naked body with frightening economy, consuming him.

Kerebos' cries rang throughout the camp.

Chapter 4

A ntiphon dismounted and gazed across the barren land toward the approaching horsemen.

"No use trying to outrun them, eh, girl?" he said and patted the donkey's head. "You deserve a rest, anyway."

The priest pulled a water skin from the saddle and squirted some of the liquid into the beast's mouth before allowing the mount to graze upon the sparse vegetation.

"Don't run off," he told the donkey, which raised its head and somehow managed to appear perturbed.

Antiphon parked himself on the dusty ground and waited for the closing patrol. He had been traveling west for days, and these riders were the first people he had seen.

He had seen some non-human life, though. Two nights before he had been attacked by a pack of *irbarzis*, striped desert wolves with legs three feet long. His staff still bore bloodstains where he had brained one of the lean predators, and the donkey had a gash on its right flank.

The six horsemen were almost upon him when, as though convinced of his utter inconsequence, they slowed and lowered their crossbows. Two of them even laughed at the robed *Aharoni* priest and his spotted donkey.

"Greetings, traveller," said the oldest rider, a fellow in a leather jerkin. "I'm Captain Lasaris, Imperial *Chaconni* Rangers. Who might you be?"

Imperial, is it? Antiphon thought, intrigued. It had been generations since the Old Kingdom had thus designated itself.

"I greet you, valiant captain," he replied. "I am Antiphon al-Caliph of the Order of the Flame."

"Well, *Aharoni*," Lasaris replied, motioning a man toward the donkey's packs, "I trust you know this is the king's road?"

"I do, Captain," Antiphon answered meekly. "I pray my travels have not disturbed his highness."

Lasaris' weathered face surrendered a smile. He reached for the canteen at his side, saying:

"I don't think he'll lose sleep over it, priest." He took a long draught and wiped his mouth with the back of his hand. "But there is a toll."

"Of course, Captain."

"What have you there, Ruthar?" Lasaris asked the man searching Antiphon's belongings.

The sandy-haired *Boru* shrugged. "Not much, Captain. Clothes, food, books, that kind of goat dung."

"Any weapons?"

"Nothing, Captain. Uh, oh!" Ruthar caught himself. "Here's one." He drew Antiphon's whittling knife and lifted it for general inspection. The other Rangers snickered.

"What's that for, 'father?' Cutting of bodices before the 'laying on of hands?'" one asked.

"No wonder the *Aharoni* can't protect themselves," said another.

Antiphon felt hot in the face. "I'm no soldier, but a man of God," he said slowly.

Lasaris looked thoughtful. "Isn't a good priest both?"

"Not usually, Captain."

"Let he who has not a sword, sell his mantle and buy one." the Captain quoted scripture; he turned to the *Boru*. "Leave his things. He's harmless enough."

"I thank you," Antiphon said softly.

"Don't do that too quickly, my *Aharoni* friend," an edge slid into Lasaris' voice. "You still owe to travel this road."

"Certainly." The priest unhitched his purse. "How much?"

"One silver, priest of the Flame," the Captain replied, not unkindly.

"All I have is gold," Antiphon stated, dumping coins into his hand.

Lasaris appeared startled and quickly scanned the horizon. The other Rangers shot longing glances at the shiny money. Ruthar whistled.

"Are you insane?" Lasaris berated the priest. "What are you doing with all that? A man less honest than myself would slit your throat for those coins. I might yet!" The small bag of gold easily equaled a Ranger's salary.

"Before you'd do that, I'd gladly give it to you," Antiphon assured him. "To be honest, I'm not sure why I brought it all."

"Well put it away!" Lasaris commanded. "Or I might have to protect you from my men, here. On second thought, throw me one of those goldies for the toll."

"With pleasure, Captain."

Antiphon tossed a coin at Lasaris, who plucked it from the air with thumb and forefinger, then bit it. He shook his head as he stuffed the money into his belt.

"Now what are you doing, and where are you going?" Lasaris demanded.

"I am going to your capital," Antiphon lied.

Lasaris pushed his helm back, exposing short gray hair. "Oh?" he asked. "Why Korenthis with all that gold? Going to relieve the state debt?"

Antiphon stood mute. He had not expected to see anyone so soon and had yet to work the wrinkles from his story.

Lasaris raised an eyebrow. "I'd hate to arrest you with no cause, friend," he said. "But you must convince me of your good intentions. Strange things are afoot and my orders are to let no trouble into the land."

Maybe it was the way the other Rangers stared at him which loosened Antiphon's tongue. Whatever the reason, he told the truth. "I'm on a mission to convert Kerebos *Ikar* to the one true faith," he replied.

Lasaris' men looked shocked.

"Really?" the captain laughed. "That's good. That's even funny."

I'll say! Antiphon thought. "Still, that is my mission," he replied.

"You'd do well to purchase a sword then," Lasaris said. "Or better yet, ask God to hold the bastard so you can baptize him. Convert

Kerebos *Ikar!*" he snorted.

"He'll kill you, fool," the *Boru* said.

You think I don't know that? Antiphon thought, but replied: "I didn't volunteer for this quest."

Lasaris gazed in wonder at the small, bearded priest and sighed. "He moves in mysterious ways."

"Maybe he'll frighten Kerebos into heaven with that knife, right Cap'n?" a *Chaconne* laughed.

Antiphon smiled at the Ranger.

"Perhaps you'll go in my place?" he asked. "What are you doing in the war against Kerebos?"

"We're not at war with Kerebos," came the icy reply. "Not until the king and the barbarians strike their truce, anyway. But I don't fear war either, priestling." He hefted his crossbow. "I'd love a shot at one of those black-clad renegades."

"That's the last thing you want, idiot!" Lasaris snapped. "One of Kerebos' *cohari* could level our fort in half an hour!" He looked at Antiphon. "You're braver than me, priest. May God go with you, but for now you're coming with us."

"But my mission!" Antiphon protested helplessly.

"We're heading west also," Lasaris replied. "We're completing a sweep before we return to camp, and the least service I can do God is to make sure you reach Fort Hermis. Okay?"

Antiphon bowed gratefully and said: "I am your servant."

"Grab your mighty steed, then," Lasaris nodded at the vapidly chewing donkey, "and ride beside me."

Antiphon and Lasaris talked as they rode and the miles passed quickly. Lasaris had a broad understanding of all things *Chaconni* and proved anxious to share. Antiphon learned much about *Chaconni* history, particularly the capital, Korenthis, and began to wish he was going to visit the city.

The terrain grew greener as they made their way through the Valley of three Rivers, but the scenery was marred by many ruined villages. Here and there along the highway, an occasional statue stood guard over the long-deserted towns, but the effigies had been abused in various ways.

The Black Legion had razed this province centuries before,

Antiphon learned, and the area had never been repopulated. Vykalitis *Ikar* had sworn to keep the valley free of life after the local garrison trapped and killed a Power Guard. Later *ikari* had honored his edict, preventing most forcefully any effort by settlers to secure the land. An eery quiet lay over the valley. Antiphon and Lasaris' conversation moved onto religion.

"I cannot agree with you, priest," Lasaris said, shaking his head. "The Savior was only a man; he was not God. He was a very good man, but a human being, nevertheless."

"Arios, who pioneered that heresy, was an *Aharoni* priest, you know," Antiphon replied.

Lasaris shrugged. "So? Because your order labels a man a heretic does not make him one."

"If it did, would that make us more or less right?"

Lasaris laughed to himself. The son of a merchant, he had enjoyed some schooling and had learned to appreciate rhetoric. He prized the opportunity to talk with someone other than his men with whom, having only recently been assigned, he was still on rather awkward terms. Besides, none of them were very bright. They rarely wanted to talk about anything other than wine and women.

"Very good, very good," Lasaris said, looking down from his great warhorse. "But clever words don't save the argument."

"Well," Antiphon changed direction, "do you heed the words of the Savior?"

"Of course."

"What do you make of it, then, when he ascends the temple steps and calls himself by God's name?"

"That's when the townspeople went for the stones?"

"Yes," Antiphon said.

Lasaris looked troubled. "I don't know. Maybe they thought he was being heretical."

"If he was claiming to be God and was wrong, there is no reason for you to listen to him," Antiphon said. "If he was claiming to be God *and knew he was wrong*, there's even less reason." Antiphon smiled at Lasaris. "Which interpretation do you prefer, if not the one that he was God?"

Lasaris rode in silence for a long moment.

"I'm only a fighting man and well know my limitations," he said at last. "I'd like to see you argue with a *Chaconni* holy man."

"So would I. You'd see that that apple didn't fall too far from the tree. Do you often read the scriptures, Captain?" Antiphon asked.

"Yes. I'm a lettered man."

"Have you ever read the first chapter of Xonis?"

"Many times," Lasaris admitted. "In the beginning was the Word," he quoted, "and the Word was with God, and the Word was God. And..." he slowed and stopped. "I think I know where you're going with this."

"What does the fourteenth verse say?"

"It says, 'And the word became flesh,'" Lasaris answered and fell silent. "You make your point well," he finally admitted. "But if the Savior was God, that leaves you with the three-gods-in-one problem. How can one make sense of such silliness and why would they want to?"

It was Antiphon's turn to think. Lasaris took the opportunity to turn to his men who had been very quiet.

"You fellows still alive back there?" he asked. "I haven't heard anything all afternoon."

"We're fine, Cap'n," one replied.

Lasaris appeared unconvinced and favored the priest a wry glance. "I'm afraid my men don't enjoy your company," he intimated.

Antiphon did not need to be told; he had felt the Rangers' eyes upon him the entire journey. "I apologize."

Lasaris shrugged. "No need. But how do you *Aharoni* come to grips with the three-in-one principle?"

"We've a number of ways," Antiphon said. "But did the *Chacconi* ever stop to consider that God is, must be, by definition, beyond our comprehension?"

"We believe that."

"Then why denounce every theological question you can't answer?" Antiphon asked.

"Just because a proposition's difficult doesn't make it true," Lasaris retorted. "The Trinity may simply be a bad idea."

Antiphon appreciated that one. Lasaris was improving at debate before his very eyes. Antiphon said:

"My good Captain, there are many things we simplify, which we should not. We cloud the truth that way."

"Like what?"

I hope I don't butcher this, the priest thought, having done exactly that back in the seminary.

"Take the mind," Antiphon offered.

"What about it?"

"Like God, we often consider the brain to be a single entity, but it is obviously composed of separate parts acting in concert."

"Yes?" Lasaris said, unconvinced.

"Let's say that you were trying to remember your first love's name, but couldn't at the moment."

"Yes?"

"Of course you know that you know it," Antiphon continued, "and you even know that you're going to remember it, but for whatever reason, you can't grasp it at the moment."

"I understand," the Captain replied, nodding. "Things of that sort often happen to me."

"Me too. Now, seeing that we both agree that her name is in your head, but you can't find it, this seems to imply that there is a compartment of the brain which acts as a storage bin for the intellect."

"That is not too difficult," Lasaris said.

"All right, then. How does the mind recognize this girl's name when it comes across it?" Antiphon asked. "If the intellect were consistent with the entire mind, there would not be any need to search for her name."

Lasaris pondered this.

"We *must* have a memory that recognizes her name when it goes into the intellect to search," Antiphon insisted.

"Go on," Lasaris said softly.

"And besides the intellect and the memory you must have the *will* to seek your sweetheart's name. Without any of the three factors, the intellect, memory or will, your brain would not function, yet we still tend to think of the mind as a single entity."

Lasaris suddenly shook his head, saying: "But all those things are only part of a single whole!"

35

"That is my point exactly."

Lasaris looked perplexed but Antiphon knew he would arrive at the proper conclusion. "So you're equating the workings of the brain with the Trinity?" Lasaris asked.

"Yes. I'm trying to show you how multi-leveled propositions, like the brain, are often mistaken as flat."

Lasaris broke into a wide grin. "You're smart, my friend," he said without the slightest rancor. "I suspect you'd have little trouble with our priests. If this road were a little longer you might make a convert."

Antiphon lowered his head and thanked God that he had given a good account of the Word. "By the way, what was your first love's name?" he asked.

One of the Rangers behind Lasaris cocked a crossbow.

"That's one I'm not likely to forget," the captain laughed. "Or had better not. I married her."

Antiphon laughed along with the *Chaconne*, and there was nothing forced about it. He had known few non-*Aharoni*, and those had left unfavorable impressions, but he liked this soldier.

A Ranger loosed a crossbow bolt—through Lasaris' back.

The smile froze on Lasaris' face as the quarrel ripped from his chest in a fountain of blood. His eyes rolled and he crashed face first into the dust.

"Captain!" Antiphon cried, leaping from the donkey. He ran towards Lasaris, but was swarmed by the other Rangers. The *Boru* grabbed the priest from behind and laid a jagged dagger across his throat.

"Give that purse!" he hissed in Antiphon's ear.

"Take it!" Antiphon yelled as a Ranger stripped him of the money and sent him to the ground with a knee to the stomach. A sword rang from its scabbard.

"Wait! It's bad luck to kill a holy man," a soldier said. "Leave him and let God decide his fate."

There was some grumbling but the Rangers eventually decided to abandon Antiphon, who lay wheezing. Antiphon heard some more bickering then the clink of coins. The rangers mounted their horses and rode off in different directions.

Lasaris moaned.

Antiphon forced himself to crawl to the fallen man.

"Captain!" he cried, laying a hand near the hole in the ranger's chest. "Can you hear me?"

Lasaris opened his eyes. There was pain and deep sorrow in them.

"Priest?" he coughed.

"Yes, yes, it's me!"

"Preesht," Lasaris slurred as Antiphon tried to staunch the wound.

"Yes, my friend! Ask God's forgiveness!"

Lasaris closed his eyes and tears bled down his grimy face.

"My wife," he whispered. "My wife..."

The *Chaconne* lay still.

Antiphon knelt in the growing pool of blood, a great anger within him. He knew had not Lasaris shown compassion, he would still be alive. *And had I not been sent on this worthless mission, this good man would be returning home tonight*, he thought. *To his wife.*

Antiphon thought of his dead Khloe, and tears came. This present evil and his long grief opened a gate in his heart, forcing a sob. He pounded Lasaris' chest, which was sticky with blood.

"I'm sorry!" he cried. "I'm sorry!"

He stayed beside Lasaris until bright stars came out, wondering what purpose the captain's murder could possibly serve.

Chapter 5

Black thunderheads growled across the morning sky and a raw gale lashed the encamped legion. Kerebos gazed up the ridge at the forest of erected crosses.

A *Stalenzka* screamed as he was nailed to the last rood; the wind carried his cry over the *landesknecta* tents. Kerebos, roused by the voice, tramped up to the squirming victims and helped raise the final cross. The tribesman glared at him with a look of utter detestation.

Kerebos basked in the hatred. *But even now, the feeling fades*, he thought dismally.

Time was when such a blasphemous bloodletting would have energized him for days, but like an addict, he was requiring ever greater stimulation for ever less satisfaction.

"A beautiful sight, lord," Janus said. He dropped a mallet and licked blood from his hands.

"Hear, hear!" other legionaries agreed.

"What? Oh, yes," Kerebos said, coming to himself. He turned slowly round, noting the crucified; some were already turning blue. "Beautiful," he spat, disgusted.

"I'm proud to serve you, lord," Janus said.

Kerebos' thoughts had moved on, though.

The legion had herded the *Stalenzka* along for three days, brutalizing them while gathering wood for the crosses. Finally Kerebos had grown so tired of their pleas and screams, he had sacrificed some supply wagons to make up the deficit in wood.

Or was I near to sparing them? he wondered.

The last *Stalenzka* struggled on the cross. Blood flowed freely from his wrists and feet.

"He's trying to bleed himself to death," Janus observed.

Kerebos stirred and laughed wickedly, saying: "Tourniquet his limbs so he dies slowly."

Janus searched for rope as Kerebos stepped forward and smacked the tribesman's foot; the bearded warrior's chest had been cruelly chewed by the lash.

"After we tie you off, you'll end up suffocating," Kerebos informed the man. "Probably not for a few days, though. Just thought you'd care to know."

"Goddamn you!" the tribesman cried. "You will answer for my wife and children!"

"You people had a chance to punish us on the battlefield," Kerebos said. "I was not impressed. I guess you've already answered for them."

The *Stalenzka* leaned into the nails with such vigor they began to pull.

"Temper, temper," Kerebos cautioned. "You'll hurt yourself. And your foaming mouth is most unbecoming."

"Let me down and I'll kill you!"

The *Stalenzka* howled when Janus crushed his knee with a hammer.

"Now, Janus, don't forget the other," Kerebos said.

Another blow. The tribesman shrieked again, then began bashing the back of his head against the wood.

"Seems to have forgotten his wife and children," Kerebos noted.

"Lord Triskeles!" Janus suddenly saluted.

Triskeles stopped beside Kerebos.

"Some of them have died," he observed. "See, their bowels have released."

"They didn't last very long, did they?" Kerebos replied.

"My lads could live up there for days," Triskeles boasted, and Janus agreed. "I'm sure they'd volunteer if you'd like proof, lord," Triskeles added.

"No thanks," Kerebos grumbled.

"It would be no effort, lord."

"Were your parents siblings?" Kerebos demanded. "We've just fought a major battle and you want to bleed the men again to no purpose?"

Triskeles hurried onto another subject. "What do you make of the reports the steelmen gave?" he asked.

Kerebos shrugged. "Who knows? Maybe."

"But scaly beasts and ghosts?" Triskeles pried.

Kerebos started down the ridge. "I've more pressing problems."

Triskeles followed. "Like what, my lord?"

"Think man!" Kerebos snapped, already sick of the *elhar's* company. "Neither the *Razkuli* nor the *Chaconni* produced a good harvest this year."

"That's true."

"When we get home, I want you to squeeze our neighbors," Kerebos said. "'Harsh summers past make rough winters coming,'" he cited his father.

"I understand, my lord."

"I'm sure. Start recruiting as soon as we get back, also."

Triskeles walked in silence for a few steps before asking: "So soon, lord?"

Kerebos could almost hear the grinding in the *elhar's* slow brain. He decided to test his plans.

"I'm giving thought to expanding the legion," he said as they reached the bottom of the hill. "Maybe creating a separate auxiliary, altogether."

Triskeles halted in his tracks and pulled Kerebos to a stop. "Two legions?" he whispered and looked furtively about. "What about the Scriptus?"

Kerebos smiled. He knew exactly where to strike. "Two legions *would* be a lot of men," he said. "I suppose I might even need a regent to help. Someone with experience whose loyalty is beyond question."

Triskeles licked his thin lips. "Where would you find such a man?"

"The First *Elhar*, maybe?"

Triskeles gave a sinister chuckle. "Desia is dead and Kerebos is *ikar!*" he declared. "Where you lead, I'll follow."

Kerebos slapped him on the shoulder, saying: "Very good. Now see to your men."

Triskeles saluted with the enthusiasm of a recruit and departed at a brisk pace. Kerebos watched him leave.

"Fool," he muttered.

At that moment the sky grew even darker and the earth trembled. Men cried out as their tents collapsed upon them. Some of the crosses slammed to the earth, those *Stalenzka* nailed to them wailing like the damned.

What's this? Kerebos wondered.

A flickering green light appeared in the south. It arched across the sky and left an emerald path in its wake. The legion watched in astonishment as the light descended upon them and cast an olive pallor over the camp. At the very last, however, it constricted into a narrow point and struck the earth at Kerebos' feet, sliding into the ground with a long, audible hiss.

"What in hell?" Kerebos shouted in the cold silence that followed. He stared south, toward the distant desert.

The camp had barely begun to stir when the light started again, this time moving much slower. As it grew closer, the men could see figures languishing within. Terrified faces pressed against the sides of the beam as though against glass. As they passed overhead Kerebos saw many he had known, their tongues darting from gibbering mouths opened wide in a collective, silent scream. The light bent upward and lanced into the pregnant clouds. It disappeared with an enormous thunderclap.

Kerebos was in a cold sweat when the frightened *elhari* reached him; all of them jabbered at once. He forced himself to remain calm and beat fear into the back of his mind.

"Silence!" he cried in his most menacing tone—even the wind died down. "So the men are afraid of lightning, now? Soon they'll be starting at mice!"

The *elhari* composed themselves at once, heartened by his nonchalance.

"Better," Kerebos continued. "Tell the lads that I said it was a sign, a good sign! Hell, I'll tell them myself!"

Kerebos marched toward the legion as though free from care, officers in tow. He snapped out a few orders, then summoned the *cohari*, whom he upbraided in similar fashion.

"Next time I pass gas, I want you fools to catch it in a bottle!" he commanded. He surveyed the disheveled camp. "What a mess!" he complained and jerked a thumb at the crucified. "You waiting on them to clean it up?" Before long the entire host was laughing.

Kerebos led the afternoon drills himself.

*   *   *

Antiphon rode down the swath the Black Legion had trampled through the grass. *They seem to delight in torturing His creations*, he observed. *Little wonder they live by forage.*

A vulture croaked overhead but flew on to a distant steppe, where many of its kind dotted the sky. The wind changed direction and the priest nearly retched at the stench that assaulted him.

"God, what is that?" he asked.

When he grew near enough for an answer, he did vomit. Antiphon slid from the saddle and fell onto all fours.

God save us, he thought, spitting out the last of his dinner. He looked up at the crucified *Stalenzka*. Many had already been stripped of flesh; their skulls smiled in the wan sun. The grass beneath was black with blood.

Antiphon walked the donkey toward the crosses, the cawing of vultures in his ears. He tried to curse Kerebos, but coughed on the reek. *If only I had ridden faster I might have saved some*, he thought.

"Help me," a tribesman rasped.

Antiphon found the man, a bearded fellow with limbs swollen and black; claw and beak marks dotted his torso.

"Help," the wretch begged, as a huge red vulture started on his scalp.

Antiphon knew full well the bloated *Stalenzka* was beyond succor.

"What can I do?" he asked miserably. "I can't pull those spikes without causing you greater damage." In truth he could not even see the nails, which had been swallowed as though by rising dough.

The tribesman closed his eyes, and just when Antiphon was sure he had died, coughed: "K...kill me."

Antiphon wrung his hands in dejection. He longed to fulfill the request but, as a priest, knew it was beyond his authority. *But certainly the Lord would forgive my mercy?* he reasoned.

The tribesman smiled, a gruesome sight. "I understand," he said. "Kerebos."

Somehow, the name stiffened Antiphon's resolve and he searched for a weapon. He found a sticky mallet.

"Kerebos!" the *Stalenzka* cried and stared into empty space.

"He's gone," Antiphon said.

"No. Kerebos?" the tribesman quired softly. "Help me across the water."

Antiphon watched as the *Stalenzka's* head drooped a final time. Within the moment, liquid ran down the tribesman's leg. Two vultures immediately landed on the corpse.

"Off him, damn you!" Antiphon shouted and hurled the mallet. A bird fell onto its back and lay flapping. Four more took its place.

A rage swelled within Antiphon. He reclaimed the mallet and started in on the vultures. He pummeled, punched, screamed and made such a nuisance of himself that most of the hideous fowl removed to a safe distance.

Exhausted, Antiphon slumped to his knees. It took some time before he could commence the dreary business of cutting down the dead. It took hours to detach the bodies from the encrusted crosses. By the time he had finished he was covered in filth. Knowing he could not bury so many, and lacking even a shovel, he piled them into a large pyre.

Antiphon said a prayer over the cadavers then went into a saddlebag for tinder and flint. He managed to get a small fire going but the *Stalenzka* refused to catch flame. In the end he had to abandon them to the scavengers.

It was with a heavy heart that the priest rode away. Though convinced he had done everything possible to prevent further dishonor to the dead, he nevertheless felt he had committed a grave sin.

Even witnessing Kerebos' actions soils a man, he thought bitterly. *I hate him.*

Hate, Antiphon knew, was a sin also.

*   *   *

Kerebos looked down the rocky valley, over Cemetary River and beyond to the *landesknectos'* walled castle. The sprawling, basalt structure stood dark and menacingly alone, its sharp, spired donjon stabbed into the sky.

"There she is, my lord," Janus said happily. "The trail was pleasant, but I'm glad to be home."

Kerebos nodded then asked: "Did you have the dream, too?"

"About the green light? I think all of us did, lord."

That was nearly true. Everyone Kerebos had talked to, except Triskeles, had reported visions of being swept away by the "green from the anvil". He himself, however, had suffered the usual dream of fire, whereas Triskeles had complained about nightmares of being strangled from behind.

Janus indicated the river's muddy floodplain.

"There's one of the beauties!" he said, sighting a stump-legged, amphibious shark.

The mottled beast, twenty five feet long, roared up at them then slipped into the murky water. But Kerebos knew it had not gone far. He knew that even now many sharks were gathering beneath in anticipation.

Cemetary River, wide and slow, had gained its name for obvious reasons. For nearly a thousand years the Legion had dumped the dead, both soldier and slave, enemy and friend, into its muddy embrace. Over time sharks began to appear, swimming miles upstream from the swamplands by the sea.

The early *ikari* had been most put out by the creatures, which were incredibly ill-tempered and ran down even the swiftest men. Decades of shark hunts had failed to eradicate the predators—the blood only brought more—and had resulted in the loss of many *landesknectos*. Over time, however, the legion had cultivated a relationship with their monstrous neighbors. Now known as "Legion sharks" the beasts served many purposes.

First, they kept all but the largest armed forces at a distance. Few knew or cared that the sharks only left the water for a short time. Second, the beasts were a seemingly inexhaustible food source; Kerebos himself was very fond of shark steak. Lastly, the toothy terrors played a major part in *landesknecta* rituals.

Very often the last thing a legionary saw during the yearly Winnowing was the gaping mouth of a shark. Kerebos remembered well the "cleansing day," many years before, when he had killed

Lasctakos for the *ikar's* ring. The confrontation had raged for moments before Kerebos had beaten the notched sword from the *ikar's* hand and run him through. Kerebos never forgot the look of pride on Lasctakos' face as he lay dying.

"I saw this man's potential," Lasctakos' expression had said. "I was not wrong."

The abandoned *ikar* had not even screamed as the sharks dragged him into the water.

"There's another one!" Janus cried.

"What are they doing out in midday?" Triskeles asked as he arrived.

Kerebos shook his head.

"My lord," Triskeles said, "the wagons won't be here for some time, and we already have a pontoon bridge in the fort..."

"Yes?"

"We didn't lose many men this year," the *Boru* pointed out. "And you wouldn't let my lads prove themselves on the cross. We need a challenge."

Legionaries gathered around in anticipation.

Kerebos felt trapped. He had no desire to weaken his command, but he wanted to let the men engage in something, anything, which might take their minds off the last few days.

"Go ahead," he sighed.

Triskeles winked at a subordinate, who grinned and darted off with the good news. Shouts of excitement spread rapidly through the legion.

Triskeles raised a dagger above his head and cried: "Let the baiting begin!"

Men began to unbind their armor. Before long naked *landesknectos*, knives in hand, were sprinting toward the river.

Kerebos read the disappointment on the faces of his bodyguards and said, "Oh, go ahead."

"My lord!" Janus whooped, then ordered his men to undress.

Kerebos could not help but smile as his men reached the river. There had been a time when he had enjoyed shark baiting as much as anyone.

The host came to a halt a dozen feet from the water and spread out. Blades slapped thighs as men worked their courage up. At last one man broke from the line; Kerebos recognized a *sestar* who had distinguished himself in the last battle.

"I, Daedilos, shall lead the way!" the junior officer bellowed, then sprinted for the water. Daedilos was not as good as his word, though, and slowed in the shallows before slinking back to the muddy beach.

"Janus for the First *Elhar*!" came the cry, and Kerebos' bodyguard walked slowly forth. He entered the opaque water up to his hips and slapped the surface with his blade. Other bodyguards joined him.

Those on land roared their approval as a dorsal fin sliced the surface. Syranos and twenty of his men raced to the water. More followed in twos and threes.

Janus screamed then disappeared in a spray of foam. He bobbed up again fifty yards downriver, stabbing furiously at the striped belly of what must have been a twenty footer. He was still fighting as he was dragged under for the last time.

Here and there men cried out as they were attacked, but their mates instantly jumped to their assistance. The water changed from brown to black as pools of blood spread downstream. Before long Kerebos' bodyguards had dragged a dying shark into the mud. The fish tried to stand but was stabbed time and again.

Kerebos grimaced at the number of legionaries that floated dead in the water. The frequency of shark sightings tapered off as most of the legion joined in, but here and there men were still getting pruned off the fringes. Kerebos made his way down to inspect the eight multi-colored brutes which had been wrestled ashore.

"A fine catch," he admitted. The men beamed.

A wave of laughter washed over the legion as a sole *landesknecta*, dagger buried in a shark's back, rode across the river. The legionary, one of Triskeles', was dragged under a dozen times before he abandoned ship and splashed to the far shore. He stood in the mud with hands raised high, shouting his own name.

The First *Elhar* gave a deafening round of applause as the man turned and made for the safety of the remote castle.

The legionaries set about skinning and butchering the sharks while Triskeles severed the heads with a series of sword blows. When he got to the end of the line, he straddled the remaining shark and acted as though he were strangling it.

Erebas' *elhar* arrived with the wagons and loudly protested that they had missed the fun. Erebas stomped in disgust and turned to Kerebos, who had wandered off, apparently lost in contemplation.

More legions, he thought. *We will start recruitment immediately.*

"Kerebos," the wind hissed in his ear.

"Who calls?" he replied listlessly.

The *ikar* could only watch as a rider descended into the valley. At first the man appeared a mighty knight in blazing armor, but swiftly transformed into a mere *Aharoni* in soiled robes.

Antiphon's face was gray as he halted his donkey a dozen paces from the most dangerous man in the world.

"Kerebos *Ikar*," he said.

Kerebos knew not why he trembled. "Who are you, little man?" he sneered.

The priest gave an insulting half-bow.

"Antiphon al-Caliph of the Order of the White Flame," he replied. "Your destiny has found you."

"*White flame?*" Kerebos gasped and grabbed his sword.

An unpleasant smile creased Antiphon's dirty face. "Indeed."

Kerebos was speechless.

The priest and the *ikar* stared at each other.

alf-dressed legionaries instantly surrounded Antiphon and dragged him from the saddle. He was thrown to the ground.

"A spy!" someone said.

"An assassin!" insisted another.

Erebas cast an inquisitive gaze at the *ikar*, who stood in wide-eyed indolence. Antiphon ignored the rough treatment and focused on Kerebos, trying hard to recall the exact words Dokein had fashioned for this moment.

"Fate has claimed you, *ikar*," he said at last.

"What fate?" Kerebos grated. "Why did you speak of fire?"

"The words of God are older by far than your Scriptus Brand, Kerebos *ikar*," Antiphon intoned. "And in them we've the secret that can forever end your dreams."

Kerebos winced as though slapped and stumbled backward.

"My lord!" men cried in distress.

A hawknosed *Razkul* jumped forward, scattered the men holding Antiphon, and wrapped scarred hands around the priest's neck, effortlessly hoisting him from the ground. The *Razkul* squeezed until blue veins snaked across his massive forearms.

"This roach bewitches our lord?" he demanded. "Stay your magic, or I'll pop off your head!"

"You can't hide, Kerebos," Antiphon coughed, kicking air. "Only I can heal you."

"Silence!" the *Razkul* bellowed and squeezed even harder.

"You...need...me," Antiphon gasped. His face turned pink, then beet red.

48

Landesknectos watched in amusement. Triskeles pushed through the crowd to Kerebos, who looked quite shaken.

"This priest has bewitched him!" the *Razkul* growled, shaking Antiphon like a rag doll.

"Drop him, Stilchus," Triskeles said.

The *Razkul* obeyed reluctantly, but did not go far. Men crowded around in anticipation; Triskeles' interrogations were infamous even among legionaries.

Triskeles towered over Antiphon, who lay in a panting heap.

"Who are you, dog?" the *elhar* demanded as he toed the priest onto his back.

Antiphon could only wheeze.

"Do you seek death, man? Why have you come here?" Triskeles asked.

Antiphon laid a shaky hand over his bruised throat. His chest heaved.

"Speak!" Triskeles ordered.

Antiphon tried to shake the spots from his eyes as he sat. "I've come for Kerebos, not his slaves," he choked. The effort almost caused him to faint.

"Is that so?" Triskeles snarled and flattened him with a kick to the chin.

Somehow Antiphon kept his senses. He rolled onto his side as warm blood oozed over his tongue. He coughed two broken molars into the dirt.

"Want to speak to me now?" Triskeles asked.

Something spooked the donkey and it began to buck.

"Kill that animal!" Triskeles said.

Twenty men fell upon the beast with dagger and sword; blood and flesh rained through the air. The donkey screamed as its eyes rolled white. It was dead before its butchered body hit the ground.

Antiphon turned from his fallen friend and stared into Triskeles' blue eyes. He tried to spit but the bloody saliva only dribbled onto his beard.

Triskeles's black sword hissed with satisfaction as it slid from its rune-embossed sheath. The *elhar* grabbed a handful of Antiphon's curly hair and pressed the sword against the *Aharoni's* cheek.

"This is my friend, Cattamos," Triskeles introduced the blade. He leaned close enough to whisper in Antiphon's ear. "I've raped *Aharoni* with this sword...as I shall you after I shove him through your guts. I think you'll like it."

Antiphon mumbled a prayer as Triskeles drew Cattamos for a thrust.

"Hold!" Kerebos interceded.

Cattamos came to a disappointed halt an inch from Antiphon's belly. Triskeles turned wild eyes on the *ikar*, whose usual snarl had returned.

"Release him," Kerebos said.

Triskeles appeared more perturbed than had been the *Razkul*, but obeyed. "As you wish," he said glumly.

"He will not die yet," Kerebos promised. "Not until he has been properly chastened."

Any confidence Antiphon had possessed dissipated beneath Kerebos' wilting gaze. Whatever uncertainty the *ikar* might have experienced had obviously passed. Perhaps Kerebos had been toying with him all along?

God, why have I been brought to this end? he thought. An image of Lasaris dead passed through his mind.

"Bind him," Kerebos ordered.

*   *   *

The audience room was large, dank and lit by only a few large candles. Mineral deposits shone luminously on the stone walls. Kerebos, seated on an iron throne, ignored the prostrate *Tantorri* chieftain's pleas.

What to do with that priest? Kerebos brooded, wiping perspiration from his brow. The *Tantor*, Haam by name, grovelled before the warlord.

"*Ikar*, it was not our fault!" he cried. "Believe me, we were vigilant as eagles!"

Kerebos nodded to a guard, who immediately left the room.

"Be silent," Kerebos said contemptuously.

For three hundred years the *Tantorri*, farmers mostly, had been under the legion's "protection." The tribe not only surrendered food to the brotherhood but also procured slaves. The system had worked well for the Legion. Only infrequently had *ikari* been forced to flex their muscles.

"You have disappointed me," Kerebos said.

Haam burst into tears. "My lord *ikar*," he sobbed, "for centuries we have not failed your trust. Give us another chance!"

Too much 'failed trust' this year, Kerebos thought. He stood, and the grayhaired chamberlain, Magos, handed over Mistaaka. Kerebos wagged the sword at the *Tantor*. "You have few obligations to me," he said. "All I've asked is for you to keep my lands and slaves safe while I'm away. Is that so much? Have you been treated unfairly?"

"No lord, but—"

"Quiet!" Kerebos roared. "Your women and children have been spared from our kennels and beds, your food has only been tithed, less than the *Chaconni* crown imposes on its subjects, and you have enjoyed our generous protection."

"You have been most benevolent," Haam whined.

Kerebos poked the *Tantor's* bald head with the sword, asking: "Then where are my slaves? You heard we had lost to the *Stalenzka* so you sold them! Is that not right?"

"No! No, by God, I swear it!" Haam insisted.

Kerebos neither knew nor cared the truth of the matter. He had already made up his mind to punish Haam most horribly. In fact, his men were probably ready.

"Now," he told Magos.

The freedman limped over and opened the heavy door. Soldiers dragged two girls into the room. One of the females, a lovely lass of twelve, with huge brown eyes and braided black hair, screamed when she saw Haam on the stone floor. The other girl, a tiny seven-year-old, burst into tears.

Haam paled beneath his dusky complexion when he saw the children. "My God," he gasped, stricken. "How did you find them?"

Kerebos chuckled as a grin crossed his face. "Your daughters? I hope my men didn't have to torture your entire family."

Haam blubbered something incoherent and crawled toward the children, but Kerebos stepped hard upon his hand.

"You have failed me for the only time," Kerebos said.

The wailing girls struggled with their captors and reached for their father.

"Let them go," Kerebos ordered and realeased the *Tantor's* hand.

The hysterical girls raced to Haam, who waited with arms wide. He wept as he assured them everything would be fine.

"*Tantor?*" Kerebos said.

"Yes, lord *ikar?*" Haam sobbed.

"Which one shall I kill?"

The girls screamed anew and their father tightened his embrace. Haam began hyperventilating.

"Please," he begged. "Kill me instead."

"You died when you sold my slaves," Kerebos answered. "All that remains undecided is which of your little sluts shall join you."

"But they're innocent!" Haam howled.

Kerebos shrugged, saying: "Rain falls upon the just and the evil alike."

"No, no, no!"

"If you don't choose," Kerebos laughed, "you'll watch both die before I kill you."

Haam closed his eyes and shook his head with vehemence. "I can't," he said through clenched teeth.

Kerebos turned to Magos. "Bring my spikes."

The chamberlain hobbled from the room but soon returned. He handed two tent spikes to the *ikar*.

"Which one dies?" Kerebos again asked.

Haam lifted a bruised palm in warding and denial. "Nooo!"

"Choose or *you* shall kill them."

Haam punched himself in agony. Kerebos had seen it all before; he knew the *Tantor* had passed the point where he was capable of making decisions.

"Take them, lads," Kerebos told his men, who tore the girls from their father. "This is the last chance I'm giving you." He told Haam.

The *Tantor* had been reduced to a subhuman state. He frothed and howled like a rabid animal. He struggled to his feet in attempt to charge his tormentor, but a *landesknecta* swept the legs from beneath him. The legionary shook his head.

"You try to be fair to people," he sniffed.

"Kill both of them," Kerebos ordered.

"Wait, ohhh, wait!" Haam choked. He turned from one daughter to the other. "Spare my firstborn, oh God, her, her, her!" he pointed at the older girl.

"Daddy!" the seven year old screamed and backed into her giant captor.

"Oh, God!" Haam wailed.

"Are you sure?" Kerebos asked.

Haam nodded a few times before he jerked and stopped moving, his mind broken.

"Kill the older, and send the little one back to her mother," Kerebos told the guards.

"My lord."

Kerebos nodded at Haam. "Kill him, too."

"Yes, lord."

The eldest girl made barely a whimper as the *landesknecta* eased her onto the ground and placed the black spike in her ear.

"I need a hammer, Magos," the legionary said.

Another soldier picked up the seven year old and gently carried her from the room.

Kerebos wiped sweat from his forehead, thinking, *I'm burning up in here.* He walked to the door and stumbled into the broad, ill-lit hall. Torches lined the wall at irregular intervals; Kerebos stopped near one of these. Magos scurried by with a hammer and disappeared into the audience chamber

Kerebos composed himself, trying to ignore the conscience gnawing his mind. *You can still stop them,* it said. He waited what seemed a long time, but still no sound from the room.

"I can still stop them," he told the empty corridor.

The sound of metal on metal rang out as a legionary began hammering. Kerebos stood with eyes closed shivering inside his armor.

*   *   *

The dungeon was large with a low ceiling, from which depended many tiny stalagmites. What light there was came from the hearth fire. Instruments of torture lined the wall opposite a dozen cramped cells. Rats scurried across the floor. The smell was like the putrescence of a hundred emptied stomachs.

Two *landesknectos* lounged outside the cell where Antiphon had spent a day and night. Bored with dice, and of playing with the fist-sized spiders, the soldiers turned their attention to the new captive.

"Are you sure he's a prisoner, Dorios?" one of them, a *Boru*, asked.

"So I was told. I heard nothing about him being a slave."

Both stared at Antiphon. Eventually the *Boru* sauntered over to the fireplace and pulled a brand from the coals.

"Let's mark him just in case," he said, hefting the brand. The Legion's symbol, a mailed fist, glowed red.

"We can't, he's not a slave," Dorios reiterated. "Do you want the world to think we're barbarians?"

The *Boru* snorted and pitched the iron back into the flames. "I want to hear him scream. I'm going to ask the *cohar* what we can do."

Dorios spread out on a bench, saying: "I don't like priests either, but we should wait for orders."

"I've heard these *Aharoni* can make magic. Maybe he can heal himself?"

Dorios sat and turned toward the cell. "I'd like to see that," he admitted. "Will your faith heal you if we burn you?" he asked Antiphon.

Antiphon, who had listened in horror, swallowed on a dry mouth. He was reluctant to admit that he believed in the healing power of prayer as the *landesknectos* would demand proof. If he looked as petrified as he felt, he looked scared indeed.

The *Boru* used tongs to apprehend a red coal and toss it through the bars. The priest just managed to scuttle out of the way.

"Speak!" Dorios commanded, and rose to assist his comrade, who groped for more missiles.

"If my faith is strong enough, I can move mountains," Antiphon replied quietly.

"*If*," Dorios laughed, "*If!*"

The *Boru* reclaimed the brand. "Let's test his faith," he said. "It will be a holy experiment."

Dorios grabbed his arm, saying: "I already told you we can't. Why do you always want to brand them, anyway?"

54

The *Boru* smiled. "I like the smell."

Dorios pulled the dagger from his belt. "We can do other things."

The *Boru* swiped the dagger from his companion. "Give me the keys," he said.

Antiphon backed into a corner as the huge *Boru* fumbled with the brass lock.

"What's the matter?" the *landesknecta* feigned surprise. "I've heard your 'Savior' even raised men from the dead." The lock clicked and he filled the doorway. "But that was a long time ago, huh?" he asked. "Perhaps it never even happened?"

Antiphon looked about for anything he might use against the mailed behemoth. There was nothing.

"Hey, Dorios!" the *Boru* called, his eyes glowing like coals. "Ever notice how all the miracles happened a long time ago?"

"I guess God ran out of spells," Dorios chuckled and leaned against the bars.

Antiphon took some abortive steps toward the door but fell back. He was close to screaming.

"Where's God now, little bunny?" the *Boru* chided, ducking as he entered.

Antiphon's knees turned to jelly as the legionary approached. He lifted his hand and improvised a number of bogus magic passes. "Wait, I've a trick!" he cried as the *Boru* lunged for him.

"Let me see it!" the jailor said and grabbed Antiphon's hair.

Antiphon mumbled some gibberish, and clapped his hands before his closed eyes. *Dokein, protect my son…* With that thought, he buried his thumb into the legionary's eye. The *Boru* howled and shoved him into the wall, where he slumped to the floor.

When Antiphon awoke, he was stripped to a loincloth. Dorios was standing on his elbows and the *Boru*, eye swollen shut, was sitting on his chest.

"I think you put my lamp out for good," he told Antiphon. "That's damn bad for you."

The legionary wiggled the dagger into Antiphon's left pectoral muscle and sawed across to the nipple. Antiphon screamed.

"How's that feel?" the *Boru* asked. "Good?"

"Cut the other one," Dorios suggested. "Let's keep a sense of balance, here."

"I don't see any healing going on," the *Boru* said.

Antiphon howled again as another furrow was opened in his flesh. He knew he was a dead man. *You've been deserted by God*, a voice whispered in his head. *Curse him before you die.*

Antiphon suddenly thought of Dokein, and the image strengthened him. "No!" he gasped.

"No, what?" the *Boru* mocked. "You want me to stop?"

"I don't think so," Dorios told the priest. "Cut his privates off. He's a holy man and doesn't need them anyway."

Antiphon tried to throw his tormentors but their combined weight felt like a fallen tree.

"He's one of those 'White Flame' priests," the *Boru* pointed out. "They can marry." He smiled and poked Antiphon's groin. "But you've a good idea in any case."

The dungeon door swung open with a creak and they heard footsteps. A *sestar* stepped into the cell. "No more games!" he snapped. "The *ikar* wants to see him. Clean him up."

The *Boru* spat a stream of obscenities.

"I guess he keeps his stones," Dorios said.

"For now," the *Boru* amended.

Now that's a miracle, Antiphon thought through the pain.

wo *landesknectos* marched Antiphon through a seemingly endless maze of dim corridors. Bruised, bleeding and exhausted, he had trouble with the pace. His head swam and something crept up his throat, which surprised him; he had not eaten for days.

The legionaries kicked open a door and entered a broad hall, dragging Antiphon after them.

Your time has come, he thought. *They're taking you to Kerebos and he's going to chop you into chunks!*

The warriors halted before two great wooden doors and announced themselves. A peep-hole slid open.

"For the *ikar*?" a man asked.

"Yes."

The peep-hole slammed shut and the iron-rimmed valves swung open. Antiphon was pulled through the First *Elhar's* spartan barracks. The quarters were empty but for a group of men shaving each others' heads. They glared at the foreigner.

Antiphon was hurried up some uneven stairs into a small room where a man sat behind a desk. An impressive chandelier hung overhead. Antiphon nearly fainted when Triskeles looked up from some scrolls and said: "About time!"

"Yes, sir," the guards replied.

Triskeles waved them to the next door. "I hope he rips the little rat's heart out," he grunted as they passed.

"Me, too," a *landesknecta* agreed.

They crossed a brief parlor and entered a most foreboding room.

The ceiling was at least thirty feet high and a number of skeletons hung from the apogee. Weapons and skulls adorned the black walls. Twin fireplaces faced each other from opposite ends of the chamber, and iron maidens served as posts for a giant bed. Three suits of armor lined the far wall.

"The prisoner, my lord," a guard announced.

A berobed Kerebos glanced up from the small table where he was taking a simple dinner. Magos left the *ikar's* side and limped behind the priest, who dared not turn around.

Kerebos broke into a toothy smile. "Hello!" he said.

Magos kicked the back of Antiphon's knee and dropped him to the stone.

"Mind the blood," Kerebos cautioned with a chuckle. "I've been entertaining lately."

Antiphon inched away from a pool of the liquid but Magos cuffed him in the head.

"Don't get it on your robe," Kerebos said. "It won't come out easily. I know."

"I'm sure you do," Antiphon replied.

The remark earned another slap. Antiphon gazed at the *ikar* who still smiled, but no longer seemed amused. Hopelessness weighed upon Antiphon like a wet blanket.

"Does a stranger's blood stain as indelibly as a father's?" He asked quietly.

Kerebos' expression darkened and he pointed to the door, saying, "Out."

Magos and the *landesknectos* left at once; Antiphon stayed. Kerebos pulled Mistaaka from somewhere beneath him and laid the blade onto the table. Antiphon grimaced as he recalled what Triskeles had promised to do to him.

Kerebos seemed to relax a bit and nodded to himself. "You're deliberately trying to goad me," he said. "You know you're dead and want me to lose my temper and get it quickly over, hoping I'll forget to torture you."

Antiphon was horrified by Kerebos' perception. The *ikar* was exactly right. *Am I so easy to read?* he wondered, appalled. *Maybe I should have kept quiet...*

"You're surprised, I see it in your face," Kerebos said. "You're regretting your bold words, and are contemplating the futility of your situation, right?" Again he smiled. "You also hope you haven't made things worse."

Antiphon was ill with dread but stayed his course. "No, Lord Kerebos, you're wrong," he replied. "After pulling your victims off those crosses, I couldn't care less about maintaining your good graces."

Kerebos shook his head. "Lies. I see you priest. Do you think that I've killed thousands of men without understanding them?" He laughed. "I know them only too well. That's *why* I kill them."

Antiphon answered with a forlorn stare.

Kerebos smirked. "New tactic, or have I cowed you? Do you know how many men, *and priests*, have given me that very same look before they died?"

"I can only guess," Antiphon said.

"I can't even do that."

Kerebos stood and walked behind his bed. He swept a woolen sack from a shelf and upended Antiphon's belongings onto the floor. He picked up and thumbed through a book.

"In *Chaconne*, no less," he said.

"I didn't know you could read."

"Magos taught me." Kerebos hefted the tome and read. "'He shall be known to the Order at the end of days. A soldier of hell, a break-er of God's laws and a patricidant unrepentant...'" He turned to another dogeared page. "'God, in his infinite mercy, shall give the clearest of signs...when the guardian of the gates of hell abandons his own cause, look to your soul.'"

Kerebos gazed at the *Aharoni*. "Shall I go on?" he asked.

"It's easier to read than comprehend," Antiphon said.

Kerebos tossed the book at him. "Oh I understand, all right!"

"What is your understanding?"

"I see a ploy to prevent my destiny," Kerebos replied.

"What destiny?"

"It's obvious," Kerebos continued. "The world knows I shall be its master and it is afraid. Somehow your holy men have learned enough about me to concoct this." He kicked another book into a fireplace, where it immediately ignited.

"That book is thousands of years old and exists in every nation," Antiphon reasoned. "How would we have planted it just for you?"

Kerebos ignored the remark. "Your plot fails," he said, watching the flames. "I'll do what I must."

Antiphon was impressed by the incorrect analysis. The *ikar* was definitely not stupid. *Would that I knew that ahead of time*, he thought ruefully.

"Why would we hope that you would believe us?" Antiphon asked. "Even if you did, why should we think it would sway you?"

Kerebos looked upon the priest with pity. "What other choice do you have?"

Antiphon racked his brains. "Kerebos *Ikar*," he started at last, "you deceive yourself if you think you can subdue the entire planet. Your legion is impressive, certainly, but what is that compared to God?"

"*Legions*, with an 's'," Kerebos corrected. "I'm creating more. And where was your God when I nailed that little girl's head to the floor? Same place he always is: Nowhere."

"Good question," Antiphon sighed. "Nonetheless, you won't prevail. You've no real power base, and with the world aligning against you, cannot possibly win."

"I have faith."

"But all Pangaea?" Antiphon countered. "It can't be done."

Kerebos shook his head. "You're wrong. One of mine is worth a hundred of theirs, and the kings will fall piecemeal because they will not stand together." He stared at Antiphon. "Division is the natural state among monarchs."

Antiphon remembered something Dokein had told him; he wished he had paid closer attention. "Have you seen an *Aharoni* longbow?" he inquired. "The *Chaconni* king is hiring my people to instruct his soldiers in its use."

Kerebos looked amused. "I need no lessons in warfare from you, fool."

"The longbow can skewer an armored man at five hundred paces."

"I know, that's why I'm going to have them, too." Kerebos laughed. "Really, your masters should have sent someone smarter, or are you their best?"

The ironic remark caught Antiphon off guard. "I'm certainly not the best," he allowed. "Just expendable."

"That's good." Kerebos picked up his sword, saying: "Cheer up little man! At least you won't live to see me murder your loved ones!"

Antiphon desperately tried to redirect the conversation. "'Murder' implies a moral standard," he said. "Do you accept God's law?"

"There is no God, there is no law," Kerebos replied, annoyed. "Why try that weak tack on me? Shall I believe now what I've never believed because some skinny priest weaves a web of words?"

He's hooked! Antiphon thought. *Oh, if only I don't ruin it!* "You've always known right and wrong," he said smoothly. "Your conscience is God's law etched on your mind."

Kerebos waved off the comment. "My conscience is dead."

Antiphon fashioned his response for maximum effect. "Then why do the flames still chase you, and how would I know if my God were false?" he asked.

That one stuck. Kerebos swallowed a riposte.

"Killing a loved one is a terrible thing," Antiphon said gently. "Set down the burden."

A silent moment crept by.

"I loved my father," Kerebos murmured. "That's my conscience."

Antiphon felt a twinge of pity, even for Kerebos. Then he remembered the *Stalenzka*. "Then ask His forgiveness!" he roared. "And forgive yourself! Stop punishing the world!"

Kerebos rocked on his heels. "There is nothing..."

"Ask Him!"

"Ahhh!" Kerebos screamed and covered his eyes. He pounded his breast, shrieking: "Why, why, why!" He rushed suddenly forward, grabbed Antiphon's robe, and hoisted the priest into the air. "Do you think I don't know what I've done?" he demanded, shaking Antiphon. "Do you think you can come to me, now, and fill the void? Where were you when I needed you? And if you people knew for a thousand years, why did you wait?"

Antiphon saw madness in the *ikar's* eyes and once again gave himself up for dead. Again he was premature. Kerebos unexpectedly dropped him and stumbled back to the table. He slid into his chair.

"Your God won't even protect you," he sighed. "Why would he ever shield me?"

"He—"

"Magos!" Kerebos shouted.

"Wait!" Antiphon cried.

Magos appeared. "Yes, lord?"

"Get the priest his own quarters."

"In the dungeon, lord?"

"No, up here."

"As you wish, lord," Magos replied.

Kerebos stared through Antiphon. "You had your chance," he muttered. "Now it is *I* who shall convert *you*."

*   *   *

Kerebos whistled for the soaring hawk, which immediately repaired course for his outstretched wrist. He carried the bird to the edge of the castle roof and gazed out between two sawtoothed crenelations. He looked down into the grassy bailey and beyond to the distant curtain wall.

A *cohar* of Syranos' men herded some new slaves through the castle gates. Some of the prisoners wept openly as the doors boomed shut behind them, but the *landesknectos* only laughed.

We're all prisoners, Kerebos wanted to scream at them.

"My lord," Antiphon called and approached from behind. He was dressed in black, Kerebos' orders, and walked as though beneath a great weight.

The *ikar* greeted him with a smile. "Little man! I want to show you my favorite hawk. This is Iaga." Kerebos displayed the preening animal.

"I love birds," Antiphon said. "Except vultures."

Kerebos stroked the Iaga's neck. "Me, too."

"Your men still ignore me after these weeks," Antiphon declared. "Why?"

Kerebos chuckled. "I've commanded them to avoid you. I won't have you filling their tiny minds with sedition. That's exactly what you would do, eh, you little bastard?"

Antiphon looked down at the new slaves. "I haven't had much luck with you," he replied.

Kerebos glowered. "You're not likely to, either."

Antiphon sensed that something nasty was about to happen; Kerebos was steeling himself to do something awful. "Another lesson, *ikar?*" he asked.

Kerebos nodded.

Antiphon heard a scream down in the bailey. He looked to see *landesknectos* tying someone to a stake. The soldiers tore the hairshirt from a captive.

"Watch," Kerebos told the priest, then to Iaga, "Kill!" The bird took flight and swooped down onto the bound slave.

"Please, *ikar*, no," Antiphon said, but knew it was already too late.

The victim screamed as Iaga buried her talons into his face and thrashed wildly in an attempt to dislodge her, but to no avail. Blood flowed.

Antiphon placed a hand over his mouth and turned away but Kerebos pulled him back. "See how she goes after the eyes!" the *ikar* said proudly. "Do you know how long it took me to teach her that?"

During his time with Kerebos, Antiphon had grown accustomed to gruesome sights. He had been forced to watch the dismembering of slaves and had seen women beaten to death with the bodies of their children. He had even seen the *Elhar* Satyrnos pleasuring himself with corpses. And always he wondered where God was.

The priest's throat tightened and he felt hot tears. *Why have you abandoned me?* he thought. The slave eventually stopped struggling, but the hawk persisted.

"She'll hold on until sure the prey is dead," Kerebos said. "Just like me."

Antiphon thrust off the *ikar's* hand; he had learned when it was safe to do such things. "I pity you if you take pride in this," he growled with contempt.

Kerebos grin was sincere. "Anything worth doing, is worth doing right." He whistled for Iaga, who reluctantly returned to his arm. He tried stroking the bird's bloodstained beak but she pecked at his gloved finger.

Antiphon was struck by the likeness of hawk and master. Both were handsome, intimidating and vicious. Antiphon studied Kerebos' profile, and wondered: *But who holds your tethers?*

Kerebos walked a short distance and struck the small gong which hung from Iaga's perch. Magos rose from unseen steps.

"Bring my tidbit," Kerebos told the chamberlain.

Magos disappeared back down the steps. Kerebos tied Iaga to the crossbar.

Down on the grass the First and Second *Elhari* were assembling for evening drills. Antiphon watched as men checked their armor and padded their shields. The legionaries taunted and joked with each other and behaved most commonly. Antiphon wondered how they could be so banal one moment and so bloodthirsty the next.

When does their sanity cease and their fanaticism begin? he asked himself. He noticed Kerebos eyeing him.

"What are you thinking?" The *ikar* asked.

Antiphon cleared his throat. "I was wondering how your men broke the monotony of these evening drills?"

Kerebos shrugged. "With morning drills."

Antiphon shook his head.

Kerebos embarked into a short account about how he had once lost a wager to two men and paid his debt by wearing their armor and drilling in their places.

"Back to back to back exercises," he went on. "I was young but even boys can't fight all day. I was so sloppy by the end of it that Lasctakos punished me by sending me to the river for a pail of water. And I RAN, I assure you. Night was coming down and the bull sharks were emerging from the river."

Antiphon once again found himself engaged by the *ikar*. "He didn't punish you for deceiving him?"

"Punish me? He would have killed me if I revealed myself. And he would've been right; we can't have men skipping drills."

"I suppose you slept well that night."

Kerebos laughed. "Actually, no. When I got back with my bucket of water, Lasctakos said I'd run too slowly and gave me the first three watches. I don't need to tell you what happens if you're caught sleeping at the gate. Anyway," he concluded, "I never again played cards."

Antiphon gazed at Kerebos. It was moments like these he had learned to dread most. *Just when I relax the slightest bit, he does some-*

thing terrible, he thought. *It must be on purpose.*

"You might have made a fine *landesknecta* had you been tall enough," Kerebos said. "You've tenacity."

Antiphon started to voice a vociferous denial, but caught himself. Was that meant as a compliment? "I don't think so, *ikar*," he replied. "I've no belly for violence."

"Sure you do, we all do. Did you enjoy sex your first time?"

Antiphon was taken aback. He recalled his first experience. "It wasn't what I had hoped," he admitted. "But we were just wed."

Kerebos got a faraway look in his eyes. "My father found me choking her in the barn," he said wistfully. "I swear I was not forcing her, she said she liked it that way." He sighed then continued, "I was seeing red, and was out of my senses when he grabbed me. He shouldn't have done that."

Antiphon could only stare.

Moisture glistened in the *ikar's* eye. "How would you heal me, priest?" he demanded, then instantly turned away.

Antiphon caught his sleeve. "You're sorry, aren't you?" he asked anxiously. "Repent!"

At that moment Magos and two *landesknectos* brought a young girl onto the loft. Kerebos hurriedly wiped his eyes as they approached.

"I guess I'm not sorry enough," he said and conferred the tiniest smile. "It's theological tutoring time."

Antiphon felt the moment slip away and his disappointment, so close upon the heels of a chance unexpected, drained him of any desire to press forward. Kerebos walked toward the *landesknectos*, gaining composure with each step. By the time he reached Magos he was again whole.

But Antiphon could still see the cracks. Indeed, he had never seen a man so shattered. How had Kerebos kept himself whole all these years?

Kerebos had the lass, a little blond, bound to the steel rings which stuck from the basalt. Dark stains beneath the bands suggested frequent use.

"Oh, you will hate me, priest," the *ikar* lamented and drew Mistaaka. "That I promise you."

65

Kerebos dangled Mistaaka over the whimpering girl's blue eyes. He grinned at Antiphon and asked, "Do you think I could chop her in half?"

Antiphon did not answer.

Kerebos beamed at the child. "She's so scared she couldn't even run, bless her!" he said. "She'd do anything I asked, and still I'll kill her. Where's the justice in that?"

Antiphon could not look. *God stop him!*

"Do you have any of these at home?" Kerebos asked and prodded the child. "Answer me."

Antiphon shivered. "One son."

"How old?"

"Twelve."

"Perhaps someday I'll make his aquaintance?" Kerebos replied. He laid Mistaaka across the girl's heaving chest, saying, "Hold that, lovely." He turned to Antiphon. "I barely remember twelve. Can you?"

The priest nodded though he did not take his eyes from the girl, whose woeful expression wounded his heart. *Yes, where is justice?* he wondered.

"Guess I'm farther removed from innocence," Kerebos said with a laugh. He turned to the chamberlain, who looked stoic. "Magos, you and the lads go below. I don't want the priest to be able to comfort himself by saying there was nothing to be done against so many of us."

Magos and the swordsmen departed.

Antiphon's knees were so weak he doubted he could move, but he contemplated a move for Mistaaka. He glanced at the sword.

"Don't even try it," Kerebos chuckled. "I'll break your back over my knee, then hers."

Antiphon licked his lips in painful indecision. He gazed at Kerebos' thick limbs; the *ikar* could certainly fulfill the promise.

"Where was I?" Kerebos said. "Oh, yes, twelve. Your son, is he a bright lad?"

Antiphon thought of Yeshua but Kerebos' presence allowed no pleasure. "Yes."

"Did you ever wonder why a child's mind is inferior to an adult's?" Kerebos asked. "I'm not talking about experience, either, but intentional talent only." His brow furrowed. "I suppose that may be tied to experience."

Antiphon was again impressed by the *ikar's* erudition, and his expression communicated the fact.

"I read a lot," Kerebos explained. "Not all *landesknectos* are fools. Only those who follow me."

"I believe you." Antiphon said.

"A nasty little barb!" Kerebos replied. "But back to the present question. I'd say the answer lies in the fact that the mind and body are one. As one grows, so does the other. When one fades, the other follows."

There were many ways for Antiphon to attack the comment, but he wanted Kerebos to talk. Maybe he would forget the girl. "I'm familiar with Desian Uniformity."

"As well you should be. You're living through its cycle."

"How so?"

"When you are old and decrepit, won't your capacities desert you?" the *landesknecta* asked.

"Yes," Antiphon allowed, "but only because I am old and decrepit."

"I know what you'll say next," Kerebos ventured. "You're going to propose that the soul's departure causes the body to fall apart, right?"

"Something like that, though more complicated."

"No doubt," Kerebos replied, smirking. "You holy men have had thousands of years to chop the problems. Why is it, though, that they're still not sure of anything?"

"There is much of which we're certain," Antiphon insisted, pleased that Kerebos had ignored the child for some time.

"For instance?"

Antiphon gave the *ikar* a cold stare. "That evil exists."

Kerebos looked thoughtful. He worked his gloved fingers as though he missed something then reclaimed his sword. "I agree," he said. "There's so much evil, in fact, that if your God lives, he himself must be wicked. 'Maltheism' I think they call it."

Antiphon snorted. "One so well read must know of original sin."

"I'm familiar with the concept, I just don't believe it." Kerebos grinned wickedly. "Though I myself have helped many men lose grace."

"You beget nothing," Antiphon answered. "All you do is release potential." *I've got to get him away from her*, he thought. "Can't we argue this over a bottle?"

Kerebos' smile broadened. "We could, but I can lay the question to rest right here and now." He turned to the girl.

"No!" Antiphon cried and took a step. Mistaaka was instantly in his face.

"Back!" Kerebos barked. "Or by Desia I'll take a month to kill her!"

Antiphon withdrew. Kerebos placed a foot on either side of the child's narrow chest. "Really now," he said without taking his eyes from the girl. "You must admit that when it comes right to it, faith is the only thing religion has to go on."

"Not at all, reason is faith's handmaiden."

"We'll get to that later," Kerebos said. "For now, consider my proposition. Even with all your theologians and ceremonies—I assume you have them—and with all your books, the cornerstone must be faith."

"It is."

"If so," Kerebos plowed on, "you must admit that there isn't any substantial proof with which to proceed. Belief for belief's sake."

"That's not a fair interpretation," Antiphon complained.

"Open your mouth, kitten," Kerebos told the girl, then slid the black sword in. He looked at Antiphon. "Admit it," he said.

God stop him, Antiphon prayed.

Kerebos wiggled the blade and the child gagged and coughed. "Admit it!"

"Yes, yes!" Antiphon cried.

"Now we're progressing. Don't you agree?"

Antiphon nodded mechanically.

"But where does unsupported belief get you?" Kerebos asked as he

68

drew the sword from the girls mouth. "It seems a waste since 'the rain falls on evildoers and the righteous alike.'"

"As it must. God cannot interfere with free will." Antiphon sounded perfunctory even to himself.

"God does not interfere," Kerebos stated slowly, "because he does not exist."

Antiphon was numb. He felt battered mentally, emotionally and physically. He felt ashamed as well, fully aware that he was not giving a good account of the Word. Dokein had been foolish to send him here...

The girl yelped when Kerebos accidently stepped on her arm.

Save us! Antiphon thought.

Kerebos raised his sword above his head, saying: "I'm the highest power you'll see, priest."

"Please, *ikar!*" Antiphon begged.

"Where is God now?" Kerebos scowled. "Make Him stop me! Have Him save this girl!"

Antiphon was beside himself and raked his cheeks with his fingernails. The girl loosed a thin shriek.

"Denounce your faith and I'll spare her!" Kerebos thundered.

Antiphon's mouth moved soundlessly. Finally he managed to sputter: "I, I can't."

Kerebos' dark eyes blazed. "I can!" he replied, and clove the girl's head almost in half; blood squirted into the air. He stepped away from the small, quivering corpse.

Antiphon fell onto his knees. The world spun around him.

The *ikar* ran to the gong, struck it, and roared: "Magos, bring another one!"

Landesknectos immediately dragged a screaming boy onto the roof.

"Tie him on top of her," Kerebos panted. They did and he straddled the boy, who whined as the bloody Mistaaka was lifted above him.

"Denounce your faith!" Kerebos ordered the priest.

Antiphon felt trapped in a nightmare. His entire body seemed nauseous. "I can't," he whispered, unheard.

Kerebos made as though to slash the boy and looked at the priest.

Antiphon lifted a trembling hand. "All right, I renounce my faith." *God, Forgive me!* his tortured mind begged. *It's for the boy!*

Kerebos' face cracked into a mad grin. "I knew you'd agree."

Antiphon fell onto his back, utterly spent. He shook his head and tried to console himself.

"Now that wasn't so bad, was it?" Kerebos asked and sheathed his sword. "One little lie for a child's life? Your God'll forgive you," he laughed. "Don't worry, though, eventually you'll mean those words."

Magos freed the hysterical boy and carried him from the roof.

"You can go to your room now, Antiphon," Kerebos said gently. "Today's lesson is over."

In the end, however, the *Aharoni* had to be carried.

That night, Kerebos decided to risk a few chunks of the drug, *heretos*. *Because I need it,* he thought, slipping the sticky clay under his tongue. His senses dulled quickly. He sprawled out on his bed and stared at the stone ceiling, which seemed to swirl above him.

As Kerebos sorted through the day's events, he recalled the slave girl's wide eyes and the horror therein.

*Pools of blue on blue on blue…*he thought.

A knock on the door.

"What?" he demanded.

Magos peeked in, saying: "My lord, I've cleaned and oiled your armor. May I take your sword, now?"

"No," Kerebos grunted. "I'm not going to be alone tonight."

Magos departed and Kerebos stared down the length of the blade. The girl's unspoiled visage appeared above him and he closed his eyes. It did not help; he could still see her. Again he hoped the *Aharoni* were correct about eternal damnation. He tossed another piece of *heretos* into his mouth and chewed until it stuck to his molars.

"Hell's too good for me," he muttered.

Some time later he rose and made his way across the cold floor, Mistaaka in hand. Magos was in the antechamber perusing the *Tantorri* crop tally.

"Go to bed," Kerebos said, grabbed the chamberlain's torch, and went down the steps.

Coming to the bottom, he pushed a saluting legionary aside and marched from the *ikar's* wing, across a huge atrium and down six flights of stairs. Passing through a chilly wine cellar, he came to a webbed-over door, unbolted it and descended into the clammy catacombs.

A carpet of dust covered the clay steps. The torch crackled as it singed cobwebs. At the bottom of the steps a wooden sign read: "Only the *ikar* may enter this chamber where his fathers sleep."

Kerebos peered across the extensive graveyard. The torch illuminated only the first few sepulchers, but he knew that hundreds lay hidden in the shadows. He approached the sarcophagi. Each bore the likeness of the man buried within. He stopped to pay silent homage to his favorites.

There was of course, Desia, the first in line. And there was Parikles II, the first to sack Korenthis. Kerebos bowed to Titos, who had ruled but one day before falling in battle; the story had always struck his fancy.

Kerebos found Lasctakos' grave. The carving was a superb likeness, right down to the wounds suffered on that fateful day long ago. Kerebos felt melancholy. Even now it pained him to think of Lasctakos.

"Where are you now?" he asked the graven face, which frowned in the torchlight. He sat on the tomb and looked around. Demonic caryatids supported the ceiling with clawed palms. Granite megaliths, engraved with the names of distinguished *elhari*, stood proudly beside the pillars. Kerebos remembered a time when nothing had seemed as important as getting his name on one of the stones.

"But where are you now?" he shouted. The question echoed.

Kerebos, a voice whispered. A hot breath blew through the chamber.

Kerebos dropped the torch and jumped to his feet, gripping Mistaaka with both hands. "What?" he yelled.

Suddenly a plume of white flames exploded from Desia's tomb and swept towards him. Kerebos dived for cover as fire roared overhead. He cowered beside Lasctakos' tomb. Frantic shadows told him the fire was working its way around the room.

Then complete darkness. Even the torch had gone out.

Kerebos lay still in his terror, silently swearing off *heretos*. Moments passed. He waited so long for something else to happen that he was able to convince himself that the drug alone had tricked him. Still trembling, he gained his feet and fumbled in what he hoped to be the right direction. He felt his way by running his hands

71

over the tombs, which were icy to the touch.

Then the graves began to slide open.

The sound of stone on stone was so loud Kerebos could not even hear himself scream. Stone lids fell with a deafening thud, shaking the ground. Green figures began to rise from the graves. Kerebos threw himself prone as spectres floated by and collected *en masse* on the ceiling. The forms began to stir from their long sleep, when a sudden gust whisked them from the catacombs.

Kerebos covered his eyes. "Not real, not real!" he cried.

Kerebos, the voice repeated. *I called you.*

The *ikar* wanted to slay himself, but his body would not obey. Against his will, he stood. At the far end of the chamber sat the translucent form of Desia. A nacreous light played about the Great *Ikar,* who beckoned to his heir.

Terrified though he was, Kerebos could not refuse. Desia smiled and raised a hand to stop Kerebos, who was now at arm's length.

"*He* came and harrowed me," Desia said.

There was a blinding flash and when Kerebos could see, he was alone. The ignited torch was again in his hand and as he looked over the *ikari,* he saw the graves were undisturbed.

Kerebos bolted up the stairs.

*   *   *

In his own tiny room, Antiphon heated water and scoured himself clean, then prayed until dawn. Kneeling beside his pallet, he recited his priestly vows, begged for forgiveness, and humbly requested a chance to redeem himself. But even after hours of vigil, he still felt covered with slime. He had failed God.

The legionaries were already drilling when Antiphon finally sagged onto the straw mattress, but sleep eluded him. Eventually he was forced to admit that Kerebos had injured his faith. In fact, it seemed the *ikar* had exposed those precise doubts Antiphon had always tried to suppress.

He closed his eyes and resumed his orisons. *Lord, strengthen me,* he begged. *I am perishing and need a sign.*

But God was silent.

 riskeles fidgeted with his swordhilt, avoiding Kerebos' darkening gaze. "So you see, my lord," he told the *ikar*, "when the recruiters arrived, all they found were dead lads. *Aharoni* arrows riddling the lot of them."

Kerebos drummed his fingers on the desk. "And our men?"

"Two emissaries were beheaded," Triskeles replied. "With their own weapons, by the look of it."

Kerebos shook his head in disbelief. It had been a bad day. *First Erebas' betrayal, now this*, he thought gloomily. He felt a growing weight across his shoulders. "What about *Boru?*" he grumbled. "Your people have always replenished the legion."

Triskeles seemed distraught. "It looks bad. I think they're already on Korenthis' payroll." He grimaced at the proposition; his people were ancient enemies of the *Chaconni*. "Kyonig Tryggva kusse arst Kakkoni, nin!" he cursed in his native tongue.

Kerebos could not translate, but suspected he would agree. "This is bad, Triskeles," he said. "Aren't we getting any new blood?"

The *Boru* frowned. "Satyrnos has secured a number of *Tothmecs* and *Razkuli*, though most of the *Tothmecs* look too short. Anyway, I'm leery of admitting too many of either breed."

"Why? Few tribes are as fierce as those from the steppe. Desia, is there no one you like?"

Triskeles muttered something about reliability.

"What? Speak up!"

"They are dogs who run wherever the crumbs fall," the *elhar* said. "They are also uncouth and stupid folk. I don't like desert people. Besides, we'll have to supply them with armor."

The last comment had weight, considering the recent elimination of the *Stalenzka*. "You're right about the armor," Kerebos admitted. *The flame god wars against me*, he told himself. *Ever since that night in the catacombs, everything I try brings new frustrations. I should kill the priest...*

Kerebos could not pinpoint when he began to suspect the genuiness of Antiphon's god, but the suspicion had steadily grown on his mind. The realization only solidified his resolve, though. Now he could personify the cosmos, and hate it all the more. He eyed Triskeles, who looked unusually subdued.

The God must be evil, to create such men, Kerebos concluded.

Triskeles broke the silence. "This abuse from the *Chaconni* cannot be borne, my lord. Let us march on Korenthis."

Kerebos longed to sack the huge, rich capital, but knew he lacked the troops, unless he first destroyed Pontis' army in the field. Once taken and populated by his men, the innermost ring of the city might be made impregnable. It was tempting, but not yet possible.

"We could enter through the sewers and river," Triskeles prodded. "The Old Kingdom has long been fat and their sentries lazy."

"No," Kerebos said at last. "Blood will flow in due time, but we've yet too few swords to take those walls. Anyway, their scouts will spy us long before we reach Korenthis, and the city will bottle up."

Triskeles took a deep breath. "I hear you, lord," he replied. "Yet may the holocaust be swift in coming."

Kerebos smiled, thinking: *It will, idiot, and your blood will also be required.* "Triskeles, if this recruiting dearth persists we might need to conscript," he said.

The *elhar's* eyes widened. "*Ikar*, no man has ever worn the black who hasn't begged for the privilege," he said. "We should not change that. We can't."

"I'm not going to make them brothers, dolt," Kerebos replied. "They would be squires, runners and such. Maybe archers and horsemen, too. Just think how many men could be freed for action."

Triskeles was obviously unconvinced. "How can we trust such men?"

"Victory breeds trust. Besides, we'd take hostages."

Triskeles stood mute.

"Keep up your morale, for we shall win," Kerebos said. "What I must do for victory, though, I will. If I have to bend a few Scriptus edicts or break a few necks, it shall be. If I must cheat Desia to kill his enemies, so be it."

"I understand," Triskeles monotoned.

"Look at me," Kerebos ordered. "My sub-*ikar* must understand these things."

A smile slowly brightened Triskeles' skull-like face. "Two legions, my lord?"

Kerebos smiled in return. "Haven't I said so? Now bring in that traitor, Erebas."

Erebas' unabashed sedition disturbed Kerebos, who fought to control his emotions. *How dare he preach to me about the Aharoni God!* he thought.

"Erebas," Kerebos said, "you took an oath to me and I will not be cheated, your conscience or no."

The *elhar*, arms tied to the spear across his massive shoulders, did not shy from his commander's gaze. "I understand that, my lord," he said. "Still, I'm done bearing arms for the brotherhood."

"Then I'll chop off your arms," Kerebos threatened. Triskeles moved behind Erebas.

Erebas shrugged best as he could. "You know that won't cow me."

That I do, Kerebos thought, depressed. *Damned boy, you were one of my favorites.*

Though Kerebos had long suspected the black warrior's desire for the *ikar's* ring, and testimony from subordinates affirmed this, he could not help liking Erebas. He was everything Kerebos respected—clever, ruthless and ambitious. Erebas was a first rate legionary.

Now he's a convert to the White Flame, Kerebos thought. *The legion's being chewed away by a cancer and it must stop!*

Kerebos looked at Erebas' empty sheath. "Again you've lost that sword, first to Kyros, now to me."

"You would've killed me this Winnowing Day, anyhow," Erebas admitted.

Kerebos drew Mistaaka. "Give us a moment, three-legs," he told the *Boru*. Triskeles left.

Kerebos approached Erebas, who tensed. For the first time Kerebos noticed something new in the *elhar's* eyes. Humility. He did not wear it well.

75

"Why have you betrayed me, dark one?" Kerebos implored. "I had such plans for you."

Erebas turned away. "I'm sorry, my lord," he said softly.

"Why?"

"I love the legion," Erebas replied. "But I've been called to a higher purpose."

"What purpose demands you die when there are so many wars left to fight?"

Erebas shook his head. "I'm not sure. All I know is once I stumbled in darkness, and now I can see."

Kerebos looked about then leaned closer. "Did you dream of fire?"

Erebas looked surprised. "How did you know?"

"I've dreamed the same thing."

An expression of warmth crossed Erebas' face. "You must surrender to the flames, Kerebos," he confided. "I've been scaled and gutted," he slowed and groped for the adequate words, "but I'm clean, now."

Kerebos snorted. "Clean, is it? Have you forgotten your deeds, rapist? The children's skulls you've busted open?"

Erebas hung his head.

"You may yet be scaled and gutted," Kerebos chuckled cruelly and pressed Mistaaka against Erebas' chest. "Clean you will never be."

"Perhaps."

A suspicion crossed Kerebos' mind. "Have you spoken to *that priest?*" he demanded.

The *elhar* looked momentarily startled, but composed himself.

"You have!" Kerebos cried. "You're protecting him?"

Erebas shook his head. "I've not disobeyed you there," he answered. "But he once talked to me."

Kerebos lowered Mistaaka. "Go on."

"He was outside your room when I came to inform you about the *Boru* whores," Erebas explained. "I had blood on my brassard from drills and he asked if I were in pain."

"Is that it?" Kerebos sneered. "Miraculous."

"He said he'd pray for my quick recovery," Erebas ended.

"So, that's all it took? Did the wound heal any faster than normal?"

"I don't think so," Erebas confessed. "But though I would have killed him for sheer spite, he lamented my discomfort. I've not been able to forget that. Why would he do that?" he ended hollowly.

Kerebos had heard enough. "What manner of death frightens you most?" he asked.

The *elhar* pondered the question. "Drowning, I suppose. The seas are rough near my homeland, and the thought of dying in water has always bothered me."

"Really?" Kerebos said. "Triskeles! Syranos!"

The *elhari* entered. "My lord?" Triskeles replied.

"Have this man chained and cast into the river."

Triskeles' jeered. "At once, my lord!" he said and called for the guards. Erebas looked over his shoulder as they muscled him from the room and said: "It's just for me to die like this."

"Get him out of here!" Kerebos snarled.

Syranos slammed the door behind the captive. He looked confused by it all. "Shall I pour you a goblet, lord?"

Kerebos sank into his seat.

"Sire?"

"Have you a trustworthy *cohar* to take his place?" Kerebos asked.

"Mmmm, Phaedros, maybe. He's young, though," Syranos replied, forgetting his own youth.

"Send him here. Now."

Syranos saluted and left. Kerebos was alone.

What's happening and how can I right it? he wondered, though he already knew the answer. How could he expect his men to resist the nigglings of the soul if he did not set a sterling example? *The way I've been acting, it's small wonder they're losing faith.* Kerebos' mood soured further as he realized he had caused Erebas' defection. *I can no longer afford to be a hypocrite,* he thought. *Victory over Pangaea will only happen if I first defeat myself.*

It took a while, but Kerebos eventually concluded that he could purify the legion only by murdering his troublesome conscience. He would deny God access to his mind and would thus remove the corrosive presence from the brotherhood. Antiphon, the most visible proof of that corruption, must die.

Antiphon stood on the roof brooding his situation. Premonitions of doom had dogged him all day. *Time passes and I falter,* he thought.

Every day Kerebos slays more and more, and I'm guilty by association. Dokein's trust in me was vain.

For no apparent reason, he recalled a poem he had written shortly after becoming an acolyte.

Some there are, who are born to sprint
While others to pound the long trail—
I have not yet discerned
Which it is I do best
Still, I feel God's pleasure
When I choose to run.

Dokein had liked the words and had included them in a hymn. The memory warmed Antiphon a little. Dokein spoke in his head:

When the runner falls, does he lay on the path? Certainly not. He rises and finishes the race.

Antiphon looked down into the bailey at the gathered *landesknectos*. "I must finish my race," he said and smiled for the first time in days. *Do you come to revive me, Master?*

"Priest of the one true God," he said aloud, "tender of the White Flame, do what you have been called to do!" He completed the doxology with: "I hear and obey God's will."

Antiphon felt faith renewed like a fire in his belly, and wondered why it had returned, and where it had been. *So I am still alive*, he thought. "Where are you, Kerebos *Ikar*?" he called. "I'm ready for another bout."

And Kerebos came. He rose from the sunken steps with Mistaaka in hand, his face a mask of hatred. The gold and purple dusk receded behind him as he strode toward Antiphon with grim purpose. His lips were twisted as though closed over a bitter seed.

"So today's my last," the priest whispered, curiously relieved. *Goodbye for now, Yeshua, but don't cry, your father has made his peace.*

Kerebos towered over the *Aharoni*. "It's time to leave, holy man," he said. "Your witchcraft has poisoned me long enough."

"I didn't think I'd live this long," Antiphon confessed.

"You've already died," Kerebos retorted. "When I struck your faith, I dealt a mortal blow."

"You're almost right, but you weren't strong enough," Antiphon said, taunting the *ikar*. "Get it over with."

"Do you want to see it coming?" Kerebos asked. "Why don't you turn around?"

"I'm fine like this," Antiphon said and stood tall as he might.

Kerebos raised the sword. "Goodbye, little man."

"Farewell," Antiphon replied and looked heavenwards. "I forgive you."

The blow never fell. Eventually Antiphon risked a peek. Kerebos was still standing there, sword held high. His face betrayed both fear and doubt.

"How can you forgive me?" he demanded.

"Because you send me to a better place, and because you're no better than a fool." Understanding dawned on Antiphon. "You're going to let me live?"

Kerebos nodded slowly, as though even he was surprised. "Our games are over. Go protect your boy."

God of miracles! Antiphon thought. "I don't understand," he gasped, elated, confused and frightened. .

"Neither do I. Go now. Spread your death elsewhere." He pointed toward the castle gates. "If you're not through them by dark you'll never see the dawn."

"Kerebos—"

"Silence!" the *ikar* cried. "Or by that God you hold dear, you'll regret it. You and every slave I lay hands on!"

That said he struck the gong. Magos climbed onto the roof.

"Lord?"

Kerebos pointed at Antiphon. "Have him escorted past the river. Slay him if he speaks or tries to return."

"Yes, lord!" Magos nodded vigorously.

"But you must come with me and fulfill the Scriptures!" Antiphon insisted.

Kerebos' punch lifted Antiphon into the air then laid him senseless on the stone. Blood seeped from the priest's mouth and nose.

"Get rid of him!" Kerebos shouted, then stormed off. He hit the steps at a run.

Later Kerebos mulled the irony that the only man he had ever spared was one that neither asked for, nor wanted, his mercy.

Chapter 10

Kerebos was dismayed by the appallingly bloody Winnowing Day. Forty men, nearly a an entire *cohar*, had died. With recruits scarce, and war looming, he grieved to lose so many to the elevation process. The legion's chain of command had been badly damaged, too. Contrary to convention, many subordinates had ousted their commanders, weakening the officer corps. Kerebos blamed God.

Free will or not, He's trying to bleed me. He fears me, the *ikar* thought as he watched Triskeles lop off a *cohar*'s arm. The *cohar* fell to his knees, then onto his face.

Damn, another one, Kerebos mused. *Is there no way to halt this stupid tradition?* He studied the cheering legionaries. *Probably not. Perhaps Lasctakos was right—Winnowing Day prevents mutiny.*

A messenger handed him a scroll and said: "From Magos."

Kerebos read the report. Syranos, who had been injured by the last of his challengers, was expected to recover from a blow to the head. The surgeon suggested three days bed rest. Kerebos sighed relief. At least he had lost no *elhari*.

Triskeles chose some spectators to strip and dispose of his opponent. The legionaries lugged their senseless comrade toward the eager sharks that had gathered in the shallows of Cemetary River.

Triskeles doffed his helmet and wiped grimy sweat from his brow; he smiled at Kerebos. "I never expected that one to challenge me," he confided. "But I'm not displeased. He was a good fighter but a poor leader." The *Boru* glanced around. "I think that's my only victim for the day."

Kerebos frowned. "We lost too many men."

"Everyone's anxious to fight the new commanders," Triskeles pointed out. "Young Syranos was lucky to pull through."

"The recruits will just barely replenish us," Kerebos griped.

"*If* they survive the branding," Triskeles reminded him.

Kerebos nodded. He would probably lose a third of the inductees to the Scriptus; men often developed gangrene after the extensive burning. Those who survived, however, would forever wear Desia's commandments. "Start breaking them in," he ordered. "Your *elhar* shall take most of them."

Triskeles looked unhappy. "*Razkuli* desert rats," he muttered.

"Have the *elhari* join me for lunch," Kerebos said. "I'll dispatch my challengers this evening."

Triskeles saluted and called for a runner.

*   *   *

A few hours later the legion reassembled to watch the battle for the *ikar's* ring. A giant circle was formed in anticipation. Even the very wounded hobbled out from the hospital to witness the sacrament. A charge was in the air.

Men cheered as Kerebos swaggered onto the scene, blade in hand. He glared at the *landesknectos*, hoping to cow prospective aggressors. The applause grew progressively louder, but nobody stepped forward to face him.

Maybe I won't have to kill, he thought hopefully and silenced the legion with a raised hand. "Who would fight me?" he cried. "Who desires the *ikar's* ring? Let him step forth!" He turned in a circle, letting them all get a look at him. "Come forth and die."

Still nobody.

Good! Kerebos thought, sheathing his weapon.

"I challenge Kerebos *Ikar* for the ring!" a legionary shouted and leaped forward. Kerebos recognized the man, a *sestar* and a former bodyguard. The *sestar*, a barrel-chested *Chaconne*, approached and saluted. Kerebos scowled.

Triskeles cried: "Skewer the dolt, lord!"

Afraid you might lose your legion? Kerebos thought, grimly amused.

He studied the legionary, trying to recall having seen him fight. He had. The *sestar* was an excellent lefthanded swordsman.

"What's your name, boy?" Kerebos asked.

"Alpheios."

"*Chaconne?*"

"Yes, my lord. We're from the same town."

"Oh?" Kerebos asked. His had been a tiny farming hamlet in the poor province of Ios. It was entirely possible he had known Alpheios' family.

"I used to pretend I was you when I was a boy," Alpheios confessed; his expression suggested second thoughts.

He's terrified, Kerebos concluded. *Too bad I can't spare him. I need every man*. But to show weakness would only encourage others. The youth must be killed quickly and in impressive fashion.

Kerebos crossed his arms in disdain. "You should have stuck to fantasizing, boy. Start when ready."

Alpheios' eyes flashed murder. He drew his sword with astonishing speed. Kerebos, a man not easily impressed, was impressed. He made a show of fumbling for his hilt, before faking a slip and landing on one knee. Alpheios closed quickly, lowering a head shot.

Kerebos burst into action. He tackled Alpehios and threw him onto his back. As they tussled, Kerebos dealt Alpheios a powerful punch to the temple. Spiked knuckles screeched through helmet and skull; Alpheios went limp. Kerebos rolled the legionary onto his back, sat on his chest, and pounded his face with a dozen more blows. When Kerebos was finished, blood and flesh clung to his gauntlets. Kerebos stood, found Alpheios' sword, and pinned the *sestar* to the ground. The vanquished convulsed like a stuck insect.

Kerebos studied the mess that was Alpheios' face. "Leave him here for the sharks," he told his audience. The legion burst into applause. Kerebos soaked it all in, pleased by the embarrassingly easy victory. He thought, *That should prove the old man can still fight.*

"IKAR! IKAR! IKAR!" men cried.

Triskeles rushed up and clapped him on the shoulder. "Superb!" he cheered. "Maybe next year none will challenge you, hmm?"

Kerebos smiled. "Maybe next year there will be nobody?"

Triskeles looked puzzled as Kerebos waded into the heart of the host. "Brothers!" he bellowed. "The Winnowing is over—let us feast in honor of your new officers!"

Kerebos protested mildly as he was hoisted off the ground and carried into the castle. The *landesknectos* sang along the way.

That night the legion devoured a small herd of *Tantorri* cattle and a river of wine. Kerebos, whose usual diet consisted of fried grains, suffered indigestion so severe he could not sleep. He spent an uncomfortable evening looking out over the moonlit plain where stump-legged sharks battled over the remaining morsels of Winnowing Day. The sharks were the last thing on his mind, however.

Why in hell did I free that priest? he wondered time and again.

The next day Kerebos and Triskeles watched from the roof as rookie *landesknectos* repaired worn-out wains. Kerebos tried to tune out the droning *elhar*.

Such a bore, like all my men, he thought. *How I hate them all. Times like these, I almost miss the priest.*

Triskeles seemed oblivious and displayed a daunting ability to ramble endlessly about inane subjects. He concluded a monologue about feet.

"So you see, lord, it's almost impossible to travel any distance through the jungle without ruining your feet, you've got to keep them dry."

Kerebos, who felt bludgeoned, merely nodded.

A short silence.

"It's sometimes amusing, my lord," Triskeles started again. "Why, once a man begged me to kill him after the rot started on his toes."

"You don't say."

Triskeles embarked on a lengthy description, complete with dialogue, of how he had ended his comrade's discomfort. Several times he stopped in the middle of the story and started over.

All right you buggered God of Fire, Kerebos thought. *If you really exist then close this fool's mouth.*

Triskeles droned on.

I knew it.

"What's that?" Triskeles' asked, his tone suddenly sharp. He pointed toward the river. "Horsemen at the bridge!" he cried in disbelief.

The mist cleared from Kerebos' mind. He followed Triskeles' gaze. At least twenty riders were riding hard for the castle. The *Chaconni* king's standard, red lion on a gold field, snapped atop a cavalryman's lance. A great anger welled within the *ikar* as he stared at the flag. Never in his lifetime had the Old Kingdom sent soldiers over the river. Stunned guards shouted from the walls.

"Desia's blood!" Triskeles growled. "What do they here?"

Kerebos made his way down through the castle. Triskeles followed. Kerebos climbed the outerwall; legionaries swarmed around him.

The horsemen halted a stones' throw away. A tense moment passed. A moustached cavalier in red jupon approached the gate to within fifty feet. He lifted a glove hand.

"Hail Kerebos *Ikar!*" he cried in a loud voice. "I am Count Vasilex of Thibis! I bring greetings from his majesty, King Pontis Alexius Grasmilios III!"

Kerebos leaned dangerously over the wall and bawled: "How dare you ride in my lands, you perfumed fool!"

Vasilex looked indignant. "King Pontis informs you that this is no longer your land," he said. A collective gasp escaped the legionaries. "His gracious majesty allows your band one moon to vacate this territory which your predecessors stole from the crown during the years of its uncertainty. You may take your slaves, but must leave his castle, walls and livestock intact. So says your lord."

Kerebos' face darkened. "My lord? Fat Pontis gives *me* this command?"

The horsemen muttered behind Vasilex; one even drew his short sword. The nobleman's smile was insolent. "Leave or face the consequences," he charged. "Either way, your days have ended, auxiliary."

It was the *landesknectos'* turn to grumble. "Auxiliary" was clearly an insult. Even a thousand years had not clouded the fact that Desia had commanded a *Chaconni* auxiliary legion. Vasilex was implying that the *landesknectos* were faithless mercenaries, uncultured commoners, or both. The horsemen, tall on their chargers, looked smug and laughed among themselves.

Never had Kerebos endured such treatment. He trembled visibly. Triskeles grabbed a shoulder as though to prevent Kerebos from leaping down at Vasilex.

"Little man," Kerebos grated, "I know that your incestuous, sister-tupping king thinks he's grown strong. I know of the foolish treaties he has made with the *Boru* and the *Aharoni* and the other vermin he has seduced into his bed, and if you think that scares me, you've less sense than he. Our legion fought for this land and will never release it. Tell fat boy that he should stick to poisoning his relatives and fondling sheep because there's no victory for him here."

Now Vasilex's face grew livid. His eyes blazed as he leaned forward in the saddle. "Victory? Victory! You think you can hold back time you, you, mercenary!" he stammered. "Great God above! Too long has your parasitic 'brotherhood' tortured the world, but His justice reaches out to your wretched perch! You," he pointed at the *ikar*, "should have passed long ago, and it is testament to *landesknecta* unimagination that you've not planned for this day! You will not leave, you say? Then you will die! My lord will starve and sap you from your holes! Not one of you blackclad bastards shall be spared!"

As though on command Kerebos stopped shaking. He laid a calm hand on Mistaaka and smiled, thinking, *Nobles are so easy to goad.* "I cannot believe you are from impotent Pontis," he said. "You must be a renegade who wants this castle. Do you have the signet with you as proof? No." Kerebos shook his head. "Vasilex of Thibis? No, I can't say I've heard of you."

Vasilex tore a scroll from beneath his cape and held it aloft. "Here is the mark of his majesty!" he cried.

"Let me see it," Kerebos replied and started for the stairs. "Open the gates!" he roared, pushing men aside. "All of you stay put!"

Kerebos stalked onto the plain. Vasilex shook off a concerned companion and spurred his horse; he reined the roan to a halt and threw the scroll onto the grass before the *ikar*. "Here, if you can read, gain wisdom!" he said.

Kerebos did not slow for the parchment, but rushed the horseman. Too late Vasilex realized his error. Even as he tried to escape, Kerebos grabbed the reins, drew a dagger, and slit the horse's throat. The mount crashed to the ground as Vasilex jumped clear.

Before the startled cavalrymen could respond, Kerebos had thrown Vasilex over his shoulder and was stomping back toward the gates. The *landesknectos* howled and hooted. The *ikar* entered and the gates were slammed shut. Outside, a horse screamed as it was struck by a pilus.

Kerebos dumped his captive to earth. "Where's Satyrnos?" he cried above the commotion. The summoned *elhar* soon arrived.

"My lord?" he asked as Vasilex cringed in terror.

Kerebos placed a boot on the *Chaconne's* chest, saying, "Satyrnos, you and your friends take this lad and entertain him in your special way." He grinned evilly. "I know you'd prefer him dead, but you'll just have to settle for a man with a heartbeat."

Satyrnos licked his lips. "My lord, can I hurt him, just a little?" he asked as six smiling, eager legionaries crowded behind him.

"Of course, but leave him strength enough to ride side saddle." Kerebos gazed at Vasilex, who wiggled beneath his foot. "Tell Pontis this is my reply. I think he'll 'gain wisdom.'"

Vasilex screamed as Satyrnos' "friends" hoisted him into the air. "Make way!" the legionaries cried as the thrashing victim was rushed to the nearest barracks. Satyrnos ran beside Vasilex, shouting obscene promises.

Kerebos nearly laughed himself sick. "You!" he eventually called a guard on the wall. "Tell them their master will be with them by-and-by."

The legionary smiled and relayed the message.

Standing alone, Kerebos' thought of coming battle. *If the Aharoni God feeds on life, then I'll steal his food. Victory or defeat, many are going to die, and that pleases me mightily.*

The *ikar* hummed all the way to his bedchamber.

Chapter 11

ntiphon rapped briefly on the study door before peeking in. "Grand Master?" he called.

Dokein was dozing behind the desk, an open book before him. His face looked wan and gray, Antiphon thought. Older.

"Master?" Antiphon repeated, louder.

Dokein opened his eyes and dark circles appeared beneath them. He chuckled. "My dear boy. Or am I dreaming?"

Antiphon strode into the room, smiling from ear to ear despite his great fatigue. Dokein rose and embraced him with surprising strength.

"Ani!" he cried. "Ani, lad!"

Antiphon, his face still crusted from the road, held on like a lost boy who had found his father. Eventually Dokein stepped back and looked him over.

"It does my old heart good to see you," he said, then arched a bushy, white eyebrow. "Why wasn't I told of your return?"

"I've just arrived," Antiphon replied. "It took me some time to get through the gates."

Dokein looked apologetic. "All the new soldiers, right? I've hired a gaggle of them to keep the peace. Our population swells every day."

Antiphon eyed a wine decanter.

Dokein laughed. "Take all you want. Pour me some, too."

Antiphon quickly drained two draughts. Dokein had again seated himself and studied his visitor over the rim of a goblet. Antiphon turned to the old man, saying, "Thanks for watching Yeshua."

Dokein waved him to a chair. "Take a seat. Have you seen the lad?"

"Yes. I stopped by his room. He must have grown four inches," Antiphon said proudly. "He'll eclipse me before his next birthday."

Dokein's expression was inscrutable. "My daughter has also spent time with him," he said. "It's strange. I never knew her to like children."

Antiphon felt fulfilled. *It's good they get along*, he thought. Old dreams, long obscured by duty, nagged him. He hoped Selah would quickly accept his proposition of marriage. "Has she missed me?" he asked, stroking his mustache, which had grown unruly.

"Ani, I won't venture a guess as to what goes on in that head of hers. Men have called on her, though, and not all of them *Aharoni*. Shekkinah, the house-mother, has given me no end of grief about it, too."

Antiphon stiffened. "Called on her?" Then he thought of the last time he had seen Selah, how her eyes had shone after he kissed her. "No matter," he concluded confidently. "I'm home now."

"Of course, my son."

The Grand Master pulled the knotted cord which hung from the ceiling. Presently, a bleary-eyed acolyte in a short, blue robe bowed into the chamber.

"Grand Master?" the youth said.

"Get Master Antiphon something to eat, please."

The boy departed.

Dokein's dark eyes grew suddenly sharp. "Now, my son, we must discuss your journey," he said. "And Kerebos."

Antiphon's heart skipped a beat. He shook his head emphatically. "I failed, Master," he declared. "You shouldn't have placed such faith in me."

Dokein looked thoughtful. "Oh, why?"

Antiphon had trouble formulating an answer—he'd done so much wrong. Had he overestimated himself or underestimated his opponent? *Or was it my fragile faith?* he wondered.

"He bullied me from one end of the fort to the other," he conceded. "And when I laid a rare blow on him, he swiftly bounced back."

"That's very vague. Explain yourself."

"I struggled with the philosophy," Antiphon said. "It's hard to discuss Relativism and Natural Law with a sword at your throat...or at a little girl's."

88

The scribe returned with a plate of cold pork and some dark bread. He handed the food to Antiphon then hurried out.

"Ani," Dokein said, "I didn't expect you to manhandle Kerebos *Ikar*. If that's what I wanted, I would've gone."

"I did miserably," Antiphon insisted. "Worse than usual. And when I was finally ready for him, he dismissed me. Told his men to kill me if I returned."

Dokein shrugged. "Sometimes, we drop seeds and move on. I'm not unhappy with your performance. As I said before, I felt *you* were meant to go, no one else."

"You told me to bring him here."

"I never expected you to, however. Old, rotten trees snap in God's good time, as will Kerebos *Ikar*. But your breeze shook him a little."

Antiphon starved for an answer. "How so?"

"He didn't kill you, did he?"

"Obviously."

Dokein gave a toothy grin. "Then first blood is ours."

Antiphon pondered the words. Until now he had never really considered why Kerebos had released him. At first he had been too anxious to get away, then too discouraged over his failure. Kerebos had certainly not surrendered him out of kindness. Or had he?

Impossible, Antiphon thought.

Dokein stood and opened the stained glass doors into the courtyard. "You lit a candle under the giant's rump and have put him in motion," he said firmly. He whistled along with the birds that greeted the coming dawn.

"If that's the case, it was a tiny candle and he won't move far," Antiphon replied.

"Kerebos shall come to me, his *landesknectos* behind him," Dokein said quietly. "I have seen it."

Antiphon leaned back into the cushioned chair, the untouched meal on his knees. "How do you know?" The floor shook with a slight tremor and the birds scattered.

Dokein faced Antiphon. "My scouts report that his force set out five days ago," he said. "The Black Legion marches this way. God's will be done."

"How many *landesknectos* did you kill, father?" Yeshua demanded as they walked to the center of the domed conservatory. Antiphon found a soft patch of grass and sat. The boy plopped down beside him.

"I didn't kill anyone," Antiphon said. "That's not how men of God behave."

Yeshua raised a finger. "Yes they do! The men of Kwan Aharoni have always been valiant warriors, Juntha says!"

"He did, eh? Did the Savior ever kill anyone?"

"No," Yeshua admitted, somewhat deflated. "But Juntha says He whipped blasphemers who marketed in the temple."

I must have a talk with this Juntha, Antiphon decided. "The Savior said 'Be imitators of me,'" he said.

"So I may whip my enemies?"

Antiphon could not help but laugh. "Only if they're moneylenders in the temple," he replied.

Yeshua remained defiant. "Many priests have been warriors," he said.

Antiphon felt a twinge of pride at his son's tenacity. He touched Yeshua's nose with a forefinger. "When you are a priest, and the time has come, I'll tell you when to fight. Agreed?"

Yeshua's eyes narrowed as though he had been tricked, but was unsure how. "Okay," he said at last.

Antiphon rustled the boy's dark hair. "Let's walk over to the fountain."

As they approached the spring, which was circled by a low marble wall, Antiphon was appalled to see Montanus seated by the water. Hairs rose on Antiphon's neck.

Montanus, repulsive at any time, looked even uglier than usual. Large red veins shone on his bulbous nose, and acne peppered his cheeks and forehead. He smelled as though he had not bathed in a month.

Montanus' pock-marked face slid into an oily grin. "How was your trip among the heathens?" he asked. Even his voice was unpleasant, thin and shrill. "Why didn't they kill you?"

Antiphon put an arm across Yeshua's shoulder's.

"I'm sharing the day with my son," he said. "I'd thank you to leave us in peace."

"Oh, so it's back to the quiet life, is it?" Montanus sneered. "You go on a glory road while I do all of your work, and now you want a little family life, with Selah's juicy rear in your bed, no doubt!"

Antiphon flinched at Montanus' crudity. *So that's the problem?* he thought. "Montanus," he said through clenched teeth, "I'll thank you to hold your tongue while my son's around."

Montanus folded bony arms across his bird chest. The bubbling fountain was the only sound for many heartbeats. Yeshua squeezed his father's arm.

"Go ahead and whip him, dad," he whispered.

Montanus turned rheumy eyes on the lad, saying, "I've noticed that Selah has spent a lot of time with that young man of yours. What has our naughty lady been teaching him, I wonder?"

A snarl welled within Antiphon and became a roar as it burst past his lips. He sprang forward and thrust Montanus into the fountain. Montanus floundered clumsily as he tried to stand; scraggly bangs hung in his eyes.

"You bastard!" he cried. "Why didn't you die out there? Why'd you have to come back?"

"Not up for competition?" Antiphon yelled. "Take more baths and maybe a woman could stand you!"

Montanus stood in the shallow pool, sagging beneath his dirty robe. His stare held hatred and sorrow.

"She loved me until you returned," he wailed. "She now says she wants me no more."

"Did you really believe she could love you?" Antiphon asked, doubting the two had ever been alone, much less that they had been intimate. He grabbed Yeshua by the arm. "Let's go!"

The boy's face glowed. "You really sent him flying!"

"Ignore what I just did," Antiphon ordered. "I lost my temper."

"Wait till I tell Juntha!"

"'Shua," Antiphon said, "the day somebody insults your son and a woman you hold dear, I give you permission to push them into a fountain."

As they reached the garden door, Antiphon glanced at Montanus, whose arms hung limp by his side. Incredibly, the soaked priest was sobbing. *First hate, then tears*, Antiphon thought, perplexed. *How is that?* Then it dawned on him that he had seen Montanus' brand of madness elsewhere. *Kerebos also desires something he can't have,* he concluded.

Antiphon found the banquet a discomfiting affair. Dokein had surrendered his own seat to "our returned hero" and had made a speech lauding Antiphon's resourcefulness. The subsequent applause was genuine, but Antiphon felt he hardly deserved it. He ate quickly and excused himself at the earliest politic opportunity, and after putting Yeshua to sleep, sought out Selah.

As he walked through narrow, dusty streets toward the Gynaeceum, Antiphon pondered what Dokein had said at dinner. Unfortunately, Montanus had been close enough to hear every word.

"My dear boy," the Grand Master had confided. "I fear you two aren't meant for one another."

Antiphon stared at his plate.

"She's grown dangerously willful," Dokein continued. "Most of the women no longer talk to her, and what's worse, she doesn't mind."

"I'm not interested in other women," Antiphon said, and looked across the wooden table. "Besides, it's her difference I cherish."

"Ani," Dokein replied, "there is nothing I would deny you, but for your sake, find a different woman."

"You have already given me permission to court her," Antiphon replied. "Do you revoke that?"

"No."

"Why, then, do you seek to discourage me?"

Dokein was silent.

"Whom should I marry, then?" Antiphon pressed.

Dokein stared as though sizing him up. "Nobody," he replied, then more softly, "I was young once. I know how you feel."

"I am no longer very young, and I've been married before. I'll handle her."

Dokein made a "we'll see" face.

Antiphon turned into the gynaeceum's hedge-lined courtyard. A red lamp shone from Selah's window on the fourth floor. Stars burned in the heavens above, though clouds were moving in from the west.

Antiphon navigated the worn front steps and entered the building. The austere drawing room was empty but for a small girl lugging a large pot of water.

"Good evening, child," Antiphon said. "I'll strike a deal with you. If you tell Dokein's daughter I'm here, I'll carry that into the kitchen."

The girl smiled and set down the pot. "Certainly, father!" she chirped and darted for the steps.

Where do children get the energy? Antiphon wondered as he picked up the pot.

"Thank you, Shusaan," Selah told the girl. "Tell him I'll be right down."

Selah waited until the door was closed, then finished her wine. She sauntered over to the mirror for a quick inspection.

Pretty good, she thought, rubbing her hips and belly. Would Antiphon suspect that she had been pregnant? *Probably not*, she decided. If she could dupe Shekkinah, she could certainly fool Antiphon.

Selah applied some perfume, though it was not really necessary; she had been pretty much ready all night. *Thought he'd come by before now*, she thought and amused at what she was sure he considered self-control.

Selah had enjoyed many adventures while Antiphon was away and had drawn some conclusions. First, that men desired her enough to hand over whatever she wanted and second, that she enjoyed such control far more than anything else. The authority lasted longer than sex, and could be wielded outside the bedroom.

And Antiphon has a future in the Order, she told herself. *What's better than mastering a Master? Certainly it'd be more rewarding than soldiers and stable boys. Or Montanus.*

Selah knew in her heart that Antiphon would make Master before long. Her father would never risk the chance of dying before elevating him and, eventually, Antiphon stood a good chance at the pontiff's seat. He was generally respected, and many now considered themselves beholden to him because of the Kerebos mission. Besides, he was the sort the Council liked—bright and solid, but nothing special. In truth, Dokein had been the only great mind to hold the see in many generations.

Selah heard women whisper as they passed her door. *Of course all the gossip will have to stop*, she decided. *I musn't be a liability to him.*

With more than a little distaste, Selah realized she would have to play the perfect wife. At least until Antiphon became Grand Master.

And then I'll turn this village into a real city. My city, she mused. *It's all falling into place*, she thought. *Let other women be playthings all their lives! I'm going to climb and dear Ani shall be my ladder.*

Selah suddenly changed her mind about the makeup and towelled it off. She let her hair down, and slipped into something more modest.

Antiphon was waiting in the drawing room. He smiled when he saw her on the steps. Selah smiled, too.

"My dear, noble Ani," she said cheerfully and stopped on the bottom step. "I've been waiting all day."

Antiphon took her petite hand.

"Well, I've been waiting ever since your father sent me after Kerebos *Ikar*."

Selah touched his beard. "It's getting bushy," she said with a laugh. "I see a little gray."

"It's been a while."

Selah could not resist batting her lashes. "Now that you're finally here, what shall we do?"

"Anything you want," he promised.

Selah pecked his cheek and replied, "I knew you'd say that."

okein joined Antiphon on Kwan Aharon's ivyed inner wall. Together they surveyed the bustling marketplace. Fruit vendors loudly advertised their goods and haggled with customers over price. The noise, colors and stench from the bazaar gave Antiphon a headache. Even so, he would brave the crowds on Selah's behalf.

But what to buy now that she's abandoned her flashy wardrobe? he wondered.

Antiphon thanked God that he and Selah were getting along so well. Even Dokein was surprised by his daughter's newfound humility.

The Grand Master cleared his throat of dust and said: "Iram will be hard to replace. As though I don't have enough problems."

Antiphon nodded. Iram, head of the Order's intelligence branch, and Kwan Aharon's foremost historian, had died of natural causes earlier in the week. The death had caught everyone off guard; Iram had lived so long it simply seemed impossible to not have him around.

"Besides," Dokein concluded, "I liked having at least one peer older than me."

"Shall you miss him more as professor or intelligence officer?"

"I'll miss him most as a friend, but also as a teacher. Think of it! He taught *me* when I was a boy!" Dokein stroked his beard in contemplation. "Besides, we hardly need scouts anymore, the way news pours in. Events are almost following the scriptures to the word."

Antiphon frowned. He was tired of talking about Kerebos. "Why didn't you tell me he was destined for Kwan Aharon?" he asked. "I almost got killed a hundred times for nothing."

"How would I make you go get him if you knew he was coming here?" Dokein replied. "And would he have come here without our prodding? I don't know. I do know, however, that I dreamed I should send you, so you went."

"*And in the last days, your sons and daughters shall prophesy,*" Antiphon pondered the Savior's words. He turned toward the desert. "When will he get here?"

Dokein also glanced beyond the walls. "Soon," he said. "Unfortunately my visions aren't specific."

Antiphon shuddered though the air was tepid and uncommonly moist. "I don't want to see him again."

"Why not?" Dokein asked, surprised. "He brings the end, and thus salvation. What else could a priest of The Flame desire?"

Antiphon withheld that he sometimes doubted redemption and justice. Anyway, why should he welcome Armageddon when what he most wanted was Selah? He skirted the subject.

"What will happen to Kerebos?" he asked.

"I couldn't say, my son. I've always assumed he would perish. The Word seems to indicate that."

"I guess it does," Antiphon muttered and turned away. He wanted to be alone with his doubts and did not feel like arguing or having his mind changed.

"On the other hand, his salvation would not be necessarily inconsistent with the Book," Dokein continued. "'Even as Pangaea breaks, the herald shall break from himself,'" he quoted. "Interesting."

They fell silent. Antiphon contemplated the atrocities he had witnessed while Kerebos' guest. *It wouldn't be consistent, either,* he mused.

"I dreamed of him last night," Dokein said. "He was holding me in a crushing grip, but screamed all the while. Said I was burning him." He tapped his forehead. "What good are such premonitions? God often tempts me with tidbits but witholds the main course."

Antiphon snorted. "Maybe He does so for drama?"

Dokein looked thoughtful. "You know, Ani," he said. "I think God would very much like a repentant Kerebos *Ikar.*"

"Why not a repentant devil, then? He's an equal chance of seeing it happen. Really, now!"

Dokein's pleasant face grew indignant. "Don't preach poison to me, boy," he snapped. "And don't judge men, either. It's not your right."

Antiphon again looked away. He felt sorry for how he had spoken, if not for his cynicism. He loved Dokein and was thankful for all he had done for him, but the Grand Master did not know Kerebos. He had not seen what the *ikar* was capable of, nor how he could ruin a man's faith. *Would I even want Kerebos to repent after all he's done?* he wondered.

It was an unpalatable question. Naturally gentle, and a healer, Antiphon could not divorce himself from the desire to see Kerebos saved. It was not a strong desire, though.

Dokein stared as though trying to divine the younger man's thoughts. "Is not a lost, soiled diamond treasured all the more when found and restored to its proper setting?" he asked with a concilatory smile.

"Diamonds may be made under pressure, but they exert none themselves," Antiphon countered. He lowered his gaze. "Forgive me for grousing at you, Master. As usual, you were probably correct."

Dokein shrugged. "We shall see. Let's speak no more about it."

*   *   *

Kerebos and the *elhari* were seated in the war room. A large map of Pangaea lay unfurled in the center of the round table. Kerebos outlined two territories with his finger.

"Pontis has taken command of the *Boru* and Western *Aharoni*," he said. "After he consolidates he will most likely drive at us from three directions." He moved his finger south, saying: "Here at the ford. Here across the *Tantorri* plain and a galley landing just shy of the mountains. He will outnumber us twenty times, I'll wager."

Triskeles, still glowering over the *Boru/Chaconni* alliance, shook his head. "Galleys? It'd be easier to march the men so short a distance."

"Yes, but he'll move his big siege engines by water. I would."

"Can we forever defend our castles against so many?" Satyrnos asked solemnly.

"We can hold!" Syranos insisted. Though his head was still bandaged, he sounded none the worse for the injury.

97

The newest *elhar*, Phaedros, nodded agreement. Phaedros, a strapping *Chaconne* with eager dark eyes and a badly scarred face, had formerly served as Syranos' First *Cohar*. He was widely known for brutality and a fanatical admiration of Kerebos. He had never voiced an opinion even remotely critical of the *ikar* and had openly stated that orthodoxy was far less important than victory. These facts, above all else, had determined his elevation.

Kerebos stared at Satyrnos, who had captured a fly and was in the process of plucking its wings.

"Are you with us, Satyrnos?" Kerebos asked snidely. Though he would much rather have Satyrnos' open support, he feared the tenacious officer would cling to the old ways. *Don't want to have to kill him before his time*, he reflected.

"Just thinking, lord," Satyrnos replied and tossed the fly into his mouth. "We've ample supplies for a long siege, but not an indefinite one. Do we really want to fight before we're fully provisioned?"

"We've plenty of slaves to eat," Syranos joked, getting a general laugh.

Phaedros smiled, exposing teeth filed in proper cannibal fashion. He had developed a taste for human flesh while enslaved in the jungles of the south.

"And when they run out?" Triskeles asked.

The room grew silent, though Satyrnos' expression was one of triumph. For his part, Kerebos was thrilled by the conversation's course. For days he had plotted to lead the discussion to just such a point, one where he might introduce his newest assault upon the Scriptus Brand. He scrambled to properly align his arguments. Even with Triskeles, Syranos and Phaedros in his pocket, he wished to proceed with caution. Better to win over the others with words than with swords.

"A valid concern, Triskeles, but we will not starve. We will not even be sieged," Kerebos said.

"Why's that, lord?" Satyrnos asked.

Kerebos placed his fists onto the map. "For we shall sack Korenthis."

His words were still in the air when the walls shook and a bass voice rumbled through the earth. Candles dropped from the chandelier and struck the table with a thud. The cries of legionaries sounded throughout the castle.

"Another quake!" Syranos exclaimed.

Kerebos waved him to silence. "We shall take Korenthis!" he thundered. "Nothing can stop us! No league of petty nations shall stand between us and a river of blood! Who doubts me?"

Triskeles smiled at the welcome audacity. "But how shall we approach Pontis unmarked?" he asked. "His mounted archers will hound us all the while."

Kerebos felt like thanking the *Boru*. "There are ways, Triskeles," he said slyly.

"Yes?"

Kerebos smiled. "We'll foil them with our own cavalry."

A moment of silence then the *elhari* began talking at once.

"What?" Kaiaphos blurted.

Kerebos had not expected friction from Kaiaphos, his dimmest *elhar*. "To meet so many mounted men in the open is to admit defeat," he explained. "But a few horses might grease the road between here and Korenthis. Think of it, man!" he shouted. "Would you rather be starved and outmanuevered in the field, or masters of the largest city in the world? What glory could be greater?"

Triskeles, Syranos and Phaedros nodded assent, but Kerebos had already tallied their support. He turned the full weight of his presence on the others.

"*Well?*"

Satyrnos slowly wilted beneath his commander's gaze. He shrugged and said, "It matters not to me where I go to fight and kill, as long as I fight and kill. Desia proclaimed we should not keep slaves, but owned some himself."

"A sound rationalization," Kerebos agreed. "Kaiaphos?"

Kaiaphos studied the map. "So be it," he said softly.

Kerebos' hand inched away from Mistaaka. *Why did I wait so long to suggest these things?* he wondered, greatly heartened by how smoothly things had proceeded.

"Anyone have a problem with using a few horsemen?" he asked sternly. "Anyone want to discuss orthodoxy with Kyros in the dark hereafter?"

No answer.

"Excellent. Triskeles, appropriate riders from the *Tantorri*. They'll serve very well indeed when we take their families hostage."

"Yes, lord."

"Uh, lord?" Satyrnos stammered.

"What?"

"You know, if we made good use of the *Tantorri* we might be able to fall on the enemy unannounced," Satyrnos said. "They'll never expect us to engage them with cavalry, nor will they be watching their backsides."

"I didn't think of that," Kerebos admitted, pleased. "Warming up to the idea, eh?"

"Well, yes."

"You're right, too. We might take out their scouts and their flanks before they even knew we're in the field. We'd only get one chance to surprise them, though."

The *elhari* passed silent gazes among themselves. Kerebos could see their minds working. They would accept the change.

Triskeles, Syranos and Satyrnos began to talk strategy while Kerebos basked in the golden future.

Once I've sacked Korenthis thousands will flock to me, he thought. *I'll have more swords then I'll know what to do with.* He envisioned an endless plain of dead and laughed. *Earthquakes, archers and God be damned, Pangaea will pay!*

"Triskeles and Satyrnos, stay here," he ordered. "Syranos, get to work on a plan for the upkeep of our lands. I want to see it tonight. The rest of you get about your business. We've a war to win."

Alone with Triskles and Satyrnos, Kerebos asked: "Do you disapprove of my plans?"

"You are *ikar*," Triskeles said and Satyrnos agreed after the barest hesitation.

"Good," Kerebos replied. "I don't want to do without either of you, my old, faithful weapons. Now I want to hear your suggestions. Satyrnos, you seemed to have ideas about cavalry. Elaborate."

Satyrnos, unused to being consulted, was delighted to share his thoughts. Kerebos was impressed, too; the *elhar* seemed to possess an inherent understanding of mobile warfare and made many astute observations. Had he underestimated Satyrnos?

Kerebos, happy with his victory, was content to let the *elhar* take ownership of the question at hand. Besides, Satyrnos' ideas were sound. A casque of wine was broached and they planned long into the night. The meeting eventually ended on a lofty note, Kerebos thought, and the *elhari* were sent forth with words of encouragement and brotherhood. As he staggered out, Satyrnos hinted that Kaiaphos had better come around, and right quick.

Kerebos closed the door behind them.

Even if I fail, and at the very least, I'll soon be rid of those two, he thought.

That night Kerebos woke in a cold sweat. He had dreamed of fire, but the images were more intense than ever, more personal. Long after he had tried to wake himself the nightmare persisted; he saw the white flames chasing him through the castle and trapping him against a barred door.

Now he sat groggily in his bed, panting. When he gathered his wits, he interpreted the dreams as proof that he was on the right path. *So the Flame God doesn't like my plans?* he thought.

For once he found it easy to fall back to sleep.

Weeks passed before the legion was ready to move but since Pontis had troubles of his own, Kerebos had extra time to ingest the *Tantorri* into his command. This proved easier than expected.

The rank and file legionaries reacted serenely to the breach of Desia's commands—at least none were willing to lose their heads over the matter. There had been some grumblings about sharing camp with non-*landesknectos*, but when Kerebos lodged the calvary in a nearby *Tantorri* village, even this complaint dried up. The legionaries still drilled, still stood watch and were still the apple of their adored leader's eye, so what had changed?

After the legion crossed Cemetary River, Kerebos had the pontoon bridge sunk in a way that it might be easily raised. He seriously doubted he would again use the bridge, but appearances had to be maintained. *If I have my way, none of us will be coming back,* he thought, as the bridge gurgled into the river. *But why give the men too much to think about?*

He called for a runner.

"My lord?"

"Tell Satyrnos to send over the *Tantorri* co-commander," Kerebos stuttered. He had almost said *cohar*!

"Yes, lord!" The runner took off at a sprint.

"Let's move," Kerebos told Triskeles.

The air was soon filled with the sounds of booted feet and the screech of wagon axles. They had not marched far when a lone cavalryman appeared. He was young, rawboned and handsome, with luminous green eyes and bronzed skin. Sword and bow hung from his ornate, leathern saddle; the *Tantorri* were reknowned tanners.

"Kerebos *Ikar*," the *Tantor* nobleman said mildly, though hatred burned in his eyes. "You asked to see me?"

"*Ordered* to see you. *Insisted* upon seeing you. *Commanded* to see you. Take your pick, Sayed."

"Yes, *ikar*. Ordered, then."

Kerebos smiled. "And understand this: If our enemies spy us, both your sisters shall die."

Sayed's face grew suddenly haggard and he slumped as though a bag of bricks had been laid on his shoulders. He seemed ready to reply, but did not.

"Now get moving," Kerebos said. "I want at least four scouting reports a day, and constant interaction between you and Satyrnos. Who have you designated your lieutenant?"

"Lord Ghazal."

"Send him to me, now. If your men fail me, I'll bathe in *Tantorri* blood."

Sayed squinted down at the *ikar*. "We will not fail."

"Go."

Sayed spurred his sleek gray charger and was gone. Kerebos smiled to himself.

"Do you think they'll manage, my lord?" a bodyguard asked.

"It doesn't matter, boy," Kerebos replied. "The outcome shall be the same."

The legionary removed his helmet and hitched it onto his belt. His sweatdrenched topknot smacked his shaved neck with every step. He began to hum, timing the melody to the beat of the topknot.

"Why do you serve me?" Kerebos asked wearily.

The bodyguard looked surprised. "Because I'm a jackal and you're my lion," he replied. "You lead me to the kill, and I feast."

Kerebos found the response somehow unnerving. As he trudged along he wondered what manner of man he might have been had fate not named him a murderer.

The legion had traveled northeast for the better part of two days. The march was unremarkable, except for the discovery of some huge claw-toed footprints. Whatever had made the tracks was headed south, which was just as well, since it must have been larger than a house, and though Kerebos discounted the sighting, he nevertheless ordered a more northerly approach to Korenthis.

The day grew unseasonably hot, and the draft animals were proving difficult to move; in fact Kerebos was about to call a short halt, when the latest, worst, earthquake struck. The initial growling tremor threw many a man off his feet.

"Yet again," Triskeles scowled as the caged *Tantorri* captives shrieked in terror.

Kerebos threw his arms out to steady himself.

"Earthquake!" men bellowed.

The march sputtered to a stop as the rumblings intensified. Wagons rattled and food jars broke against each other. Cries of confusion lifted over the legion.

A crack appeared in the prairie just north of the host and quickly branched in three directions. Then, with a sound like a giant Titan bending a sword, the cracks yawned open. Dozens of legionaries screamed as they disappeared into the earthen maw.

Kerebos was thrown onto his knees and Triskeles beside him. Another fault crept toward the *ikar* but, as though having changed its mind, turned and cut through the very heart of the legion. More *landesknectos* cried for help as they tumbled to their deaths.

Pangaea rocked with such force Kerebos thought the world was coming apart, and with it his designs. He covered his ears.

The stroke of doom! he thought.

But the earthquake soon subsided. Its report moved into the distance like a herd of retreating cattle. With a final moan the faultlines closed, leaving only smiling lips of dirt where the cracks had been.

The distressed legionaries struggled to their feet.

"Damn, I lost my sword!" a man said.

It did not take long for the runners to reach Kerebos, who managed to control his voice. "I want casualty reports, wounded and dead," he told them.

"Over there!" someone cried, and was soon echoed by a multitude of voices.

Glancing north, Kerebos was astounded to see a new range of impossibly sheer, rocky mountains. The spiny obstacles were the tallest any legionary had ever seen and ran east and west to the horizons. Nobody ventured an explanation, but Korenthis was undeniably out of the question.

Kerebos whirled on Triskeles, screaming, "Where'd they come from?!"

Triskeles was paler than usual. He shook his head. "We'll never get over them," he said. "They must be three leagues high."

Kerebos hung his head in disgust and bit back bitter disappointment. "Send out some horses, anyway," he groaned. "Maybe there's a pass." No sooner had he concluded the Flame God's culpability then a new, wonderful idea came to mind. It was beautiful. "We march!" he bellowed, then laughed.

Triskeles looked puzzled. "The castle?"

Kerebos shook his head. "East."

"Into the Anvil?"

"And beyond."

Triskeles looked as though he were carefully fashioning a response.

"Look," Kerebos reasoned. "We've lost Korenthis for now, but need not go home emptyhanded. What city is poorly defended, heavily populated and might provide us a base with which to attack Pontis?"

Triskeles gave one of his ghastly smiles. "Kwan Aharon."

"Right." Kerebos laughed again and Triskeles joined him. Men looked on as though the two had gone mad.

The Flame God has made a bad mistake, Kerebos thought. *He's laid his own city under my blade.*

Chapter 13

The legion had marched east for days. The new mountain range cast a shadow over the plain, which had turned brown some time before. Now, even the sparse desert scrub was running out. Soon there would be nothing but the wide sands of the Anvil, hellish hot during the day, freezing cold at night.

At least the shade keeps the sun off, Kerebos thought.

The *landesknectos* were down to half rations of water. Many vessels had been destroyed during the earthquake, and Kerebos had not reckoned horses into the logistics. In addition, the party Sayed had taken to find water had not returned. Kerebos was livid and fully intended to kill Sayed's sisters if the nobleman did not show up by nightfall. Still, the legion would make it to Kwan Aharon, barring further unforseen barriers, and there would be plenty of water in the *Aharoni* city.

"You'd better be dead, Sayed," Kerebos growled.

"What's that, lord?" Triskeles asked.

Kerebos looked at the *Boru*, whose blue eyes were as unperturbed as ever. Of all the men, Triskeles seemed least impressed by the earthquakes and new mountains, and continued his daily business with a disturbing singlemindedness. Kerebos was not sure what to make of it; the *Boru* was either dumber than expected or he *really* wanted his legion.

"I said I've total confidence in you," Kerebos lied, curious to see if Triskeles would believe him.

"Of course, lord. As you've never failed us, I will never fail you."

"Good."

A runner came up and saluted. "My lord!" he puffed.

"Yes?"

"The *Tantorri* have returned. They are with Satyrnos but shall be here directly."

"Is Sayed among them?" Kerebos demanded. "I haven't heard from him all day."

"It appears so, my lord."

"Order him here."

It was a few moments before Sayed and his lieutenant Ghazal arrived. Kerebos commanded them to dismount and walk beside him. A *sestar* of Triskeles' men followed. Sayed offered no excuse for his absence but began his report.

"Beat him to his knees," Kerebos said.

One of Triskeles' men cracked Sayed across the legs with a spear and the *Tantor* spilled onto all fours.

"My lord!" Ghazal cried and leaped forward, but two legionaries seized the slight *Tantor's* arms.

Kerebos smiled down at Sayed. "That's better," he said. "Where have you been? Do you think I'm some village chief you can ignore at leisure?"

"I killed my horse trying to catch up with you," Sayed defended himself through clenched teeth.

"Where were you?"

"Ambushed! Some *Chaconni* fell on us as we were filling the water barrels, caught us against a river. Most of my men were killed."

Kerebos looked hostile. "'Ambushed' implies they knew you were coming. How would they know that, and why didn't you see them?"

Sayed glared. "We were engaged with our mission and expected no enemies. We have paid."

"Not enough. When this is over I'm going to hang you. Yesterday you said Pontis was on the other side of the mountains."

"So he is," Sayed replied. "These men wore the livery of Pyrros' Royal Marines. They must have been on the river when the quake struck."

Kerebos shook his head. "Marines? Where are they now?"

"I don't know. There aren't many and they're probably hiding."

Kerebos stared through the noble. "I think you're lying," he said.

"Tell the truth or you, personally, shall kill your sisters."

Sayed's face went ashen. "By God, I speak truth," he intoned. "My men lay dead not ten miles from here. You've only to follow the buzzards." He reached toward Kerebos. "Do you think I want death for my kin? You must believe me!"

Kerebos stepped forward and ripped out a handful of Sayed's curly hair with a sound like tearing cloth. "Must I!" he growled, and threw the hair in Sayed's face.

Sayed held his head with both hands; blood oozed between his fingers. "Kill me if you will," he moaned. "But I'm not lying."

Kerebos gazed at Triskeles, who simultaneously raised his eyebrows and shrugged. Kerebos drew Mistaaka, named for a *Tantorri* town he had liquidated, and pressed the sword against Sayed's crotch.

"Your incompetence has cost me," he said. "Therefore you're responsible for replacing the lost men. Go to your people and get more cavalry."

The *Tantor* shook his head with conviction. "The elders won't listen. They've already decided to fight rather than give over more hostages."

"Then I'll send them ten heads a day until they change their minds."

"All right, I'll try, I'll try!" Sayed promised. "But they'd be more likely to help if they thought there was some chance of getting our people back."

Kerebos leaned forward as though to grab more of Sayed's mane, but composed himself. He looked to Triskeles. "What would you do, three legs?" he asked.

"Kill him. But that's my answer for everything."

Kerebos told Sayed, "I'll send eight prisoners behind you. That should help you bargain with your superiors. If it doesn't I'll call off this whole campaign and kill every last *Tantor* in Pangaea. Tell your elders that."

"On my father's grave," the *Tantor* swore, "I'll return with every man who can ride."

Kerebos nodded. "Your sisters are depending on it."

Sayed looked stricken. "But they're two I shall take home."

Kerebos laughed. "No, no, no, no. You're not picking who you take. You think I'm stupid enough to send your little bitches with you?"

Sayed wiped blood from his eye. "I understand."

That evening Sayed visited the jail cart that held his sisters and hugged both through the bars, speaking softly to them until Kerebos ordered him to mount up.

"Don't leave us!" the girls sobbed and reached through the bars.

"Go now," Kerebos ordered, his breath hanging in the cooling air. "I'll send the others directly."

Tears streamed down Sayed's face as he gave his sisters a final wave.

"One week, boy!" Kerebos' warned, pointing Mistaaka at the sisters. "Or they'll die in ways you won't believe."

Sayed's expression was one of abysmal sorrow. "There's nothing I wouldn't believe of you," he said, then spurred his horse. He swiftly passed beyond the campfires and disappeared into the night.

Triskeles sidled up to the *ikar*. "What about that company of Marines? We should kill them and get their supplies if they're only ten miles from here."

"I agree. Where's that Ghazal fellow?"

"Watering his steed," Triskeles replied. "You're not giving back any hostages," he said, more statement than question.

"Not live ones, anyway."

Three days later a starved, hollow-eyed Sayed stumbled into his uncle's house. Soon after he was brought before the hastily assembled "Council of Twelve" which had gathered in Chief Bharzhra's manor. An unemotional Sayed stood before the lords and related how he had tricked Kerebos.

"Most of my men will be arriving soon, but some few are staying with the *Chaconni*," he said tonelessly. "Ghazal shall try poisoning the Legion's water before he, too, returns."

Bharzhra, Haam's brother and successor, looked with pity upon the young noble. "You have done much, Sayed Gahrin, and it weighs upon you," he said. "I'm sorry you and your sisters were forced into this dreadful situation, but war is war. Is it your opinion that Kerebos shall release the promised hostages?"

"You know he won't, or you wouldn't have voted upon this course," Sayed replied quietly. "When the *ikar* finds I've deceived

108

him, he'll murder them all. He would have eventually killed them, anyway."

"How do we know?" Lord Atta asked. "What if Pontis can't destroy Kerebos, or the desert doesn't kill him? He shall seek a terrible vengeance."

Sayed merely stared at him.

The next day Sayed was found dead in a nearby barn. He had hanged himself.

*   *   *

Kerebos sat alone on the sandy floor of his tent and studied a map. Where would he hide if a Marine commander with *landesknectos* about? Disgusted, he allowed the parchment to roll up, then swatted it away. The new mountains had made the chart worthless. He would have to rely on Ghazal's reports, which deeply disturbed him.

The little, beady-eyed bastard. Don't trust him far as I can kick him, he thought. *But I am holding one of his children,* he reasoned.

Kerebos sprawled onto the ground and stared up at the hanging lamp. He would be happy when finally ensconced in Kwan Aharon; he felt naked in the open. It was as though mounted scouts had only given him more to worry about. Add earthquakes, apparitions and other phenomenon and he felt downright vulnerable. Maybe he would feel better after killing the Marines?

Kerebos decided to call it a night and stood to extinguish the lamp, but even as he reached for it, the flame changed from orange to white. He froze as the breath was sucked from his lungs. The flame flared up and began spitting, growing so intense it burned his eyes. A guard peeked into the tent.

"What goes, my lord?" he asked.

Kerebos burst into action. He drew Mistaaka and clove the bronze lamp in a single, smooth motion. Flames splattered the tent wall and spread quickly.

Kerebos bolted from the tent, bowling over the guard. They went down in a heap and when they had untangled themselves, the tent was fully involved. *Landesknectos* were coming from all over. Kerebos slowly inched away from the blaze.

"Are you alright, lord?" the guard asked, concerned.

Kerebos buried Mistaaka into the man's chest, and tore the blade free as the corpse slumped to the ground.

"No," he replied.

*   *   *

Dokein sat at his desk and thumbed through the Book of *Ehrim*. He prayed for the strength to meet the harsh days ahead. Somebody banged upon his door.

"Yes?" he said.

The door swung open and Masters Ahbad and Torra stepped into the room. Ahbad, paunchy and sullen, nodded a greeting. "We've received word from your mercenaries," he said in a trembling voice.

"What is it?"

Torra, an unimpressive specimen with sloped shoulders and virtually no chin, blurted, "Pontis of Korenthis has crushed the black legion west of Tharbad!"

Dokein slammed closed the book. "What!" he cried. "That's impossible!"

"More than one messenger confirms it," Ahbad replied.

"And Kerebos *Ikar?*"

"They say he's disappeared," Ahbad answered.

"Call the Council!" Dokein croaked and gestured for them to leave.

The basilica bells began tolling almost immediately. Dokein sat on his bed, stunned. Either *Ehrim* was mistaken about Kerebos, or something had gone terribly wrong. Certainly the world had not ended. Had God decided to let the world suffer another thousand years?

Dokein flexed his arthritic fingers. "Lord," he whispered. "Don't make us wait."

110

T he legion's top officers and the *Tantorri* lieutenant, Ghazal, crammed the barren command tent. Kerebos sat behind a folding table and stared at the standing horseman. The smell of *kraal* tainted the air.

Kerebos could not pinpoint exactly what had changed about Ghazal. The little man was scared, obviously, but that was nothing new. Was he uncomfortable that Sayed was gone? Sometimes seconds-in-command fell apart after the removal of their superiors, Kerebos knew. He let Ghazal sweat a little longer before replying.

"So where are those Royal Marines, then?" he asked.

"Nowhere to be seen, my lord," Ghazal replied. "Must've taken to the river."

"Uh huh," Kerebos grunted. "So we've a clear road before us?"

Ghazal looked uneasily from Kerebos to Triskeles, who stood beside the *ikar*. "Yes."

"You'd bet your life on that?" Triskeles asked.

Kerebos smiled. "He already has."

"I would!" Ghazal insisted. "They must've struck camp."

"Don't like it, lord," Triskeles said. "Maybe this little rat's trying to get us pinned against the water?"

"Maybe. But by a division of Royals? What could they do? They'd soon turn from hunters into prey." Kerebos eyed Ghazal. "Unless of course there were more than he told us."

"Why would I lie?" Ghazal asked imploringly. "Do you think I've forgotten you hold my children?"

Kerebos nodded. *There'd be nothing in it for him to lie, that's true,* he considered. *Still, there's something wrong here. Cavalry does improve intelligence, but I don't like relying on foreigners. Have to teach some of mine to scout, and soon.* "Triskeles?"

"My lord?"

"You've a few farm boys who can ride, don't you?"

Triskeles sniffed. "They'd never admit it."

"Get them on some horses and send them with Ghazal. Let's make sure his men aren't walking us into a trap. Don't want some Marines slowing us up."

Ghazal looked sick.

"You've something to say?" Kerebos demanded.

"Yes," the *Tantor* replied weakly. "As I've said, the enemy is probably on our trail."

"We'll see. Get to it, three legs."

"Yes, lord!"

Triskeles snatched his helmet off the table and marched from the tent. Kerebos glared at Ghazal, then said: "Dismissed."

Triskeles burst back into the tent, halting the other *elhari* in their tracks.

"What?" Kerebos asked, peeved.

"Dust rising in the south!" Triskeles reported. "Enemy horse, no doubt, and lots of them!"

Kerebos pointed at Ghazal, who appeared on the brink of incontinence. "Scour the road ahead," he ordered. "We're going to that high ground you spoke of. Don't fail me.'"

Ghazal bowed. "Yes, *ikar.*"

Kerebos looked at his men. "Let's get moving!"

Count Vasilex of Thibis and three generals pored over a map made unreliable by recent geographical changes. "Is this the best we have?" Vasilex growled, slapping the table.

"Unfortunately, m'liege," a general replied.

An officer poked his head into the tent, which was large enough to house a company and as lavish as a bordello. "Scouting report, lord count," he said.

"Bring it!"

Two dusty horsemen marched into the tent and saluted. The

taller of the pair wore the scarlet livery of the Royal Marines, the other was clad as one of Vasilex's own riders.

"What?" Vasilex demanded.

The marine looked smug. "Kerebos has taken the bait."

The *landesknectos* struck camp and were on the march in short order. They swiftly traversed a narrow valley and reached the open plain. Knee high grass waved in the wind. Low, gray thunderheads moved in from the west. Gentle green foothills rose in the distance.

Kerebos hated that he could not see beyond the hills, but Ghazal's report and the apparent enemy arrival convinced him there was little to fear. He would ensconce himself on those slopes, and once positioned no number of *Chaconni* soldiers could dislodge him.

The legionaries initially pushed on at a brutal pace but slowed as the plain turned swampy. Kerebos found his legs covered in mud. Clouds of stinging insects buzzed round his face. Another hour found the *landesknectos* facing a shallow depression. Cattails and ferns rose to greet them; the smell of stagnant water hung in the air. Suddenly the short hills looked much more formidable. Kerebos had a very bad feeling and passed the word that he wanted Ghazal, and quickly. The *Tantor*, it was reported, was still on patrol.

Kerebos called the legion to a halt and sent for the *elhari*. "Walk with me," he said and lead them a short distance.

"What's wrong, lord?" Triskeles asked anxiously.

"We've been duped," Kerebos said sourly.

"We'd better get to those hills, my lord," Satyrnos warned. "We don't want to be caught out here on the plain."

Kerebos shook his head. "We'll never reach them. This swamp is meant to be our tomb. Pontis' men are forming behind those hills, waiting for us to get entangled in the fens. These things work both ways, though; the bog will protect our rear."

"But all that cavalry we saw?" Syranos said.

"All I saw was dust. Anyway, when you've unlimited manpower you can use twenty thousand to maneuver."

They looked at each other in silence. A stiff breeze kicked up. Kerebos glanced at the blackclad formations, and saw the confused expressions there.

"We're going to get a storm," Triskeles said.

Kerebos nodded. "Satyrnos?"

"Lord?"

"Kill the *Tantorri* prisoners and send a *cohar* to scout the hills, just in case I'm wrong. If your men can take it, they must, but tell them to retreat immediately if the enemy is in force."

"Just a *cohar*, lord?"

Kerebos smiled grimly. "I'm not wrong."

The *landesknectos* broke out shovels and entrenched in earnest. In almost no time they had a huge, semicircular moat protecting their entire southern flank and had used excess dirt to erect an elevated "command mound" nearly ten feet high. The ditch was not deep enough to stop a cavalry charge, but would certainly slow one.

Satyrnos' reconnaissance *cohar* had not even crossed the swamp before Pontis' force revealed itself. Suddenly there were many thousands of footsoldiers on the hills. Hundreds of banners snapped in the wind.

Just as I expected, Kerebos thought glumly.

He had anticipated the enemy showing himself as soon as the *landesknectos* began digging. Before long, countless horsemen were pouring onto the plain from the distant valley. Kerebos knew that a host of infantry would not be far behind.

The situation looked grim, indeed. Pontis' army surpassed all rumor and, even without tricking Kerebos into the bog, held the better ground.

I'm going to die here, Kerebos told himself.

*   *   *

A desperate and bloody battle had raged since midday but now purple dusk was afoot. Thunder rolled overhead and lighting jumped from cloud to cloud.

The latest flood of messengers crowded Kerebos. "Lord! Lord!" they cried above the din of arms.

The field reeked of sweat, blood and viscera. The screams of dying men and horses rose from the trench, long since filled with bodies. The battle would have ended long before had it not been for

114

the legionaries' incomparable ferocity and skill-in-arms.

"Silence!" the *ikar* bellowed atop the flattening mound, arms outstretched. "One at a time!"

Kerebos fought hysteria. His mind, so long on a descent into darkness, was fraying at the last. He could feel it coming unwound inside his skull, pushing against his eyes, distorting his vision.

How could he possibly be defeated before fulfilling his schemes?

Feathered legionaries littered the ground, but the lines held. *Landesknectos* crowded behind bodyshields and wagons, awaiting the next charge. The *Chaconni* lit bonfires against coming night and struck some flares; nonetheless, their shooting became erratic. The storm of arrows grew steadily lighter then ceased altogether. *Chaconni* swordsmen, newly arrived from the heights, were ordered forth. The legionaries maintained a three deep formation and braced for the assault. Pontis' men howled and charged; edged weapons shone dully in the firelight. The *landesknectos* leaned into the wind.

"Let them have it, lads!" Kerebos cried.

The crunch of shield on shield was followed by deafening screams. The crash of swords lifted above the plain. Kerebos frantically indicated a runner.

"You, Satyrnos' boy!" he called.

"Yes, lord!"

"Tell the fool to douse his torches!"

The runner bolted off, forgetting even to salute.

"Next!" the *ikar* shouted.

A trio of runners jumped forward. "Lord!" they cried.

One of the couriers suddenly doubled over, a flaming ballista bolt in his stomach. Kerebos cast aside the stricken man and grabbed another runner.

"Have Triskeles broaden his line by going two deep," he shouted.

"Yes, lord!"

Kerebos turned to another messenger.

"Have Syranos lend Triskeles his strongest *cohar!*" he cried. "They'll be the third row!"

Damn! the *ikar* thought, and wiped sweat from his eyes. *Why couldn't this storm have started an hour ago?*

Some rain drops pelted Kerebos, who tore off his cape before it grew heavy. More breathless runners arrived. Kerebos made tactical adjustments, positioning each *elhari* for maximum lethality. He gave no indication of knowing the battle was vain, though a flood of curses spewed from his mouth.

"Damn!" he concluded a stream of profanity. Satyrnos men were being overrun, and there were no more reserves; the line began to give. Kerebos turned to his bodyguards and laughed, and as he did the heavens opened. "Let's go kill!" he cried.

"*Ikar!*" they shouted.

Kerebos pried a greatshield from a stubborn corpse and stormed toward Satyrnos' faltering *elhar*. He reflected upon the unreality of it all. Somehow, he never thought he would end like this.

"Cover up!" he shouted as his guards muscled into the wall, which adapted smoothly. "Now it's our turn. Shields high and go get them! Odd *sestari* kick the flanks!" Officers relayed the command, their voices faint above the wind. Kerebos called men by name.

"Vaxtis, Petros, Heraklis! Show them how it's done!" he roared.

The *elhar* regained lost ground then fell on the enemy with renewed fervor. Kerebos forced a wedge into the *Chaconni* and held firm while the odd-numbered *sestari* pressed the flanks. A brief exchange laid low hundreds of Pontis' men before a thousand others broke and ran. Soon the entire *Chaconni* sector was in disarray. A horn called Pontis' divisions back onto the steppe for redeployment.

Kerebos brought his men to heel and they reformed the shield-wall, howling like fiends and stomping their feet on the spongy ground.

"Kerebos!" came the cry.

Restored confidence accompanied the *landesknectos'* chant. How could they possibly be defeated by common soldiers with their invincible *ikar* in command?

"Kerebos! Kerebos! Kerebos!"

Balls of lightning tore across the sky with a sound like that of a thousand drums. Kerebos stood with arms lifted, laughing like a madman.

*   *   *

Triskeles grabbed the runner by the throat. "What?" he demanded; his gauntleted fingers drew blood.

"Kerebos says attack!" the messenger yelped. "Their flares are almost spent and darkness will cover you!"

"I need more men!" Triskeles shouted.

The runner indicated the arriving unit. "These are from Syranos!"

A riderless horse, speared through the throat, crashed the phalanx. Triskeles severed the creature's head with an awesome upward swing. The decapitated animal ran a dozen steps before it collapsed. Somewhere in the gloom, a *Chaconni* horn sounded the retreat.

"Good!" Triskeles said. "Return and ask for even more! They're so bottlenecked they won't be able to maneuver!"

"Yes, lord!"

Triskeles squinted into the dimness. A flash of lightning revealed Kerebos as he deserted the command mound. The *elhar* winced. He again throttled the runner, demanding, "Where's he going? Does he think we've already lost?"

"Don't know!" the runner gasped.

Rage and frustration racked Triskeles. *Kerebos seeks death*, he thought. *He's leaving me*. A feeling of betrayal weakened his grip and he released the runner, who stood holding his neck and wheezing.

"I demand to know what he's doing!" Triskeles suddenly said. "Tell him just that!" he finished and shoved the man.

Triskeles' First *Cohar*, another *Boru*, shouldered by some pilum carriers.

"My lord!" the *cohar* called with excitement. "Now's time for an offensive! Let us use the wagons!"

"Yes, Markos, so Kerebos commands."

The *cohar* touched his commander's arm. "What's passed?"

Triskeles shook off the friendly hand. "Nothing," he pointed toward the lended troops. "I'll take them under my personal command. We move forward."

The *cohar* saluted and departed. Triskeles motioned toward a lurking runner and issued orders for his other officers, then looked toward Satyrnos' sector. By sound more than sight, he followed the first seconds of Kerebos' charge. Triskeles saw his career, his entire being, disappearing with the *ikar* into the sea of swords. The only man Triskeles had ever admired had abandoned him. Feelings of devotion bled from his heart.

The First *Cohar* approached. "My lord, why not use the wagons in case they start shooting?" he suggested.

"I know, Markos. Group the men behind the wains. Tell them I expect them to fight like gods and if any quit on me, I'll find them."

Markos' smile showed faintly.

"My men are *landesknectos*, first and last," he promised.

Triskeles waved his sword overhead and cried: "Attack, little brothers! By Desia's sacred blood, attack and kill!"

Wheels creaked as wagons were pushed over the filled ditch. Baying like hounds, the *landesknectos* charged a division nearly twenty times their number. So began the most magnificent offensive in the legion's impressive history.

Triskeles' charge gained momentum and soon the wagons were rumbling forward at a great pace. Wheels groaned over trampled grass and *Chaconni* stragglers.

Why aren't they shooting? Triskeles wondered as he labored behind an empty water cart. The enemy obliged and arrows squeaked into the moving mantlets. Here and there lucky shots hit *landesknectos*. Markos took an arrow in the shin and, howling, fell from the ranks.

"Faster!" Triskeles ordered.

At that moment the legionaries plowed into a mass of calvary. Many of the horses bucked and threw their riders who shrieked as they were run over. Those horsemen not instantly killed were soon hacked to pieces.

"Let them have it!" Triskeles cried.

The *landesknectos* stopped pushing, unslung their shields, and burst from behind the wagons. They fell upon and sliced through a battalion of breastplated, Royal Marines as though through wheat. Triskeles' vicious heart sang; Pontis' men were dreadfully positioned.

"Kill!" he urged. "And keep it tight!"

The command was unnecessary since the blackclad warriors had already cut a sizable swath through the enemy. Triskeles intended to hack his way through to the king.

If Pontis has come for a show, I'll oblige him! he thought.

Confusion ruled the *Chaconni*, who were hampered by their numbers. Formations collided and mixed. Leaderless cavalry trampled infantry in the attempt to stem the *landesknecta* advance. A *razai* of *Aharoni* archers, positioned near the bonfires, suddenly found themselves face to face with the enemy and accidentally skewered many of their confederates before beating a hasty retreat. Rain came down in torrents, and untended campfires hissed and sputtered.

A succession of lightning flashes lit the field and Triskeles identified a redoubt of footmen being arranged in the distance. The *Boru* liked what he saw and ordered another shieldwall, which materialized as smoothly as during drills. Those *Chaconni* caught in no man's land scurried for cover.

The *landesknectos* pressed forward at double time.

There was further chaos among the *Chaconni*. One of the Marines' beacons was accidentally toppled and the signal corps inexplicably horned the "attack" command. The middle of the Royal Division pushed forward while the flanking cohorts dug in. Another bolt of lighting revealed the fear and bewilderment on the Marines' faces.

Wonderful! Triskeles thought. *Oh, how easy!*

The comparatively small force of legionaries smashed through the *Chaconni* line without breaking stride. Shrieking Marines found themselves mortally wounded before they could level their first blows. The *landesknectos* were already disposing of the third line before the fourth knew what had happened to their mates. Those *Chaconni* in the rear were appalled by the speed with which the blackclad giants bore down on them.

Triskeles, ever in the fore, hacked through his first six antagonists without thinking but eventually the sheer number of *Chaconni* bogged his headlong sprint through their ranks. Then the real butchery started.

Men who had heard horror stories of *landesknecta* ferocity learned the truth of these tales befores being hewn down. Pontis' Royal Marines were mauled like dolls in a tiger's teeth. Almost every legionary thrust increased the bodycount. Superbly trained, motivated and armored, titans in stature and skill, the proud *landesknectos* embarrassed the flower of Pontis' army in what might be best described as martial rape.

Two grizzled non-commissioned officers attacked Triskeles, who absorbed a blow on his shield from one before slamming his pommel spike through the other's chin. Wrenching free the sword, he chopped the first *Chaconne's* shoulder, slicing through the entire torso and out below the forth rib. A tapering scream was followed by a sound like that of a ham dropping into mud. Thunder shook the earth.

Triskeles plunged forward.

A, young, wide-eyed spearman lunged at him, but Triskeles swatted aside the pike, leapt forward, and crumpled the lad's face with a spiked fist. The Marine collapsed as though his bones had jellied.

Triskeles kicked a fallen man in the temple, then felt a sharp pain in his leg. Looking down, he realized a kneeling *Chaconne* had pierced his shin guard. Triskeles stabbed the offender through the spine, then kneed him in the face.

Moments passed. The red flares grew ever dimmer. Pontis' casualties mounted.

The Marines began to pull out, first by ones and twos, then by entire companies. *Landesknectos* pressed their advantage and stabbed the foe in the back. *Chaconni* bodies piled up until further pursuit became difficult. The brotherhood eventually turned its attention to the enemy wounded, who begged for mercy, but were massacred where they laid. Screams trailed off, replaced by the screech of iron, and the slurp of blade in flesh. The cold rain came down.

Triskeles took a short rest. He looked to the rear and saw a mixed force of infantry and cavalry being handled by a mass of *landesknectos*. More horns sounded and Triskeles turned to see two pristine *Chaconni* divisions reforming the shattered line. Arrows fell among the legionaries.

Triskeles clapped down his short visor and bellowed: "Fall back fifty paces and reform! Let them come over the dead then hit them in Trident Formation! Hold your shields high!"

The legionaries promptly withdrew a short distance, leaving their comrades on the field. Another wall was constructed. Pontis' army got the signal and advanced. Triskeles gave a long howl and started toward the enemy; his men kept pace.

Somehow the *Chaconni* were again startled by *landeskecta* audacity. Javelins fell among the legionaries, but Pontis' men seemed less anxious to kill than to prepare for a collision.

"Spears!" Triskeles warned even as one screeched off his shield with a burst of sparks. The *elhar* slowed and fell in behind one of his men; another fell in behind him. The rest of the unit acted similarly, forming numerous "tridents".

The *Chaconni* immediately voiced their vexation. The blackclad enemy was hard enough to see without resorting to this! Triskeles rumbled the last few yards toward the enemy, his feet slapping the muck. He had no fear.

"NOW!" he screamed and jumped from behind his partner and became a "left prong". Scores of other tridents smashed the enemy line. The *Chaconni* were quickly thrown into confusion.

Perhaps the Trident Formation was not tailored for such a situation—it was used primarily for break outs—but its fluidity further baffled the enemy. The left and right "prongs" engaged the *Chaconni* with the "shaft" throwing in against the point of greatest resistance. Once this resistance was overcome, the prongs withdrew and the trident pressed forward.

Triskeles smirked at a spear thrust and chopped the pike in half. He feinted at the *Chaconne's* face and, as he had anticipated, another spearman saw an opportunity and lunged. Triskeles' shield took the pike and he killed both men as they fumbled for their swords.

The tridents tore through the *Chaconni* with ease. It mattered not that Pontis' men were fresh, they fought as though entranced. Triskeles was almost disappointed by their lack of spirit.

The *landesknectos* fanned out and plowed through Pontis' ranks like an accelerated cancer. The infantry divisions were pruned with such speed their commander, Duke Zathos, took precautionary measures and retreated with his staff to a safe distance.

Though he would later be executed for incompetence, Zathos did move decisively on one point and ordered all marksmen to form an ellipse between himself and the bloodshed. These archers, *Aharoni* mercenaries armed with the desert longbow, had orders to "discourage" either a *landesknecta* advance or a *Chaconni* retreat.

Back in the battle Triskeles wielded his sword like some myth of legend, beating lives from bodies as easily as he might snuff out candles. He had lost his helmet and had been stabbed in the shoulder, but fought on with unabated fury. Time passed and the *Chaconni* were thrust back. And back.

Then came that hissing sound the *landesknectos* had learned to respect. A legionary gargled blood as an arrow passed through his throat. Soon a score were down. Some complained bitterly that their brilliant stand had been profaned by inglorious, unmanly arrows.

The *Chaconni* were stricken, too, and their entire "offensive" was thrown into chaos. The infantrymen surrendered the field, all but those too brave or weary to run, only to be shot by their allies.

Triskeles saw the ghostlike forms of the robed *Aharoni* as they advanced through the rain. Those *Chaconni* who had not yet fled called upon the archers to spare them. The *landesknectos* finished those foes who could or would not run before turning weary gazes on the bowmen. The *Aharoni* positioned themselves at a distance of fifty paces.

Most of the exhausted *landesknectos* lifted their greatshields, but some few refused to acknowledge the enemy. Triskeles was one of these. He stood tall and sneered with contempt. An arrow pierced his mail and latissimus dorsi, but he ignored the wound.

A new hail of quarrels killed half the remaining legionaries. Even heavy greatshields were not invulnerable against the double-curved bow at such range. Gradually, the bombardment slowed and stopped. The *Aharoni* had run out of arrows.

An *Aharoni* officer cried in a loud voice, "Do you surrender?"

Triskeles gazed over his remaining men. Only a fraction were still on their feet. "Get up!" he ordered. Some fell in behind him and they lumbered toward the enemy.

"Our turn!" Triskeles shouted and broke into a run.

The *Aharoni* were not prepared for this. Armorless and equipped with empty quivers and knives, some fled. Most drew daggers and stood their ground with grim determination, trusting God and their numbers to carry the day. Breathless prayers were uttered.

Triskeles' *sestari* plowed into the haphazard line. The *elhar* threw his shield into an archer's face then wielded his sword with both hands. He fell upon the robed men, hacking and slashing. The *Aharoni* were astonished by the swiftness of such large, armored men.

Bows were swung desperately overhead, knives thrown or thrust, but the archers were very overmatched.

Triskeles sent a man flying with a kick to the chest and shoved his blade into another's stomach while elbowing yet another in the throat. The *elhar* tore free the sword and clove a bearded *Aharoni's* head to the teeth, some of which dropped onto the ground.

The *landesknectos* disposed of the bowmen with a casualness that sent Pontis' command post into a frenzy. Formations were reformed and ordered back onto the field. Horns blared and officers yelled. The rain tapered off to a drizzle.

Triskeles broke his sword on a victim's jawbone, but continued to fight with the hilt and twelve inches of steel. The weapon grew slippery in his hand, but he doggedly continued the red work. He grabbed the robe of a fleeing *Aharoni* and yanked with such force the bowman was pulled off his feet and onto Triskeles' blade. Someone else took the blade in the chest and another had his knife arm apprehended in midair before he felt the *elhar's* sword slip into his armpit and between two ribs.

The *Aharoni* wanted no more and raced off in all directions. The *landesknectos* were too tired to give chase but leaned on their swords and sized up the fresh army heading their way. Triskeles was nearly doubled over with fatigue and rubbed where his sticky gambeson chafed his side. He looked back toward Satyrnos' sector, which seemed to be holding its own. For the first time he noticed the rain had stopped.

"Did we win?" Markos asked as he stretched out on the ground.

"No," Triskeles replied softly. "The enemy is still very great." *Where is Kerebos?* he wondered.

Other legionaries eased onto the wet earth. One of them was snoring before he even lay down.

More horns. The rumble of hooves. Triskeles grimaced at the approaching columns of horsemen and many hundreds of torches.

"By Yotan's league-long member," he muttered.

"A thousand of them," Markos said, unimpressed.

Triskeles spat. "Stand, men," he mumbled. "There's more bloodwork to do."

A peculiar, metallic thunder boomed across the sky though the clouds had moved on; Triskeles gazed at the washed heavens and the bright stars. The mounted force surrounded the little band of legionaries.

Triskeles raised his broken sword in weary challenge. Horses whinnied as they were reined to a halt. Bows and crossbows were lifted. Triskeles gazed eyed the firelit faces of a vengeful enemy and laughed.

A torch-bearing *Aharoni* chieftain spurred forward to within a dozen feet of the *elhar*.

"Where are the others?" the *Aharoni* asked. "Those who sent my men dashing?"

"Gone."

"Gone where?" the officer snapped.

Triskeles looked vaguely amused as he pointed his broken blade at the horseman's breast. The *Aharoni* raised a fist.

"When I drop my hand, you and your men die," he said.

Triskeles limped toward the officer.

"Ask me what I've done to *Aharoni* with this sword," he replied with a chuckle.

In that instant, the sun was in the sky. To say it rose would be incorrect, as it did not ascend, merely one instant it was dark, and the next it burned brilliantly overhead.

Triskeles stopped in his tracks and dropped what remained of his weapon. He stood dumbfounded, blinking stupidly at the white ball of fire.

Aharoni babbled prayers. Some fell from their saddles, or accidentally shot their comrades. Torches tumbled to the ground, and lay hissing on the wet grass.

"Mother of God!" the chieftain gasped.

Chapter 15

Kerebos slipped in mud but planned his next move while falling. A *Boru*, naked from the waist up, gave a victory howl and charged. Kerebos kicked a kneecap and the *Boru* dropped with a groan, impaling himself on Mistaaka. Strong arms lifted the corpse and two bodyguards helped Kerebos to his feet.

"This damn rain!" one apologized for the *ikar's* fall, then whirled to parry a swordthrust. The legionary lunged forward and chopped the *Boru's* neck, which sprayed hot blood in a wide semicircle.

Kerebos again bolted from the pocket of bodyguards and pressed into the battle. Thus he had fought for hours but, seek as he might, death had eluded him.

I am here God of Flames, he thought. *Come take me.*

A *Boru* took a murderous axe swipe at Kerebos' face and missed by an inch. The *ikar* rushed the off-balance warrior and shoved him backward into two others. All three barbarians went down and Kerebos drove Mistaaka through the squirming, cursing lot of them. Their harsh screams lifted over the field.

Kerebos was unable to reclaim his sword before more enemies charged, so he drew his dagger. The newest assailant, a man of some importance by the quality of his armor, swiped at Kerebos's ribs and connected. The *ikar* felt his armor give, but knew the blade had not pierced flesh. He slammed the dagger up under the *Boru's* chin and nailed the lower jaw into the palate; the exiting point split the tribesman's nose. Kerebos yanked free the knife, did a swim move over the falling body, and slammed chests with the second attacker.

This *Boru* had a long blond ponytail, which Kerebos pulled an instant before he opened the man's throat from ear to ear. Kerebos walked back and pulled Mistaaka from his victims, who now lay still.

A *landesknecta* puffed to Kerebos' side and cried: "Satyrnos is dead!"

"Have you any water?" Kerebos asked, matter-of-factly.

The legionary looked bemused and fumbled the length of his belt. "I lost my canteen!" he replied.

"Get another, then."

Kerebos returned to the bloodshed and found his bodyguards awaiting him. "Lead me to the war or get out of the way!" he growled.

It was not long before they hacked into a platoon of pikemen. No *Boru* tribesmen these, but Royal Marines in full armor. It took the legionaries more time to dispose of the spearmen, but the end result was the same. Confused, cramped and, eventually, cowed, the *Chaconni* went down by the score. Kerebos saw two Marines spear each other. While sinking onto their knees, the hapless pair continued to drive deeper their pikes.

Kerebos suddenly found himself face to face with Syranos *Elhar* and a sizable number of *landesknectos*.

"My lord!" Syranos shouted, pleased.

"Syranos! Why have you left your post?"

"This is my post!" the *elhar* replied.

Kerebos laughed for no reason. "Bring your men with me," he said. "Let us kill."

Syranos' weary smile showed in the gloom. "I think my arm's going to fall off. Pontis' men don't fight well, but there are many of them!"

"So kill them all," the *ikar* said. With that, he snatched a shield from a *sestari* and worked his way back into the action.

A giant *Boru*, large even by *landesknecta* standards, suddenly loomed before Kerebos. The tribesman brandished a two-handed sword above his shaggy head.

"Your eyes, legionary!" he taunted in heavily accented *Chaconni*. "I will have them!"

Kerebos raised his shield and positioned Mistaaka overhead, point forward, as though preparing a vertical swipe. The *Boru* lowered his weapon in anticipation.

"Can't see this black sword, can you?" Kerebos asked.

The tribesman grunted something obscene.

"Watch!" Kerebos cried. Still holding Mistaaka overhead like a giant scorpion's tail, he jabbed the blade into the *Boru's* forehead. Mistaaka squeaked through skull and the tribesman crashed backward like a falling tree.

Word quickly passed that Kerebos had killed the *Boru's* greatest warrior, and something like a wail rose from the enemy. The *ikar*, who spoke their harsh language, mocked his victim's poor swordmanship and promised similar treatment to anyone who crossed his path.

"You lads should've stuck to raiding the Old Kingdom!" he berated them. "You'll find too much fight for you here!"

Perhaps they agreed. In any case, their assault lost its fire.

Kerebos severed the fallen giant's neck with a single stroke and hefted it by its oily hair. More *Boru* fled into the night.

"Cavalry!" Syranos warned.

Kerebos looked over his scattered men. *How few*, he thought wrestling guilt.

"Ahhh!" a *landesknecta* screamed as he was run through by a lance. Mounted men, Pontis' own knights, burst through the *Boru*.

"Formation, quickly!" Syranos roared.

Soon I'll be gone also, the *ikar* thought.

Then the white sun burned in the sky.

Screams burst from every throat. *Chaconni* soldiers cast themselves prone in terror, or fell to their knees in supplication. *Boru* invoked heathen gods and ran hither and yon. *Landesknectos* shrunk from the sun like guilty children. A legionary beside Kerebos slew himself.

Kerebos threw back his head and laughed. "You arrive at last!" he cried.

Men threw themselves face down into the mud. Kerebos hefted Mistaaka. "Come, come, come!" he shouted, raged, cackled. "How will you beat me when you couldn't even save your own son? Come fight! I COMMAND YOU!"

And God came.

127

Two burning hands shot from the star and hissed across the blue sky, running eliptical paths toward Kerebos, who readied himself to strike. In the instant before they seized him, Kerebos saw open mouths in the palms, and flames within the mouths. The hands circled and crushed him in a burning grip; he felt the most excruciating pain imaginable in the flash before he passed out.

For a heartbeat Kerebos' mind was erased, turned inside out, spun round the other way. He felt himself rotate while the universe stood still. He saw everything and nothing at once, and himself between them...

The next thing the *ikar* knew, he was stumbling across the prairie, blinded by tears and babbling in tongues he could not understand. He hardly noticed the men he tripped over.

Syranos tackled him from behind. They wrestled atop some dead horsemen.

"My lord!" Syranos cried. "Calm yourself!"

Kerebos screamed nonsense and grappled with the *elhar*. "The hands! The hands!" he whined.

"What hands?" Syranos replied.

Kerebos unstrapped and tossed his helmet; he scuttled backwards into a dead horse. "Syranos, the hands!" he said. "They came from the sun!"

"I saw nothing, lord."

"You lie!" Kerebos insisted, covering his face.

"My lord, I saw nothing, by Desia's sacred blood!"

Kerebos tried to stand, but stumbled over the carcass. He tried again and gained his feet. "Then you are a blind fool!" he screamed. He staggered toward a living horse, grabbed its reins, and swung himself into the saddle—something he had not done since a boy.

"My lord!" Syranos wailed, floundering after him. "Where are you going?" He grabbed the *ikar*'s leg.

Kerebos bent an insane gaze upon the *elhar* and croaked: "Let go."

"Lord, where are you going without your sons?"

Kerebos tried to shake him off.

"You mustn't!" Syranos pleaded.

"Unhand me!"

"Master, don't go!" Syranos sobbed. "There's work for us, battles to be won!"

Kerebos sent him sprawling with a kick to the chest, but Syranos managed to hold onto the reins.

"You are the *ikar*! Kerebos *Ikar*!" he shouted angrily.

"Let go!"

"Father, please!"

Kerebos stiffened, then pulled his sword and buried it into Syranos' heart. Mistaaka slid between Syranos' bleeding hands and sprang from his back. Kerebos wrenched the weapon free and blood sprayed the horse.

Syranos' dying eyes revealed infinite sadness. "Father," he sighed and slumped against the horse, then slid to the ground. Kerebos slapped the mount with the flat of his blade. "Move!" The horse reared slightly then darted across the littered plain.

*   *   *

Kerebos appraised the seeping wound in the horse's shoulder. "Yah!" he urged, striking the mount.

He glanced back to see Pontis' men gaining on him. The King's Guards, besides being expert riders on fresh horses, wore little armor. They would catch him before long.

A streak of red hissed by Kerebos' ear. *Damn close*, he thought of the arrow, and risked another look at the Guards, who drew their bows even as they rode.

Kerebos cursed and spanked the horse. Froth spewed from the animal's mouth as it gave maximum effort. Kerebos leaned forward as another arrow whizzed past. The horse labored up a slight hill. Once on top, Kerebos could see trees in the distance. He was shocked, having no recollection of forests in these parts. He lay flat in the saddle and made for the woodland, his cheek on the horse's neck.

More arrows fell. Kerebos did not turn, but grit his teeth and waited for a quarrel in the back.

Come on, horse, just a little further! he thought. More arrows. One bounced of his left shoulder.

"A little more!" he cried.

The last hundred yards seemed to take an hour but finally the horse labored across the threshold. They were out of the sun and beneath a dark canopy. The forest was dense with considerable underbrush. Kerebos reined the steed and slipped off its back. The horse stumbled into a copse and fell with a snort.

"In here!" a *Chaconne* cried and burst into the woods.

Kerebos leaped at the rider, severing the Guard's sword arm at the elbow. The horseman screamed at his gushing stump until Mistaaka shaved off his face. More Guards burst through the trees; leaves and brances flew.

"Kalenis?" they called.

Kerebos pulled a new arrival from the saddle and rode him to the ground, head first. The Guard's neck snapped upon contact. Another cavalrymen charged the *ikar*.

"Death to Kerebos!" he cried, lifting a sword.

Kerebos sliced the horse's eye then spun out of the way. The animal threw the rider who, amazingly, landed on his feet. Kerebos hewed the Guard a half dozen times, dropping him in a shapeless heap atop the leaves.

Another Guard rushed Kerebos, who ducked a sizzling sword swipe and opened up the passing horse's flank. The Guard mastered his screaming mount and wheeled about as Kerebos threw Mistaaka. The sword crunched the Guard's nose and he wavered drunkenly in the saddle, then fell hard. Kerebos drew a dagger and gave the man a "legionary's smile"—a throat slashed from ear to ear.

Kerebos retrieved Mistaaka and backed against a tree. He strained to hear above the pounding in his ears. He thought he made out the *Chaconni* word "shoot" and flung himself to earth. None too soon! Arrows zipped overhead and thunked into trees.

"Again!" came the cry. "Lower!"

Kerebos turned and slithered deeper into the forest. When he had placed some trees between himself and the Guards, he got to his feet and lumbered through the underbrush. Branches slapped his face, but it was too dim to close his visor.

The crunch of hoofs followed in the distance. "Dismount and chase him on foot!" someone shouted. "A thousand in gold for his head!"

"Head, head, head!" echoed through the forest.

Kerebos pushed on though his lungs burned and his legs felt heavier than iron. "Desia!" he roared as a thorny trailer caught him across the face.

"That way!" and "Over there!" Guards shouted.

The cries were some way off so Kerebos stopped for a rest. He fell to a knee and gulped for air. *Might as well fight them here*, he concluded. *We'll see how happy they'll be to find me.*

"This damned brush," he moaned. "Oh, help me!"

The Guards went wild and zeroed in on him with bloodthirsty enthusiasm. *Come earn your thousand gold pieces, lads*, Kerebos thought with a small smile as he crouched behind a shagbarked tree.

A Guard sprang into the thicket and Kerebos slashed the man's unprotected kneecaps. The screaming soldier flew forward without his legs.

As he jaunted past, Kerebos asked: "Was that worth money?"

The *ikar* found another good hiding spot, a huge tree nearly six feet wide. Pontis' men found their dying companion and shouts of anger lifted over the forest. Kerebos was unmoved by their threats; he had heard it all so many times before.

Something caught Kerebos' eye and he looked down to see a long, striped snake crawling over his foot. He let the serpent pass, reminding himself he was armored, and watched the reptile disappear into a hole in the tree.

The Guards were moving his direction, chopping the brush in an attempt to flush him. They were still some distance away.

"Here!" a Guard yelled, almost in his ear. The *ikar* wheeled to see a sword closing with his face and just managed to duck in time; the sword bit into the tree.

"Fool!" Kerebos snorted and grabbed the *Chaconne's* wrist. The Guard could do nothing against the *ikar's* great strength. Kerebos lifted Mistaaka. "Heard of him?"

Another of Pontis' men, an officer in gilded mail, arrived. "Kerebos is here!" he cried and lunged.

Kerebos parried then booted the man in the groin, all without releasing the wrist. The officer went crosseyed and puffed to his knees.

Kerebos turned to his captive and kicked out his legs. He grabbed the fallen man and shoved his head into the snake hole. A muted rattling preceeded a shriek loud enough to shake the tree. The Guard thrashed so wildly Kerebos let go; the horseman gained his feet and tore off through the forest, screaming.

Kerebos walked over to the officer, who was still collecting himself. Kerebos stepped on the Guard's hand and said: "Call your mates."

The *Chaconne* shook his head. "To hell with you and all *landesknectos!*"

Kerebos pushed the officer onto the ground, jabbed Mistaaka into his ear, and started turning the blade. Howls of agony filled the glade for the long moment before Kerebos stabbed the Guard through both lungs.

"Come get me, king's men!" Kerebos challenged, his laughter filtering through the trees.

A Guard ran into the tiny clearing, and Kerebos threw a spiked fist into his face. The Guard flew backwards, trailing blood. Kerebos heard others arriving and charged.

Four Guards bellowed when they saw him.

Kerebos took a blow on the shoulder, slid beneath another strike, and shoved Mistaaka through a stomach. He backpedaled from a singing swordstroke and buried his pommel spike into an advancing man's jawbone. The Guard clutched his broken jaw with both hands as a gush of red streamed through his fingers.

Kerebos gave the remaining combatants no time to coordinate but opened one's throat with a blindingly fast slice, and caught the other in a headlock. A few vicious uppercuts left the horseman's face a dripping mess of blood, brains and sinuses.

Kerebos dropped the quivering body at his feet.

"Who's next?" he taunted. More men scuttled through the undergrowth. Away from him.

Kerebos leaned on his sword and listened. He wiped grimy sweat from his lacerated brow.

Horns blew, first a few in the forest, then dozens from the plain. Kerebos shook his head in disgust. At least a regiment of Guards had arrived, probably more. Certainly more, with a thousand in gold on his head.

Kerebos jogged back past the snake tree and headed deeper into the forest. The horns were blowing wildly now, and men answered with hoots of joy.

Sounds like an entire ala, he thought.

Kerebos loped on and the symphony gradually faded. He ran for a long time through endless thickets and windfalls and made no attempt to cover his trail. Once he startled a sleeping auroch, but the bull only snorted a challenge before crashing through the brush. At length Kerebos felt comfortable enough to risk a short rest. He found a small stream and drank a bit before propping himself against a tree. He resumed the trek before his joints had a chance to lock up. Eventually, the trees thinned out a little.

Nightfall found Kerebos stumbling through a sparsely wooded grassland beneath a new moon. His lungs seared with each breath, but still he staggered forward, reflecting upon his abandoned men, and the Flame God. Would the sun come up this night, also?

Eventually the *ikar* stopped beside a wide, fast river. He stared over the dark water to the ghostly-lit weald on the other side. He was too tired to swim so he sat on a crop of rocks and dimly contemplated his next move.

The moon made its way across the sky and still Kerebos pondered his ill deeds. *I'm all worn thin and empty*, he told himself, and it was true. He had nothing left; no hopes, no hates, no wishes for tomorrow. And there was the Flame God. *Don't want to close my eyes and see him anymore*, he thought.

"I just want out," he sighed.

Kerebos groaned to his feet and fumbled with his armor buckles. His cuirass went first, then his arm and shin pieces. He threw them all into the water and watched them make barely a ripple. Boots, gambeson and mailskirt went next; they left no lasting impression, either.

Like my life, he thought, dejected. *A long war fought for nothing.*

Kerebos wanted to cry, but was too exhausted. He strapped Mistaaka round his bare waist then leaned onto his knees. The river rolled past.

"It doesn't matter," he whispered.

Kerebos jumped into the water, touched the muddy bottom, then pushed his way to the surface. The flow was faster than he had suspected, but its coolness soothed his wounds. He breaststroked with the current for a while, sweeping by the trees at great speed.

As the forest petered out the *ikar* reflected upon his many battles, especially the most recent one. He felt a strange, distant mixture of longing and apprehension. He felt outside himself, and the break brought an unbearable loneliness.

This is a place to die, he thought.

Kerebos exhaled and ducked beneath the black surface. He rolled over and over with the muddy current, surrounded by darkness at last. *At least the flames never got me...*

*   *   *

King Pontis' throneroom was huge. A single, marble hall stretched nearly a quarter mile from its gilded doors to the monarch's dais. The ceiling rose to a dizzying, domed height and its depending chandeliers were broader across than many a house.

The castle at Korenthis had been constructed by the *Chaconni* at the apex of their power, over a millenium before, but showed few signs of age. Rather, recent tribute from foreign kings dressed up the place to the point that its splendor recalled that of ages past. With the crushing of Kerebos *Ikar*, Pontis was even considering an additional wing. But that had to wait; there was unfinished business to attend.

Pontis, a stout, formidable looking man of middle age, settled onto his throne and spread his scarlet robe for greatest visual effect. His bearded face was pensive as his dark, penetrating eyes took inventory of the many, standing nobles. Some he held in his gaze, weighing their worth or intentions. How many would question his desire to absorb the Brotherhood?

They dare not defy me on this, he thought. *Shall I place their sons between us and the Boru?*

Pontis nodded to the rotund majordomo, and all chatter ceased. "Praxis, bring in the prisoner," the king said in a disaffected tone.

"Sire!" Praxis bowed deeply, impressive for a man of his girth, then knocked his brass staff against the marble floor. "Bring in the renegade!" he cried, indicating the far doors.

The lords and ladies turned to the great valves, which swung noiselessly open. Four officers from the Guards, resplendent in scarlet jupon and with swords drawn, entered at the quick step. Next came a cohort of soldiers and one prisoner, chained hand and foot.

Triskeles, clad in a slave's tunic, sneered at the entire congregation as he was ushered past. He was inches taller than any man in the room, a fact exaggerated by his erect carriage and raised nose. The soldiers quickly marched him toward Pontis, who did not quite manage to appear bored. Pontis could be excused his excitement, perhaps, as it had been centuries since his nation had bested the *landesknectos* in even the smallest skirmish.

Triskeles was brought before the elevated dais. Praxis smiled cruelly.

"The famous First *Elhar*," he chuckled. To the guards he said, "Make him kneel."

Triskeles' laughed. "Yes, do that fat boy, and I'll wrap these chains around your throat before I rip it out!"

Angry shouts issued from the crowd. Even now they had to endure *landesknecta* arrogance?

"Discipline him!" Praxis snarled.

Triskeles head-butted one of his captors and sent the man sprawling. A dozen swords rang from their sheaths and were pressed against the *Boru*.

"Give me one of those stickers and I'll teach you how to fight!" he cried.

Pontis' face displayed more emotion then he had planned; the legionary certainly was not making things easy. Praxis looked over the nobles. "One thousand years ago we lost our Tenth Legion to a renegade general's sedition," he said in a loud voice. "It has been a thousand years to rue."

Triskeles laughed again. Pontis continued.

"Not only did the Empire lose an army, but the traitor, Desia Klokonis-Varra, savaged his own country. Now, one of his sons has been brought to heel."

The *elhar* looked amused. "History bores me, great king," he shouted. "Why not give up a dagger so me and your boys can sort it all out?"

More appalled glances from the nobles. This *landesknecta* certainly lived up to his billing! A soldier smacked Triskeles in the head with a spear. The *Boru* staggered but righted himself, though his eyes glazed with water.

"Desia betrayed his people," Pontis addressed the *Boru*. "Have you anything to say?"

Triskeles shrugged. "Might makes right, or at least the *Chaconni* have always proclaimed."

Pontis smiled and nodded; he rose from his seat and started down the steps. "Do you believe that?"

"No man agrees with that more than I."

Pontis nodded. "Good," he said, "Then you must know I'm your king and master."

Triskeles' eyes blazed, but only for an instant. There was more here than a taunt. Why did Pontis waste words on him? *He wants something*, Triskeles concluded. *What?* Then he sniggered with understanding. *Pontis wants the Legion!*

"I serve no man while in chains," Triskeles said boldly.

Some of the nobles grasped what was going on and murmured disapproval. Some of the ladies moved away in fear.

"You will not long be in chains, if you swear fealty to me," Pontis replied. "Your fealty and that of your *elhar*."

"Six *elhari* make a legion," Triskeles snapped. "That's what you want, eh, a legion?"

Some of the *Chaconni* looked very uncomfortable now. His guards turned menacingly toward Triskeles.

"Earn your *elhari*, then," Pontis replied. "March under my banner, and bring me the head of Kerebos."

Triskeles smiled broadly. "Nothing would please me more. My king." *Kerebos!* he thought. *I will kill you and yet get my legion! Then I'll butcher this little fool.*

"Good," Pontis answered and started for his throne.

A dapper young man emerged from the crowd and gave a quick bow. "My lord!" he cried. "You can not enlist the services of this mindless aberration! Remember how his legion tormented us, I beg you! Remember the walls of Korenthis and your own brother before Pharazos' Gate!"

Others took up the cry. "Kill him lord! Torture and kill him!"

Pontis' face froze over. "Am I your king, Count Knossis?"

The count knelt. "Sire!"

"Then be silent. I decide what's best for my nation."

Knossis bowed hastily and melted back into a crowd grown suddenly silent.

"My Lord Trygg!" Pontis raised his voice. "Bring me his sword."

A tall, middle-aged *Boru*, forked beard stabbed into a silver belt, emerged from behind the throne and pushed his way through the Guards. His kneelength mailshirt chimed softly as he walked. His eyes, steely gray on a pale and weathered face, were devoid of emotion. He placed the hilt of Triskeles' sword, Cattamos, into Pontis' hand.

Triskeles stood erect as a spear and eyed first his sword, then his sire. "I greet you, father," he said.

Trygg nodded slightly. "My son, it is good to see you this side of the Allfather's halls."

"The ways of exile," Triskeles replied softly and glanced at his feet. "How fare my mother and sister?"

"Your mother lives," Trygg replied somberly.

Pontis hefted Cattamos and approached the *elhar*. "Free him," he told the guards. "Kneel, Lord Tryggvason," he bade Triskeles. "Accept your duty and commission."

Triskeles made to kneel but stopped. "I am an Earl's son," he insisted. "No mere lord."

Grumbles from the *Chaconni* nobles.

"In my country, an Earl equals one of your Dukes," Triskeles pressed.

"My lord!" a duke cried.

Pontis frowned. "I shall not dishonor that tradition." he replied, visibly displeased. "See that you don't, either," he warned.

"I won't," Triskeles promised loudly, then knelt.

Pontis quickly tapped the *elhar* on either shoulder with the flat of the sword. "Rise Lord Tryggvason," he commanded.

Triskeles stood, but his thoughts were elsewhere. *Kerebos!* his mind screamed.

Chapter 16

The five men stopped beside the river. The mercenary commander squinted at the sun then at Antiphon, who drove a two-mule wagon. The soldier shook his shaggy head.

"All the way out here to find Kerebos?" he asked. "Are you certain the Grand Master's correct? I'm familiar with Harat, but I haven't recognized a thing since we crossed the valley."

Antiphon opened the sketch map. "We're heading the right way, Sergeant Genianus," he replied, none-too-confidently. "Didn't Dokein predict a river where there'd never been one?"

The mercenary contemplated the churning water. "Just because nobody etched this creek on a map doesn't make the Grand Master a wizard," he said at last and reached for his canteen.

Have your visions failed you, Dokein? Antiphon wondered, desperately hoping he would not see Kerebos again.

They started forward. Antiphon was soon lost in thought. They travelled for some time before Genianus spoke.

"Go see what it is," he told one of his men.

Antiphon stirred to see a soldier gallop off; after the rider reached his destination, he dismounted, and waved frantically. Genianus and the others spurred their horses, leaving Antiphon in their dust. The priest's heart was in his throat.

They've found him? he thought.

Sergeant Genianus returned forthwith. His weathered face was anxious. "It's him," he said. "Though it appears he's no longer living."

Antiphon felt relieved. "Are you sure? How do you know it's the *ikar?*"

"Because I've never seen such a monster," Genianus replied.

"Is he in black armor?"

"No iron but his sword. Maybe somebody stripped him?"

Antiphon urged the mules forward. He reached the mercenaries and climbed off the wagon. It was Kerebos. The *ikar*, who lay on his back, appeared to have been dragged feet first from the water. His eyes were wide open, but empty; one of his thick arms hung in the river. Antiphon, a skilled healer, felt for a pulse. None.

A soldier gave a low whistle. "Are all of 'em this big?" he asked.

"Yes," Antiphon said. He opened Kerebos' mouth and checked for a blocked windpipe, then again he felt for a pulse. *Dead*, he thought, and closed Kerebos' eyes.

"Nice sword," Genianus said and grabbed Mistaaka. "Needs a good sharpening, though."

Kerebos grabbed the sergeant's wrist.

"Get him off me!" Genianus screamed. His men jumped to help.

Kerebos' lips moved, but only water issued from between them.

"Get him off me!" Genianus repeated, his arm purpling from the *ikar*'s grip.

"Kerebos!" Antiphon yelled.

The legionary's eyes opened. He released his captive.

"Kerebos *Ikar*?" Antiphon said in a softer tone.

The *landesknecta* looked through the priest. "Not peace but a sword," he gargled, then again closed his eyes. Antiphon felt for a heartbeat and found a faint one.

"That's damnable strange," Genianus said massaging his arm.

"Lift him into the wagon," Antiphon ordered.

Antiphon reached Kwan Aharon two days later. He relieved Genianus' squad then entered the bustling city; Kerebos lay covered in the wagon. It took some time to reach the Sanctum, but no sooner had Antiphon entered the gates than priests began to crowd the cart. Very quickly the throng halted the mules' progress.

"Get out of the way!" Antiphon snapped, irritated. "Dokein needs to see him!"

Women poured from the Gynaeceum and gathered round. Selah slipped through to the cart.

"Aside, aside!" Dokein shouted as he and Master Torra hurried to Antiphon's rescue. Somebody dragged the cloth from Kerebos and a murmur passed through the crowd.

"Away from the cart!" Torra cried, then glared at Antiphon. "You should've waited until dark."

"I didn't know you posted my arrival," Antiphon muttered. It had been a long, uncomfortable ride and he was exhausted.

"Some men have mouths too big for the priesthood," Dokein said, then shooed off the onlookers. Soon only a few priests and Selah remained.

Selah stared at the muscular *ikar* with fear and approval. She held onto her father as though for protection, but never took her eyes from the great warrior.

"Daughter, why are you here?" Dokein asked.

Antiphon frowned. "To see a man in soft raiment?"

"He still lives?" Dokein asked Antiphon, who was studying Selah.

"He does."

"Bring him inside."

*   *   *

Kerebos opened his eyes.

The small room was lit by a single candle, but even that weak light was a welcome reprieve from the void from which he had come. He did not know where he had been, but had no desire to return.

The bed was too short, Kerebos' feet hung off, but was softer than any he remembered. He moved his eyes. Marble walls reflected the candlelight. A serving tray and urn rested in the far corner. The smells of sweat and rue scented the air.

Kerebos tried to sit but his arms would not obey. Even drawing breath proved a challenge, and every time he moved his head on the damp pillow, his stomach threatened to revolt.

"Where am I?" he croaked and scratched the cover from his bare chest.

Kerebos noticed the door as it swung inward. A bent, robed figure hobbled into the room and leaned over the bed, regarding him with shrewd eyes. The old man stroked a short beard while sizing up his patient.

"Who are you?" Kerebos coughed and lifted an unsteady hand. "Where am I?"

The warden turned and left, locking the door behind him. Kerebos tried to rise, but could not. He rested for a moment and tried again, but failed.

I feel like a corpse, he thought. *Where am I?*

He dozed again, but was wakened by voices outside the door. Moments later, three more men entered.

"Has he spoken, Samir?" Antiphon asked and lit a hanging lamp.

"Yes, Master," the warden replied. "He asked where he was."

"Is that all?" Dokein probed.

"Yes."

"Thank you," Antiphon said. "Please leave us with our guest."

Samir eyed the bedridden *ikar*. "Shall I call for the guards? His strength may soon return."

"No," Dokein answered.

Samir bowed and left. Antiphon approached Kerebos and felt his forehead.

"His fever has broken, Grand Master. Perhaps his evil will has, too."

Dokein looked thoughtfully at Kerebos, who gazed at Antiphon and snorted: "So you're a healer, too? Why am I here?"

"All priests are healers of some sort," Antiphon replied. "And didn't I say your movements were prophesied?"

"Antiphon found you at my behest," Dokein explained. "He brought you to Kwan Aharon."

Kerebos remembered the flight through the forest, and the subsequent swim. *I killed myself*, he thought. "How'd you find me?"

The Grand Master shrugged.

Kerebos looked at Antiphon and his eyes narrowed. "Did that man call you *Master?*" he chided. "As reward for your success at my castle?"

"I have been elevated," Antiphon admitted. "The Grand Master has more faith in me than he should."

Kerebos shook his head.

"Are you hungry?" Dokein asked.

141

Kerebos thought about it then said, "Yes. Very."

"I'll have something sent to you."

Kerebos nodded but he was not thinking of food. He eyed Antiphon. "I promised to kill you if we met again," he said without passion.

"Do you still wish that?"

Kerebos sorted his feelings. He remembered the crimes he had commited while breaking Antiphon. *I should kill him*, he thought. "I don't know," he said. "Where's my sword?"

"They sleep with those things," Antiphon confided to Dokein.

"In my care," Dokein told Kerebos.

"I want it."

"Rest first. When you are well, you may have your weapon. Truly, you may go wherever you wish."

Kerebos grunted. "Then why'd you bother bringing me here?"

Dokein lifted his hands and said, "I had no choice in the matter. It was written. Anyway, I'm not exactly sure *you* have a say in the matter." He leaned over the *ikar*.

"What?" Kerebos demanded suspiciously.

Dokein laid a hand on the *ikar*'s forehead and muttered a blessing.

"Stop!" Kerebos choked, but even as he spoke his anger smoothed, and a soft jolt of energy passed through his body. Kerebos gave the Grand Master's hand a weak shove.

Dokein smiled. "You could feel like that for the rest of your life," he said. "You may go or stay. I'd prefer you stay. Besides, Pontis of Korenthis has laid a kingly ransom on your head. You could be safe here…for a while."

Dokein nodded to Antiphon then departed. Antiphon appeared uncomfortable as he sized up the *ikar*.

"I prayed Dokein's men would kill you," he said after a moment.

"I don't blame you," Kerebos confessed. "I acted very badly."

"You are evil!" Antiphon spat, but his expression immediately turned contrite.

"Yes."

Antiphon drew a number of deep breaths. "Please forgive me," he said. "My words were unbecoming a priest of the Flame."

Kerebos gave a rasping chuckle. "Really?" he asked. "Those

flames have tickled me enough that I must disagree."

"Forgive me," Antiphon repeated. He made a gesture over the bed and mumbled something before following after the Grand Master.

Kerebos was left to contemplate the trick Dokein had played on him. Whatever Dokein's methods, the "blessing" had felt better than a good dose of *kraal*. When Samir finally arrived with a meal, Kerebos' thoughts were on Antiphon's final words. He could not remember anybody ever asking his forgiveness when they had the upper hand.

Priests, he brooded.

*　　　*　　　*

Kerebos remained Samir's patient for weeks while his strength slowly, grudgingly, returned. Eventually he could eat and dress himself.

One morning after a meal of fish, vegetables and milk, he changed into a fresh chlamys and donned the sandals Antiphon had provided him. After a short rest, he hobbled to the door.

Kerebos found himself trembling. In the back of his mind lurked the fear he would open the door and see nothing but void. He was sweating as he turned the knob.

A long glass hallway confronted the *ikar*. Treetops and hanging plants waved outside the open windows; a fresh herbal scent was in the air. Samir rose from his reading chair and closed the phlactery.

"Yes?" he asked in mild surprise.

Kerebos chose his words carefully. He wanted out of the room but doubted he had vitality enough to wrestle the old man. He chose to be diplomatic.

"I want to leave this room," he said.

The warden tucked his prayer book beneath his robe. "Please lie down," he replied. "I will talk to the Master."

Since his knees had begun to shake, Kerebos heeded the request. A half hour later, Antiphon entered Kerebos' room. The priest was dressed in formal robes and carried the air of a man called from some endeavor.

"Good morning, Kerebos," he said briskly.

"Good morning, *Master*," the *ikar* answered sarcastically. "Come to bind me while you still can?"

Antiphon shook his head. "By the Grand Master's order you are to be free in the Basilica. You may go where you like, though he suggests you not mix with the population, unless you intend on leaving us. Pontis has raised the price on you to a hundred thousand in gold."

Kerebos looked suddenly dejected. "Maybe I'll ransom myself. I'm worth more dead than ever I was alive." *My legion is gone, my dreams are gone and all honor is gone*, he thought. *Why am I still alive?*

Antiphon's countenance softened momentarily, then he remembered his internment at Kerebos' castle, the slain children. "Dokein wants you," he said.

"He expects me to stay, eh?" Kerebos replied. "Is he still convinced I'm the holy man from the 'scriptures'? The world hasn't quite ended, has it?"

"That's a matter of opinion." Antiphon said slowly. "Did you ever think you would be here?"

Kerebos recalled his plan to conquer Kwan Aharon. "Yes, though in different fashion."

"Quite different, I'm sure," Antiphon replied and turned to the door. "Samir! Get a pair of strong lads to assist our guest."

"I can walk on my own!" Kerebos insisted.

Antiphon smiled. "I'd prefer they accompany us."

Samir and two others entered the room. The "strong lads" turned out to be fully armored soldiers. Kerebos was amused by the swagger in their steps; he knew his least *sestar* could teach both these professionals a red lesson in swordsmanship.

"Help him rise, please," Antiphon bade the soldiers.

"I can stand," Kerebos growled, then proved his claim.

"Follow me, then."

Antiphon led them through the sundrenched hall to a flight of circular stairs. They descended. Kerebos slipped a little on the first step then did quite well. They exited the hospital and crossed a courtyard of trees and shrubs, then out an arched gate. There was another stairway, skillfully carved from the indigenous rock, and a short walk to a sand-colored building, which they entered.

Another hallway. A trio of Masters backed into a wall at Kerebos' approach, but said nothing. They were soon back outdoors in yet another courtyard where Dokein and a boy were pruning rose bushes.

"Grand Master," Antiphon called.

"Father!" Yeshua cried and ran to hug his sire. The boy released Antiphon and gave Kerebos a long glance. The *ikar* stared into empty space.

"Is that him?" Yeshua whispered in an awed voice.

"It is," Antiphon frowned. "Remember what I told you. Run along and get some breakfast."

Wide-eyed, Yeshua backed out of sight.

Antiphon bowed to Dokein. "Grand Master, he has recovered."

Dokein gently placed his shears against an empty flower pot and wiped his hands on a rag. "I greet you, Kerebos *Ikar*," he said.

Kerebos did not reply. Yeshua had reminded him of his own childhood, and his own father.

"Are you hungry?" Dokein asked.

"He eats enough for six men," Samir grumbled.

"Thank you, good warden," Dokein replied. "That will be all. Take the guards with you; we won't need them." Dokein watched Samir's departure then addressed Antiphon. "Ani, return to the Council."

"Uh, Master?"

"Go, my son. I'll be fine."

Antiphon looked displeased but obeyed.

Kerebos and Dokein were alone with the roses, the wind and the morning sun. The light in the Grand Master's eyes made Kerebos uncomfortable; he suspected Dokein was reading his thoughts.

"What makes you so sure I won't throttle you?" Kerebos asked.

Dokein smiled broadly. "The Order of the White Flame used to boast the finest warriors in the world," he said. "Our men were soldiers armed with philosophy, mystery and swords."

Kerebos scowled. "In order of increasing importance?"

Dokein chuckled.

Kerebos found it strange to encounter an individual who did not dread him, and even rarer to experience fear of someone else, but the look in Dokein's eyes caused in him something close to panic. He sensed an undeniable power in the Grand Master and a will that dwarfed his own. He perceived that the priest's inner strength, if leveled fully against him, might snap him in two.

"Where are those fine warriors now?" Kerebos asked.

Dokein's smile faded. "When I was a child, I thought as a child and spoke as a child, but now I have put away childish things. So has the Order—and so should you. Strong men have no need of swords."

"Then they need die upon them."

"Perhaps," Dokein replied. "You look unsteady. Shall we sit?"

"Thanks," Kerebos grunted, seething at the weakness in his knees.

"My manners! Forgive me for not remembering your condition, my son!" Dokein disappeared between two rows of autumn flowers and reemerged with a tall stool, which he offered. Kerebos plopped down. After a moment he looked up at the Grand Master, who waited patiently.

"What do you want of me?" Kerebos asked.

"It is time to put away childish things," Dokein replied. "It is time for you to be a man."

The *landesknecta* looked incredulous. "Who's more manly than Kerebos *Ikar?*" he demanded.

Dokein's eyes blazed. "Killing children is easy," he grated. "Raising them with love is not, and living by God's rules takes more manliness than both!"

Kerebos inhaled a number of deep breaths. The Basilica's bells began to toll. He lowered his head and said, "I am an evil man."

"Maybe. Are you afraid of hard words and ugly stares, *ikar?*"

"No."

Dokein laid a hand on the giant killer's shoulder. "Then you shall find peace here."

*   *   *

Two months passed.

The wet season was upon the desert. Kwan Aharon daily suffered heavy rains, thunder and lightning.

146

Antiphon, who was to preside at a "rite of manhood" ceremony for a friend's son, entered the great *Syna*. Feeling a need for privacy and purification, he skipped lunch in favor of an hour's prayer. He lit a votive candle and knelt on some steps before an icon of the Savior.

I am yours, my God, he thought. *Purge me of my sins, my pride and the lusts of my heart. Erase from me all envy. Help me accept my lot, and not dwell upon the successes of other men.*

Antiphon set the candle in a holder and placed his hands together in prayer. He closed his eyes.

Bless the Grand Master and my love, his daughter. Protect my son from harm and the foolish desires of youth.

The candle sizzled as it was doused by a cup of wine. Antiphon's eyes flew open.

"I'm sorry, it slipped," Montanus explained with a grin. He knelt beside Antiphon. "Shall I relight it, Master?"

"That's correct, Montanus," Antiphon bit off the words. "*I am a Master!* If you don't want to spend the rest of your days cleaning stables, leave me to my devotions!"

Montanus' smile faded from his pock-marked face.

"What's wrong, Ani?" he asked with mock concern. "Too important for an old friend? Show some charity. You've won. You have Dokein's heart and will soon have his daughter." Montanus clucked. "I'd say your life is improving."

Antiphon stood and backed away; his eyes burned. "Perhaps you should labor in love rather than spite," he suggested. "Then you might know respect and success."

"Just like your heeled dog the *ikar?*" the *Chaconne* spat. "May I also kill everybody I choose, then kiss Dokein's ass for absolution? Is that the *Aharoni* path to high regard and salvation?"

"If you bathed, you might be held in higher esteem," Antiphon retorted and turned away.

"Oh, certainly!" Montanus' nasal whine echoed in the great chamber. "Maybe I'd smell as nice as soft Selah? Maybe I could whore myself, as she does?"

Antiphon stopped and rested his hand on a pew. He tried counting until his temper abated but suddenly whirled on Montanus. "That's the second time you've dishonored my lady!" he bellowed.

"By God, there shall not be a third!"

Montanus oozed down the steps toward him. "She dishonors us all!" he shot back. "I for the lust she imparts, you for the stupidity she demands—*Master*!" With a kick, he sent Antiphon's candle flying. "Have you not marked her eyes on that murderer?"

"Montanus," Antiphon started coldly, "if you spread your lies any further…"

"You'll what?" Montanus interrupted. "Kill me? Maybe you can get your son to wheedle Kerebos for you? Perhaps little 'Shua can make the great *ikar* rid you of a troublesome brother!"

"Now you insult my son!" Antiphon balled his fists and stomped toward Montanus.

Montanus raised his hands in surrender. "Sorry," he said. "I'd be upset, too, if my boy cared more for a cutthroat than for me, I must admit." He smiled. "He honors Kerebos like a lord and dotes on his words like a little idiot!"

Antiphon broke into a run. He tackled Montanus by the waist and slammed him onto the steps. Rank breath whistled from between Montanus' teeth as Antiphon wrapped hands around his throat.

Antiphon wanted to throttle Montanus, to strangle the life from the cruel and impious priest, not least because his words had held more than a grain of truth.

"I'm going to kill you!" Antiphon cried.

"Master!" Montanus laughed and choked as tears of amusement streamed down his thin face. Antiphon suddenly released Montanus and sat on the *Chaconne*'s chest, breathing hard.

"You are a corrupter of hearts, Montanus," he said at last.

Montanus wiggled beneath him and Antiphon let him go. Montanus sat and massaged his throat with a dirty hand.

"The evil I uncover is there already," he answered.

Antiphon pondered this before saying, "You're an abomination." He looked dolefully at the statue of the Savior then tread heavily down the steps.

Montanus spat after him.

What sins shall I buy with Pontis' gold? he thought.

Chapter 17

amir knocked lightly on Dokein's door.

"Come in," came the weary reply.

Samir entered and saw Shekkinah, the gynaeceum house mother, before the Grand Master's desk. Hands on beefy hips, she was lecturing about the proper conduct of unmarried women. The Grand Master looked as though he wanted to melt into his chair as the house mother enumerated Selah's most recent iniquities. Shekkinah paused for breath and Dokein seized the opportunity.

"My dear Samir!" he cried. "I forgot our appointment! Shekkinah, good woman, I apologize but we'll have to discuss this later."

Shekkinah was not fooled and shot a withering glance at Samir. She made a slow production of adjusting her wimple, gave Samir another glare, then lumbered from the room.

Dokein sighed, completely drained. "Thanks," he said.

"Why does she speak to the Grand Master in such a way?" Samir asked in astonishment.

"Selah," Dokein groaned, as though the name explained everything. "Please sit."

"Thank you."

"Wine?" Dokein asked.

"No, Grand Master."

Dokein poured some for himself. "How goes Kerebos' progress?"

"The *Chaconne* improves daily," Samir reported. "Physically, he'll be quite himself in a week or so."

"Are you keeping his mind occupied?"

"Yes, Master. He's quiet, humble and studious. He can't get enough books to read."

"That's good. What subjects?"

"History, philosophy and, oddly enough, architectural texts," Samir replied. "The last one surprises me. One of the maids found some sketches under his bed, improvements for our fortifications."

Dokein's eyebrows went up. "Oh?"

"I don't think they're his," Samir admitted. "They're too good."

"Don't underestimate the man because he's not *Aharoni*," Dokein cautioned. "He's very smart."

Samir shrugged.

"Will he ever be ready to join our community?" Dokein asked.

Samir looked uneasy. "He's a barbarian, Grand Master. Besides, he terrifies people."

"But God brought him here for a purpose," Dokein replied. "We must be about that purpose."

Samir, like many in the Order, was unconvinced by Dokein's arguments about Kerebos, and had never hid the fact. "My respects Grand Master, but *you* brought Kerebos to Kwan Aharon."

Dokein stared. "Couldn't God use me for that purpose?"

Samir gave the barest nod.

"Send Kerebos to me when he has healed completely," Dokein commanded. "I'll judge for myself."

Another fortnight in Kwan Aharon worked wonders on Kerebos. His health returned with a vengeance, and his morale steadily improved. Childhood mores, long dead, were slowly revived by daily interaction with people other than deranged, depraved *landesknectos*. He no longer acted a bloodthirsty legionary but comported himself with contemplative reserve. Even his temper was brought to heel, though maintained at the price of a laconic detachment. Few eyes penetrated the shield he had erected, or sensed his self-hatred and regret.

Some complained that Kerebos had cheated justice and should be turned over to Pontis, but Dokein stood firmly behind the *ikar*. Had not God previously converted slayers and even raised them very high?

At least one man was not content to grumble from a distance;

the *ikar's* newfound restraint was often tested by Montanus. Whether Kerebos was alone at dinner or labor, Montanus took an interest in seeking out and taunting him. It was widely interpreted that Montanus gloried in a soul more tormented than his own, but whatever his concern, nobody much cared. The two *Chaconni* were the city's most despised men and somehow seemed to deserve each other. A wit dubbed them "the rat and the tiger" and the labels stuck.

"On this day four years ago the Black Legion enslaved three thousand souls," a smiling Montanus once told Kerebos. Another time he asked, "Isn't this the anniversary of town Mistaaka's liquidation?"

Kerebos' replies were never more than a nod, and Montanus took the responses as proof of a broken spirit. He was wrong. He might have desisted had he realized just how close to death the barbs brought him.

Time passed quickly for Kerebos and he gave little thought to the future. His lonely days were dedicated to physical tasks and nights spent reading. But always he remembered the past. How flat his life had become only accentuated how horrendous it had been. Sometimes he would simply sit in his little room and stare at the wall, reliving his crimes and wondering why he had been spared, if not to be tormented by a conscience deprived the drug of violence.

I know I'm the worst of them all, he told himself. *It is unjust that I still live, but how can I ask forgiveness when I can't forgive myself?*

Kerebos slept little but ate much and slaved daily. No job was too difficult or degrading, nor any request for backbreaking work denied. He pushed himself to the limit every day as a distraction. His body, long spared the most extreme rigors because of rank, bulged and rippled into the most impressive of human machines.

Kerebos grew to respect Dokein, too. He appreciated the Grand Master for treating him like a man, not as he deserved. It was not that Kerebos believed Dokein did not loathe him, but the old man never acted as such. He was never anything but genuinely patient, polite and kind. Kerebos had long since stopped complaining about being called "my son"; Dokein did not hear him.

The *ikar's* chief joy came from his talks with the Grand Master, and sometimes Antiphon. When possible, Dokein spent hours picking Kerebos' thoughts and dreams. Kerebos refused Dokein nothing as long as he reciprocated by answering philosophical questions. These the Grand Master answered frankly, which rarely satisfied Kerebos as they always arrived at the question of salvation.

Antiphon, however, was often impatient with Kerebos. Their conversations were not always polite, but they did develop a grudging admiration for each other's mind. Kerebos rapidly became so skillful in debate that Antiphon would find himself lured into feelings of camaraderie. Then the priest would suddenly remember to whom he spoke and would grow sullen.

One such confrontation almost ended in blows when Kerebos pointed out that the entire *Aharoni* religion hinged upon the unjust murder of a single innocent man. Luckily, Dokein broke up the shouting match.

Time passed and the world endured. Besides a few minor earthquakes, Pangaea returned to normal. Most people, with amazing indifference, downplayed the startling events that had preceded the crushing of the Black Legion. Since the world showed no further sign of immediate destruction, gloomy prophesies backed into the shadows. Many nations ignored Dokein's emissaries and his call to holiness. Even among the *Aharoni* states, talks of the end faded to a whisper.

Except in Kwan Aharon. The elderly Grand Master daily preached among the masses, prodding backsliders and the casually religious into godliness.

Kerebos, though, had long since abandoned hope for his soul. He found Kwan Aharon bearable, and sometimes comforting, which was more than he felt he deserved. Though he accepted damnation, he no longer desired to rob others of their spiritual options. If he could live the rest of his life without lengthening his encyclopedia of sins, that would be enough.

Or so he thought.

*   *   *

Selah gazed down into the garden where a barechested Kerebos labored between rows of budding plants. She licked her lips like a hungry lioness.

152

Since first she clapped eyes on Kerebos she had desired him, in all ways, more than any man she had ever seen. He was dangerous, but she liked that. Besides sex, Selah hungered to possess the ferocity lurking behind his eyes. Here was a man equal to her ambition, greater even. With him as lover, nothing would retard her aspirations. Kerebos had held the world for two decades, and could again.

How far he could climb with the right woman, she thought. *He could be a king.*

Kerebos hefted a hoe and struck the soil near a withered cyprus. The tool jolted cruelly and sent bolts of pain through his blistered hands. He stepped back from the tree, massaging his palms.

"Does that hurt?" Yeshua asked from his perch on a pile of red bricks.

"Don't you have studies, priest's son?"

"Could you chop off a man's head off with that thing?" the boy asked.

Kerebos grimaced. "Run along, Yeshua," he replied, a little hoarsely. "Let a worthless soul finish his work."

"Why don't you wear gloves?" the lad inquired. "You wouldn't get blisters."

Kerebos resumed work. *Because I don't deserve them*, he thought.

Two priests fell silent as they passed but soon resumed their conversation. They argued which vegetables they would seed, if it were up to them, and the worthiness of plants one could not eat. They moved out of earshot.

Yeshua flapped his legs in the air and asked, "Why don't you chop the dirt with a sword?"

Kerebos thought of Mistaaka and his heart skipped a beat.

"My friend, Juntha, says legionaries can chop through rocks!" Yeshua continued.

Kerebos stared at the boy. Selah entered the garden.

"Yeshua," she called.

Both males watched her approach. Selah carried a pitcher in one hand, and hoisted her dress above the furrows of dirt with the other. Kerebos noted the curve of her muscular calves.

Yeshua clapped his hands with glee. "Selly!" he cried and darted toward her. He gave Selah a quick hug then demanded a drink.

"Now get!" Selah commanded. "You've much to study. Azoth says your geography is terrible."

Yeshua stamped his foot in the dust. "I don't have to listen to you! You're not my mother yet!"

Selah smiled. "Do I have to talk to your father?"

Yeshua lowered his head. "That's blackmail," he said.

"Yes. Now run along."

Yeshua waved at the *ikar*. "See you tomorrow." He scurried away.

Kerebos' face lengthened as he watched Yeshua leave.

Selah smiled as she closed the space between them.

"I've brought water, lord," she said and offered the pitcher.

"Please don't call me that."

"Well, I've brought water anyway."

Kerebos lifted a bleeding hand. "I thank you, lady."

Selah smiled even wider. "Oh, don't call *me* that." She ran a gaze from his face to his chest, then further below. "You've a little blood on you, Kerebos. I'm not afraid of a little blood. Or anything else." She pushed the sweating tankard against his corded chest and giggled as his nipples hardened.

You should be afraid! he thought. *Oh Desia, you should be!*

Kerebos looked away as he took the water. "I thank you," he replied and emptied the container. He wiped his mouth with a corded forearm. "Please let me work."

Selah stepped closer and swept water from his stomach with her small hand.

"You've soaked yourself," she said, swiping the liquid downward. She grabbed his loincloth. "If I knew you were going to bathe, I would've brought a bucket." Kerebos was scared. A fever overcame him as did the desire to throw her into the dirt and take her right there. She wanted him, that was certain, and he longed to oblige. Why should he care what anyone thought? Who dared deny him? He would show this perfumed priest's daughter why she had learned to fear his name before she could walk. He might even draw a little of that blood she presumed not to be afraid of. They all thought him an animal, anyway.

No! he told himself. To which another part of him replied, *But you've done it so many times before…*

Kerebos tossed the jug and arrested her soft hands. "You wouldn't touch me, woman, if you really knew me," he warned.

Selah's eyes danced as she stepped on her toes and breathed in his ear. "You can't rape the willing," she whispered. "You won't need to force yourself on any part of me, *ikar*."

Kerebos pushed her away, though with much less force than intended. "You are Antiphon's woman," he growled. "Go to him!"

Selah closed the gap. "No, he is *my man*," She rubbed a hip against the growing bulge in his loincloth. "There's a difference." She chuckled. "I see the way you look at me, Kerebos. Maybe you are fond of my father and Antiphon, and maybe you want the boy to worship you, but it just doesn't matter. We both know what's going to pass between us, and it's going to happen again." She kissed his pectoral muscle without taking her eyes from his, "and again," another kiss, "and again. You are a *real* man! Take me!"

Kerebos felt drugged. His resolve melted. She was so obviously right.

"You are to be Antiphon's wife," he protested weakly.

Selah burst into laughter. "You are naïve, my lord," she purred. "As much as you know about taking lives, you know nothing about playing them." With that she threw her arms around his thick neck, placed her full lips on his and forced her tongue into his mouth.

Kerebos went rigid, then shoved her; Selah sprawled into the dirt. "You don't know what you're doing!" he cried and stepped back.

Selah rolled onto her side and smiled slyly. "Think about me when you're alone tonight," she said. "As though I have to tell you." She stood and brushed herself off, then made her way across the garden.

Kerebos stood frozen for a long moment then snatched the hoe from the ground and snapped it with his hands. He covered his eyes with bleeding palms. *By God, I'll never touch her!* he promised himself, but the oath was hollow, and he knew it.

The next day Kerebos woke after only a few hours sleep and helped rebuild a portion of the Sanctum's defensive wall. He tackled the job with grim determination and when some masons arrived after breakfast, he chased them away.

Antiphon and Dokein watched from a distant belltower.

155

"He's chewing through that sharded concrete as though it were wood," Dokein observed.

"He knows how to go about it," Antiphon replied. "He's ruined enough cities."

Dokein lifted an eyebrow. "But now he labors to rebuild ours."

"He's the very rock of faith," Antiphon sneered and turned a mystified expression on the Grand Master. "Why do you allow him here? The Council, even your supporters, thinks he should be expelled. Or killed."

Dokein frowned. "Is the Council Grand Master now?" he replied gruffly. "Is it God? Must I remind you, lad, that we are all sinners, and all equally repulsive in the eyes of the Lord?"

Antiphon looked away, thinking, *Some are less equal than others.*

"Shall we ignore the Savior, and ourselves judge who deserves life, Antiphon al-Caliph?" Dokein continued, somewhat gentler. "No. At least not while I lead this Order."

Still Antiphon sulked. The Grand Master had known him too long to not discern a deeper trouble.

"What's wrong, my son?" he pried. "Tell me."

Antiphon made as though to leave then whirled on Dokein, tears in his eyes.

"I just don't understand!" he cried. "I don't comprehend anything, anymore—the answers or the questions."

Dokein nodded sagely. "If you did, you'd be Grand Master, and still you'd be wrong."

Antiphon searched the blue sky. "I go away to die, or to bring this beast home," he started bitterly, "and he gores my faith like I'm some untried acolyte."

"You *are* human," Dokein replied. "You have human failings."

"How well I know it," Antiphon said with a shake of the head. He studied Kerebos. "Then he comes here and acts like a damned deacon. The bastard reads scripture and catechisms all night, then works like God's first man all day. He behaves more like a believer all the time; Samir tells me Kerebos wails like an infant at night."

"He's a tortured man and I, for one, pity him," Dokein said quietly. "You should rejoice in his repentance no matter what his sins."

"But what about the people, the children, he's killed that will never get the chance!" Antiphon thundered. "What of them?"

156

"We must pray for them as God has instructed us."

"I do," Antiphon said. "But lately I can't help but pity him, too."

"That's your job, Ani," Dokein answered stoically. "Where would we be if God stopped pitying us? Rejoice that you have such awareness."

"But Kerebos doesn't deserve it!" Antiphon spat. "You know what he's done!" He took a long breath. "But I can't bring myself *not* to pray for him. Just look at him, there," Antiphon said miserably. "He looks like some graven hero. He is quick to learn, and argues me to a standstill. Just think what he could have been to the Order."

Dokein nodded in silence. "We have him now."

"Yes, we do," Antiphon choked. "So does Selah."

Dokein's bushy eyebrows arched. "What?"

"That's the worst of it, Master," Antiphon admitted. "But our resident *ikar* is blameless in this; it's all her doing."

"I don't doubt it," Dokein agreed. "What a shame she didn't inherit her mother's good sense rather than my ambition." He laid a hand on the young Master's back. "What shall you do about her?"

"What can I do about the tides, or the moon?" Antiphon muttered. "In any case, our betrothal is over. You warned me, and I've been her fool, but I am no longer."

Dokein shook his head. "It's better this way. She'd have ruined you."

Antiphon's eyes welled with fresh tears. "She already has," he said. "Still, I love her."

Antiphon walked away, head low. Dokein sent a blessing after him. *God save him,* he prayed. *He deserved better than this, better than my daughter.* He gazed back at Kerebos. *And then there's this wasted soul. What to do with him?*

Looking toward the city spires, Dokein decided the time had come to test Kerebos' spirit.

erebos sat against the basilica wall. His expression was clearly one of disgust. "No, no," he whispered.

You've come far, but will go no farther, an inner voice said. *You can bootlick these Aharoni all you want, but the healing has stopped.*

Kerebos shook his head. "I can make it all the way."

You only deceive yourself, you're certainly not deceiving them. Why have them laugh at you while you slave at useless penance? Kill them, kill them all!

Kerebos visualized the Council behind closed doors, Dokein and Antiphon included, ridiculing him, bragging about how he patched masonry and spread fertilizer for them.

Little, weak men. Ants! the voice taunted. *How did they bring you down? They guide Pontis, and they architect your nightmares. Even their God, if He exists, dances on the ends of their strings.*

Kerebos shook his head.

You're a fool, the voice continued. *Murder is the greatest tool you've ever had, and you've given that away. Do you think they respect you now?*

Kerebos closed his eyes and cried, "I won't have it!"

You're pathetic.

Moments passed, but nobody came to investigate the shout. Even the birds ignored him. Nevertheless, Kerebos sensed eyes upon him. *Stop refusing yourself, and get rid of these people,* the voice reasoned. *It's the only thing you've ever been good at.*

For a moment Kerebos imagined taking Mistaaka to some *Aharoni* heads, and he liked the idea. He even worked up an angle to dispose of Antiphon. The priest did not care about him, really, but sought only to control him. Nobody controlled Kerebos *Ikar!* Antiphon would have to go, have to, Dokein too, and Yeshua. Kerebos bolted upright.

What am I thinking? he wondered, aghast. *How can I think such things after coming so far?* He considered cutting a hole in his head and dashing it against the wall until all the evil spilled onto the ground.

Moments passed.

"If they laugh at me, they laugh," he finally informed the voice. "What good has listening to you ever done, anyway?"

I gave you the world.

A gate creaked open and Montanus strode into the yard. The smiling priest, bony bare chest pink from the sun, carried something over a shoulder. Mistaaka. Birds squawked into flight.

"Good afternoon, brother," Montanus laughed.

"Where's your robe, priest?" Kerebos mocked. "And why do you bring that?"

Montanus stopped before the *ikar* and grinned. "You don't like my new clothes? They're so much more comfortable than those smothering sheets."

"I wore armor my whole life, and hated to take it off. It protected me."

The smile faded from Montanus' narrow face. "What good's armor that allows harm?"

"Mine rarely failed me," Kerebos replied as he stood.

"I'm not talking about you," Montanus said. "As for this," he hefted Mistaaka, "I thought you might be needing it."

"Keep it. If ever I pick it up again, I'll never lay it down."

"Oh, come now!" Montanus said in the friendliest of tones and offered the pommel. "Wouldn't it be nice to have your balls back?"

Kerebos recoiled. "Leave if you value your life, priest," he warned.

Montanus threw the sword into the grass. "Threats, now?" he chuckled. "I knew it was only a matter of time."

Kerebos' face slowly transformed into the mask he donned before committing murder. He felt something larger than himself taking over, and found comfort in the feeling. "I can do better than threats, priest," he promised.

Kill him! the voice urged. *You'd be doing everyone a service!*

Montanus' face wrinkled into a surly snarl. "I'm no longer a priest, *ikar!*" The words saved his life.

"Oh?" Kerebos asked. "Dokein has realized your worthlessness?"

Montanus wrung his hands and glanced about. "I'm standing trial for assaulting a Master."

Kerebos smirked. "And you such a gentle soul."

"I wouldn't find it funny, if I were you," Montanus threatened. "If

159

I'm convicted, it'll go ill for you."

"How so?"

Montanus' eyes glowed with secretive delight. "Ahhhhh!" he said, shaking his head and wagging a finger.

Kerebos looked baffled. "How'd you ever become a priest?" he wondered aloud. "You'd have been a better *landesknecta*."

Montanus regarded him with a curious stare. "Not all killers are born so," he offered. "Nor all priests. I'm what remains of a man who does his duty, but has no prayers answered."

Kerebos' face registered rare moral disdain. "So God owes you for your service?" he asked contemptuously. "You're as profane as me."

"Not for long."

Kerebos stepped over Mistaaka and pushed by Montanus, who grasped him with a quivering hand.

"Kill Antiphon!" he growled. "Kill Dokein! They hate us and will not rest until we're both dead!"

"Release me."

Montanus' grasp tightened. "Please!" he whined. "I'll give you gold!"

Kerebos grabbed Montanus' hand in a crushing grip, forcing him to his knees.

"Ow!" the priest cried.

Kerebos released him. "You want them dead, rat? You kill them. If ever again you ask such a thing, I'll eat your heart." He left the sobbing cleric to nurse the injured hand. *I won't return to you*, he assured the voice. *I might be damned, but I'm no longer your slave.*

For once, there was no reply.

After dinner with Antiphon and Yeshua, Kerebos returned to his room. Selah was there.

Dressed in white, she lounged on the bed, thumbing through the history book Kerebos had read the night before. As Dokein had hinted, the priests of the Flame had once been first-rate soldiers. In Desia's day *Aharoni* priests had created machines and weapons that later scientists had failed to reproduce. If the book was correct, Kwan Aharon still possessed some of these wartime wonders.

Kerebos stepped halfway into the room. "Why are you here, lady?"

Selah sat, cocked her head to one side and smiled. "Have you been thinking about our kiss?"

"*Your* kiss. Why are you here?"

"Don't worry, old Samir's away," Selah replied and patted the bed. "Come, sit beside me." She reclined onto her elbows and her full breasts strained the gossamer gown; brown nipples showed through the gauze.

Kerebos squeezed the door. "You're Antiphon's woman," he started, "and he is my…friend."

"He's broken our betrothal," Selah replied. "He knows all about you and me."

Kerebos felt pangs of guilt. "What does he know?" he droned.

"That you're going to be inside me. Tonight. Come here."

Kerebos tried to respond but failed.

"I know you, Kerebos," Selah laughed, snatching his sweaty hand in hers. "We're born for each other," she cooed. "Don't you know that?"

Kerebos nodded dumbly. He could smell her desire, and the scent maddened him. Selah pulled him onto his knees, slid her oiled legs beneath his arms and locked her feet behind him. She tongued his ear.

"I need you," she whispered. "I love you. I have from the day I first saw you."

Selah raised his hand to her lips and licked between two fingers. "Take me," she gasped and slid his middle finger into her hot mouth. She once rolled her tongue over the digit and said, "Then take me away."

Kerebos was powerless to refuse. "I will," he croaked.

At that moment he cared little about Antiphon, scripture, or his soul. He grabbed Selah's lustrous hair and pulled her close, flinging the dress up over her knees.

"Kerebos!" she squeaked.

The *ikar* stood to undo his belt, stepped forward and kicked something beneath the bed. He immediately knew what that something was and froze.

Selah pushed a raven lock from her eyes. "What?" she puffed.

Kerebos stared at the wall. "My sword's under the bed."

Selah nodded quickly. "I put it there. I saw Montanus leave it in the East Yard."

Kerebos closed his eyes and took a deep breath. "Get out."

Selah slid off the bed and grasped his waist. "Why?" she demanded, flustered. "I'm yours!"

Kerebos shoved her toward the door. "Get out!"

Selah stumbled into the jamb, but did not fall. She cast a furious gaze at the *ikar* and snapped: "It's just a piece of metal, fool!"

161

Kerebos looked through her.

"You *are* a fool!" she said scornfully. After glaring at him a few seconds, she stormed from the room, slamming the door behind her.

Kerebos calmly considered throwing himself onto Mistaaka's point.

*   *   *

Kerebos tossed another shovel full of dirt onto the pile; he wore gloves which Yeshua had provided that morning.

"Why do the *Razkuli* hate us?" Yeshua asked.

Kerebos remembered his humorless *Razkuli* warriors and grunted. "They hate everyone, even themselves."

"The Grand Master tells me we used to send them food," the boy replied. "Wouldn't they love us?"

"People often resent charity," Kerebos explained.

"Aren't all people dependent upon God?"

Kerebos stopped to straighten his aching back.

"Some people resent that, too. Especially when they don't deserve the help."

Yeshua's eyes narrowed. "You're speaking of yourself, aren't you?"

Precocious child, Kerebos thought, feeling something like pride. "Maybe," he agreed.

Yeshua picked a stone from the soil. "Why?"

"Yeshua," Kerebos said dismally, "whatever your father, or the all-wise Juntha has said about me does not approach the truth."

Yeshua threw the rock then plopped onto the dirt mound. "Father told me you killed people," he replied. "So? You're sorry, aren't you?"

Kerebos felt weary. "More than I can say," he answered sadly. "But I've done far worse than kill men in battle."

"You've stopped doing those things, though," Yeshua reasoned. "Just don't do them anymore."

A miniature Dokein, Kerebos thought, wiping sweat from his eyes. "I have, lad, but sometimes that's not enough."

Yeshua appeared unconvinced. "Our greatest apostle's first career was to kill the Savior's followers. Why then did God allow him to write so many of our holy books?"

Kerebos was touched by the boy's persistence. "You'll make a good theologian someday," he said.

"Not if the world ends, I won't," Yeshua replied carelessly.

"Hope for the best," Kerebos counseled, though the advice was the sort he himself never followed.

Yeshua giggled. "I do."

Bells began to toll.

"Uh-oh!" the boy jumped up and dusted himself off. "I was supposed to do the candles at second session!"

"You'd better be about it, then."

Yeshua darted off but stopped at the gate. "I'll pray for you!" he shouted. "You'll be all right!"

Kerebos waved. *Don't count on it*, he thought.

Later in his room, the *ikar* heard a soft knock on his door. "Selah?" he called.

The door creaked open and Antiphon entered. "No," he said bitterly. "Sorry."

Kerebos folded the book, one of Antiphon's, and stood. "No, I'm sorry," he apologized. "She came here, Antiphon, but I sent her away."

The priest shrugged. "Of course."

"Antiphon!" Kerebos barked as though at a recruit. "I denied her." He raised a hand. "I swear."

Antiphon considered the pledge and broke into uneasy laughter. "That sounds most peculiar coming from you."

Kerebos looked at his raised hand and laughed, too. "It does at that."

"Let's not talk about her," Antiphon suggested.

"Fine."

"Dokein needs you."

"When?"

"Now, I suspect."

"Where?"

"Where do you think?" the priest muttered. "That damned garden of his. I think he sleeps there."

Kerebos grabbed his sandals. Antiphon prepared to depart.

"Has he finally decided to hand Pontis my head?" Kerebos asked.

Antiphon stroked his beard. "I hope not," he said at last. "Peace be with you, Kerebos."

The *ikar* looked uncomfortable. "And also with you."

"He wants to ask about 'the rat'," Antiphon offered. "No one's seen him since yesterday."

Kerebos gave a cold laugh. "I guess Dokein wants to check 'the tiger's' belly."

Chapter 19

Triskeles sat in his new barracks and revised the tactical organization sheet for his remaining three hundred men. He started scrawling *"ikar"* beside his name, when someone pounded on the door.

"What?" he groused.

"My lord, *elhar*," Markos replied, "Pontis requests your presence in the War Room. It's urgent, the messenger says."

Triskeles frowned. *This stupid little king*, he thought. *Always troubling me with "urgent" summons, which never are.* "Oh, all right," he growled. "Let me get dressed."

"The Scarlet Guards await you," Markos replied.

Royal Guards? Triskeles pondered. *Maybe it is important.* "I'll be a moment."

"Yes, lord."

Triskeles slid on his gauntlets, swordbelt and cape then left his private quarters for the common room. He looked down the rows of beds. Every fourth pallet was empty; he always had at least a quarter of his men on duty. He knew the *Chaconni* itched to revenge themselves the beating he had dealt them mere months before, and had no intention of being caught off guard.

Markos, armored and bearing a torch, marched back into the building. He looked relieved when he saw Triskeles. "My lord, are you ready?"

"Don't I look it?"

Markos lead his commander out to the waiting buggy, which bore Pontis' coat of arms. Night had fallen, and the beacons were

164

being lit on the distant walls. Though Pontis had quartered the legion outside Korenthis under the auspices of "protecting our incomplete barriers," Triskeles knew the king kept them at arm's length from prudence. This was wise of Pontis; the *landesknecta* had often considered slaying the monarch.

Markos cast a hostile eye at the Guards. "Shall I come with you?" he asked the *elhar*.

Triskeles smirked at the twelve escorts. "I'm sure these ladies will do fine by me," then whispered, "Keep the men ready."

Markos saluted and went back inside. A Guard opened the carriage door and the *elhar* climbed inside. He was still trying to get comfortable on the fluffy cushions when the driver cracked the whip and the carriage dashed toward the city.

Kerebos was right to want to sack it, the *Boru* thought as Korenthis grew in the window. Gilded towers and elevated aqueducts stood bravely against the golden sunset. *Korenthis would've made a good home for the legion.* Triskeles' face grew grimmer than usual at the thought of the *ikar. He's just like this Chaconni king*, he mused. *Untrustworthy and, very soon, dead.*

The Guards ushered Triskeles through a side gate and down a residential street of palatial homes. Moments passed before they pulled through the castle gates. Triskeles kicked open the door and leaped from the carriage while it was still moving. He stared up at the formidable defensive positions. The machicolations were much bolder than any he had seen, but that could also work to an attacker's advantage.

With a full legion and siege equipment, I could take it in a week, he concluded.

"Lord Tryggvason!" a Guard called, intentionally avoiding the *landesknectas'* "battle name". Triskeles followed him into the castle and the others fell in behind.

The *elhar* was led down hall after marbled hall, around corners and up stairs. He suspected they made the trip more confusing than necessary but did not mind. He would have done the same. At last they reached the War Room. Triskeles did not wait to be announced but barged into the chamber.

Pontis, who sat at a huge round table, was flanked by a score of nobles. Triskeles recognized Count-General Fidelis Pyrros as that man looked up from a map of northern Pangaea. Lack of sleep had etched rings beneath Pyrros' dark eyes.

"Sit, Lord Tryggvason," Pontis said.

He seems cheerful enough, Triskeles noted. He felt keenly the eyes of the other men, most of whom had lost sons or brothers in the recent hostilities, as he unsheathed his sword and slapped it onto the table. He plopped down opposite the king and asked: "Why have you summoned me?"

"In a hurry, Tryggvason?" Pyrros demanded with a sneer.

Triskeles studied the *Chaconne*. "Wars are lost while commanders play out pomp," he replied. "Leaders should move before the worm fastens on them."

Pyrros tapped his signet ring onto the table, but absorbed the insult.

"May we begin?" Pontis asked coolly.

Triskeles bent his head.

"Sire," Pyrros replied.

"Good," Pontis said and poked the map. "Our wishes have been fulfilled," he told Triskeles.

"Are we all immortal, then?"

Pontis ignored the comment. "Today an *Aharoni* priest arrived, claiming important news," he continued. "He was granted an audience with Pyrros' lieutenant." He smiled hungrily. "We've found Kerebos *Ikar*."

Triskeles' grin was at least as ravenous as the king's. "My men can march tonight," he said.

Pontis and Pyrros were alone in the War Room. The king ordered wine and Pyrros emptied a decanter into bejeweled goblets. Pyrros, a long-time confidant, noted Pontis' puzzled expression.

"What disturbs you, my king?" he asked. "You seem troubled, even as victory races to greet us."

"Just thinking," Pontis replied. "How many men would you need to destroy what's left of the Black Legion?"

Pyrros sat up in his chair. "I hoped it might be something like that," he admitted. "These *landesknectos* are incapable of becoming housebroken. I've dreamed you'd make this spring their last."

166

"How many men?"

Pyrros' eyes glazed over as he imagined such a battle. "Five thousand." he said. "Six thousand to be sure. Plenty of mounted archers."

"Then take three divisions to Kwan Aharon."

"My lord, that was only a hypothesis," Pyrros demurred. "I had hoped for five times that number to pacify the *Aharoni* and grab their largest cities."

Pontis shook his head. "I can't spare that many. I've a bad feeling about the *Boru*, and recent intelligence has done nothing to allay my suspicions," he explained. "They might attack Korenthis if we drained it of manpower."

Pyrros' mouth made a silent "o".

"My spies say Lord Trygg has been in constant contact with his son, our would-be *ikar*," Pontis continued. "They're up to something."

"Still, we should take the *Aharoni* trade routes while we can. Give me five divisions."

Pontis scowled. "You don't sound properly worried about the capitol," he accused. "Or is it my life you don't value?"

"Sire! How can you say such things?"

"Then do as I command. Take just enough men to kill Kerebos," Pontis huffed. "We'll grab Kwan Aharon, permanently, later."

Pyrros fell into the mien of an inferior forced to obey an undesirable order. "As you wish."

"Please, don't pout!" Pontis said. "If you were the *Boru*, wouldn't you attack us?"

"Maybe, Sire," Pyrros acknowledged.

"Well, good. Let the *landesknectos* do the dirty work, then kill them when they're weakest. They would have been useful, but it seems we don't have time enough to bring them along."

Pyrros emptied his goblet. "Shall we provide them war machines?" he asked then burped.

"Of course. They're our allies aren't they?"

Pyrros rubbed his square jaw.

"What is it?" Pontis grated.

"I wonder if we should not kill Tryggvason now," Pyrros said. "Some accident, or such."

167

"I've pondered that many nights," the king conceded. "But the *landesknectos* wouldn't fight if they suspected we'd killed him, and with you marching tomorrow how would we exterminate him without obvious foul play?"

"A fair question, Sire." Pyrros stood. "May I go? There are preparations to attend."

Pontis was all smiles. "By all means. See me in the morning."

Pyrros bowed. "My lord and king."

"And Pyrros?"

"My lord?"

"Take that traitorous priest, what's his name, Montanus, along as a guide."

"He must know Kwan Aharon inside out," Pyrros replied.

"Use him well, then kill him," Pontis ordered. "I shan't waste funds on a traitor's reward." He chuckled. "Ahh, the joys of complicity."

Pyrros nodded then left.

I'm coming to get you Kerebos, Pontis thought as he stared into his goblet. *I shall forge the "Old Kingdom" into a new Empire.*

Pontis polished off the draught.

*   *   *

Kerebos found Dokein in the garden. The flowers were in full bloom and the cloudy sky's light lent the sanctuary a soft, unreal quality.

"My son," Dokein greeted, lifting a single, blood red rose. "I guess Ani found you."

"I greet you, Master."

Dokein nodded at the flower. "Beautiful, huh? They say all God's wisdom is observed in a single one."

Kerebos tried to look interested. "Nice."

Dokein looked beatific. "But of how much greater worth is a man?" he inquired. "Even a man who denies his value?"

Kerebos shook his head. "It's useless, you know."

"What?"

"Seeking my salvation."

168

Dokein chuckled. "I was talking flowers, and you bring up theology. But, since you've broached the subject…"

Kerebos gave a tired smile. "You'll never quit, will you?"

Dokein shrugged. "You're my greatest task. Besides, sometimes salvation reaches us despite our wishes."

"You forget to whom you talk," Kerebos sniffed. "There's no mercy reaching me. I've thwarted God at every turn, and on purpose. He doesn't want me, and I can't accept him."

"There's nothing that says you must be damned," Dokein countered. "God doesn't work that way. He won't violate your free will."

Kerebos only stared at the old man.

"If you could have things your way, what would you have?" the Grand Master asked.

"Since I can't repent, I'd follow the course I've set," Kerebos replied. "I'd do what little good I can without hope of reward here, or hereafter."

Dokein nodded thoughtfully, saying, "You know, a saint couldn't have put it nobler."

"I am no saint," Kerebos ground out.

Dokein looked over the courtyard. "We're alone," he said. "Not even a bird in sight." A single raindrop smacked his cheek.

"So it seems."

"This garden is special for many reasons," the old man proceeded. "I interview acolytes here and listen to their sins, for one thing."

So that's where this is going! Kerebos thought, alarmed. He felt like running. "And now they're white as snow?"

Dokein considered the remark. "Yes," he said.

Kerebos looked away. "I don't believe that. I can't."

"'And the lord gave unto his apostle the power to forgive upon Pangaea what he would, and to hold that bound in heaven what he would not forgive,'" Dokein quoted.

"I've read that," Kerebos replied dismally. "It just doesn't apply to me."

Dokein shrugged. "Either it will or it won't." More drops hit the ground. "Strange to get rain this late in the season. Oh well, it's good for the flowers."

Kerebos slowly grew pale. "Can we go inside?"

"Give your confession first."

The *ikar* trembled so badly he thought he might fall. "May I sit?" he croaked, appropriating Dokein's little pruning stool.

"Of course. Come, share your burden," Dokein urged.

Kerebos shook his head. "It won't work!"

"It will if you believe."

Kerebos leaned onto his knees. He tried to speak but managed only a grunt.

Dokein laid a light hand on the *ikar*'s shoulder. "Tell me, my son," he said. "You can't go on the way you are."

"What must I do?" Kerebos asked miserably as a light shower commenced. Drops, like tears, dripped from his nose.

"Which sin most troubles you?"

Kerebos snorted. "When dying of a thousand diseases, why diagnose just one?"

"Which weighs the most? Tell me."

Kerebos' eyes fluttered. He cleared his throat. "I've killed many men."

"I know," Dokein replied. "What else?"

Kerebos rubbed his knees. "It's futile," he choked.

Dokein nudged the *ikar*. "Continue."

Kerebos took a deep breath then cleared his throat again. "I've killed many women," he sobbed. "I've raped many, too."

Dokein withdrew his hand. "Go on."

"I've killed—tortured and maimed—children," Kerebos droned. "And I enjoyed it."

Dokein felt sick. Tears started in his eyes. "Yes. Go on."

Kerebos looked miserably at the old man. "It's pointless. Even you don't think it'll work, do you?"

"Finish your confession!" Dokein ordered.

Kerebos was turning a deathly white and lifted a warding hand. "I can't."

"Open your heart. Don't you want to see him again?" Dokein asked.

The *ikar* nodded a few times then burst into tears. He slid onto all fours as sobs racked his great frame. "I killed my father!" he wailed. "I killed my own father!" He slammed his forehead on the ground. "Why would God forgive that?"

Dokein shook his head in revulsion and pity. Kerebos' loathsome crimes were made worse by the prospect of absolving them. How could such a man exist and why had God brought him here?

Kerebos lay motionless in the mud, awaiting judgement.

"Fortunately," Dokein started somberly, "God does not demand justice, only reconciliation." He lifted a hand over Kerebos and said in a weakly: "By the keys of the kingdom of heaven, I absolve you. Go and sin no more." He paused a moment and added in a surly tone, "Don't abuse what God has given you, *landesknecta*."

"You're finished?" Kerebos sputtered.

"Yes."

"It was too easy," the *ikar* decided, shaking his head.

"That's the way it's supposed to be," Dokein groused. "You can't purchase God's forgiveness, so He gives it for free."

Kerebos' heart dangled between hot and cold, hope and hopelessness. The chill won out. "I wish it were true," he said forlornly.

"It will work if you let it. All healing starts from within." Dokein hobbled from the garden, utterly spent.

171

K erebos' hands were behind his back as he paced outside the classroom. His sandals squeaked on the highly polished floor every time he changed direction.

Antiphon's voice floated through the latticed transom. He was teaching Dokein's "Morality" class, the topic: "inherited sin".

Was I born to act this way? If so, will God punish me less, or more for it? Kerebos wondered.

The opening door suddenly struck him. The emerging boy saw him and disappeared into the classroom.

"Kerebos is here!" he told the other students in an excited voice.

Antiphon tried, unsuccessfully, to quell the subsequent disturbance, but eventually had to dismiss the students. Two dozen boys filed by Kerebos, eyeing him with awed disdain. At last Antiphon poked his head around the door.

"Was just thinking about you," he said dourly. "Come in."

Kerebos entered. There were forty or so chairs facing the Master's desk, behind which hung a chalkboard and a detailed mural of Pangaea. Kerebos eyed the map.

Antiphon slid onto his desk and sniffed, "Is it accurate?"

Kerebos indicated the north central region. "Actually, there's a few mistakes, or would have been mistakes before the earthquakes."

"A born geography teacher," Antiphon derided.

Kerebos squinted at the priest, who hoisted a hand of truce. "Forgive me, I'm very, very tired," he said. "I haven't slept in days."

"I know the feeling."

Antiphon motioned toward one of the small chairs. "Please, sit."

Kerebos pushed two together; they groaned as he eased onto them. His serene face changed to one of fury.

"Today some fat 'Master Torra' refused to let me see Dokein," he said, as though Antiphon were somehow responsible.

"I heard. The Grand Master is ill," Antiphon explained. "I fear many in the Order blame you."

Kerebos half started from his seat. "Me! I'd never do anything to the man! How long has he been ill?"

Antiphon looked away to conceal his emotions. "A few days."

Kerebos' face indicated disgust. "You think I did it, too, don't you?" he demanded.

Antiphon had forgotten just how menacing the *ikar* could be; he shifted uncomfortably on the desk. "I didn't say that."

"No? You're in the Order aren't you?"

"Why do you look as though you want to kill me?" Antiphon asked.

Kerebos glowered for a long moment then averted his eyes. "Forgive me," he said gruffly. "I'm angry at Torra, or whatever his name is. The little pig. I'd like to strangle him with his own guts."

Antiphon nodded. "I don't much care for him, either," he admitted. "He spoke against my elevation. Said I was 'unwise'."

Kerebos rubbed his knees. "I *must* see Dokein," he insisted. "He musn't die because of me."

"Who said anything about dying?" Antiphon asked, alarmed. "Did Torra?"

"No."

Antiphon relaxed. "Dokein's old and tired, but he'll pull through. He must."

Kerebos stared at his hands. "Everything I've ever encountered, good or bad, I've destroyed," he sighed. "That doom I'd spare Dokein."

Antiphon looked compassionate. "He's pretty wonderful, isn't he? A father to us all." The priest tensed. Had Kerebos caught that last part?

The *ikar* leaned back and stared at the ceiling. Veins bulged in his throat. "I told him it was useless," he said. "Curing me is too much for any man. Torra!" he scoffed. "He'd better watch himself…"

173

Antiphon felt as though the temperature had dropped sharply. He had seen this side of Kerebos before and knew only fast action would prevent something violent from happening. He mustered his courage.

"Don't flatter yourself," he said. "Let Dokein get sick in peace. Anyway, are you too big a task for God? That's who healed you, you know, not the Master."

Kerebos looked sideways at him. "I'm not healed."

"Dokein is old," Antiphon continued reasonably. "His body does what an old man's does. You're not responsible for his health."

Kerebos lips curled into an ironic smile. "I felt the power drain out of him," he said. "I hear the Council thinks my death might heal Dokein."

Antiphon shook his head enthusiastically. "That fool Ahbad! Does he really believe in heathen bloodlettings when God has already shed his own? *Dokein is an old man!*"

Kerebos was still smiling. "Please," he begged. "Tell them to kill me."

Antiphon pointed at him. "I will not allow such blasphemy to assuage Ahbad's stupidity and your guilt! God in heaven!" he raged. "Honor Dokein by obeying his commands! You want to please him? Then listen to him, goddamn it!"

Antiphon's hands flew to his mouth. "I can't believe I just said that," he gasped, wide-eyed. He snatched some books off the desk and dashed from the room.

Kerebos balanced himself on the chairs' hind legs. The chortling noise issuing from his throat might have been laughter, but sounded more like he was being garroted.

*   *   *

Antiphon sat quietly beside the Grand Master's bed, pondering dark thoughts. Dokein had been unconscious for days and many feared he would never wake again.

The shuttered room smelled of incense and herbs. Silent attendants, masters of healing, discussed Dokein's condition in frantic whispers. Thunder shook the basilica. Another storm was brewing. The air was pregnant with moisture.

Dokein opened his eyes and turned toward the window. "God weeps for us again, eh?" he asked, his first words since a delirium caused him to speak about giant lizards and comets.

Antiphon was too stunned to call for a doctor. "Yes, Master," he replied. "It's been a gloomy, gray week."

"I bet the wells are overflowing." Dokein stirred and sat. He scratched his head. "What's the date, my son?"

"The seventeenth of Aleph," Antiphon replied, excitedly waving over a warden. "Please lie down."

"We're almost out of time," the Grand Master said and lay back on his pillows. "So is Kerebos."

Antiphon swabbed the old man's forehead with a damp cloth. "Forget him for the moment," he suggested. "Save your strength."

The Grand Master's eyes closed. "I've dreamed about him," he whispered. "Free will. He's the only one here who really has it..."

One of the wardens leaned close and asked in amazement: "Did he speak?"

Dokein smiled. "I said I'll be needing no more healers, Gimel."

The doctor stared at Antiphon. "He knows me?" he asked. "I never met him." Gimel, a renowned physician from afar, had only just arrived.

"Ani, send them all away," Dokein said.

"Master?"

"Away!" Dokein began to rise.

Antiphon grabbed Dokein's shoulders. "Please, Master, lie down!"

"It would be best, Grand Master," Gimel agreed as others hurried over.

"I'm still alive, no?" Dokein asked.

"You are," Gimel replied.

"Then you and the others can leave. I'm not dying until tonight, and then there will be no stopping me."

Dokein eyed the ring of concerned attendants. He smiled but said firmly, "Gentlemen, leave me in peace. Send in Torra if he's lurking about, that you can do for me."

They looked at each other. Gimel made a "what should we do" face. "Somebody get Torra, anyway," someone said.

Dokein swung his feet off the bed.

"Master!" Antiphon protested.

"Get some food, Ani, and bring my daughter," Dokein commanded. "Where's Kerebos?"

"Torra won't let him in," Antiphon said.

Dokein shook off helping hands, and strode over to a flagon. He drank greedily and belched. "Ah! Ani, want some?"

Antiphon fidgeted with his robes. "Perhaps we should listen to the healers," he advised. Gimel nodded anxiously.

Dokein looked amused. "What do they know? They couldn't even tell I was dead."

Antiphon began fearing the Grand Master had lost his mind and his expression betrayed him.

Dokein chuckled. "No I haven't, my son. Do as I said, and get Selah. We must help both of them."

Antiphon started to speak but Torra burst into the room. The Master's wrinkled face revealed anger. He stuck a finger in Antiphon's face, asking, "What have you done to him?"

Dokein dismissed the doctors then turned a grim face on Torra. "Did I correctly hear that you suggested a human sacrifice to the Council?" he demanded.

Torra was taken aback. "It was Ahbad, really," he said. "We did such things in the old days. Ahbad and I thought…"

"No."

"But Kerebos must go," Torra stammered. "Look what his evil has done to you."

"Again no," Dokein replied. "Praise God that he has lent me back to the Order to excuse you two the burden of commanding it."

An impenetrable expression crossed Torra's fleshy face. "Praise be."

"I'll have just enough time to declare Ani my successor," Dokein continued. Antiphon gasped.

Torra's eyes narrowed. "Oh?"

"Yes," Dokein replied. "You'll never see the high seat."

Torra's face curdled. "You'll never push that past the Council," he said confidently.

Dokein laughed. "Want to wager?"

"Master, I'm not worthy!" Antiphon interrupted.

"Correct!" Torra agreed wholeheartedly.

Dokein studied their faces. "You don't want it, Ani," he said at

176

last. "That's why it's yours. Once again you'll pull more than your weight."

"He's too young," Torra insisted. "You can't deny my experience."

A majestic light was in Dokein's eyes. "I see many things," he intoned. "God wants Antiphon at the helm these final days."

"Final days?" Torra sneered. It was no secret that he disagreed with Dokein on the subject.

The chamber door flew open and Master Ahbad, Torra's steadfast ally, entered. "Grand Master?" he called in surprise.

"Call the Council," Dokein ordered.

Ahbad glanced at Torra but turned to obey.

Torra shook his head. "You've gone mad."

Dokein smiled. "Ani will edge you by a single vote."

"How do you figure that?"

Dokein tapped his forehead. "Dreamed it."

Torra looked skeptical. "You've dreamed no such a thing."

"I have indeed, Master of burnt offerings," Dokein replied. "Leave me."

"You're mad!"

"Maybe, but my dreams are sound," Dokein said. "If you run fast enough, you'll reach the gates in time to greet Pontis' emissaries. Now leave us."

Torra stormed off as Dokein poured another goblet. "I don't think there's wine up there," he sighed.

"You're scaring me, Master," Antiphon said.

"And myself," Dokein chuckled. "But either I *am* mad, or the world *is* ending!"

"Maybe both?" Antiphon proposed nervously.

"Maybe." Dokein patted Antiphon's arm. "Now, please find Selah. I must say goodbye and try to talk sense to her."

Antiphon nodded dumbly.

"It's too bad you haven't slept lately," Dokein replied. "You won't get any now."

Antiphon stared in wonder. "Are you really back from the dead?"

Bells began to toll.

Dokein's eyes sparkled. "I thought you missed that remark."

177

Dokein entered the Council Hall with a sheepish Antiphon at his heels. Men leaped to their feet and clapped in welcome. The applause was loud and sincere.

Dokein, decked in new robes, proceeded to the first table. He took the high seat and forced Antiphon into Torra's chair. "Sit brothers," he said, clear and loud. "Join me in silent prayer while we wait." He pressed his hands together and closed his eyes.

After a few moments Antiphon whispered: "What are we waiting for?"

The Hall's tall doors swung open. Torra, Ahbad and several others entered.

Dokein opened an eye. "Him."

Torra made a meandering path to the Grand Master. He was so subdued he did not even notice Antiphon in his chair.

"How did you know?" he asked the old man.

Dokein nodded toward the assembly. "Tell them."

Torra lowered his head. "I submit, Grand Master. May God forgive me for trying to thwart his plans." He drew a deep breath and addressed the congregation.

"I've just spoken with Pontis' messengers," he said. "Though the main force is still days away, the King has made demands of us and expects immediate compliance. Even now his envoys await our decision." His nose wrinkled as though at some foul smell as he added: "Montanus, is with them."

The Council erupted. Dokein had to raise his voice to silence the gathering.

"Pontis demands Kerebos *Ikar*," Torra concluded in a noncommital tone.

"Give him up!" or variants thereof were the most common cry.

Ahbad raised his hands, shouting: "And they want us, the Order, to leave Kwan Aharon. Forever. Both must be done. Surrendering Kerebos is not enough."

Shocked silence.

"Unthinkable," someone scoffed.

"Never!" The Masters at the First Table protested.

Many of the younger men called for war. Debates raged for a time but eventually everyone wanted Dokein's opinion. The Grand Master, who had suffered the discussions in dignified silence, rose to his feet. "I have seen the future," he declared loudly. "We must fight."

Bursts of clapping and screams of affirmation followed.

"If there are any among you without a sword, sell your mantle and buy one!" Dokein proclaimed, leaning on the table. He then lifted a cautionary finger. "But remember, our hope is not in victory, but in God." That said, he swayed and crashed onto the floor.

"Master!" Antiphon cried, jumping from his chair. He grabbed Dokein, who croaked, "Brothers, Antiphon al-Caliph shall lead you! Listen to him!"

"Where's Gimel?" Antiphon screamed, trying to cradle the old man.

"Lay me down," Dokein groaned, going pale; the Order crowded around. "Borrowed time," he confided to Antiphon. "Didn't think it would be so little, though."

Antiphon gently laid the old man flat. "Master, don't leave me again," he entreated.

More shouts for the healers. A general commotion ensued as Gimel and the others made their way to the patient.

Dokein coughed. "Save them, Ani...my son," he said. "That is your victory." His distant gaze grew wide. He cocked his head to one side and said, "Singing. How nice."

The one hundred and forty-third Grand Master of the Order of the White Flame died with a smile.

"Master!" Antiphon sobbed, shaking him. "Master!"

He tried to revive Dokein for a moment before burying his face into the Grand Master's chest. He wept loudly in despair. The healers had to pull him from the corpse.

Later that night Antiphon al-Caliph was elected Grand Master by a single vote, making him by far the youngest in history. Surprisingly, none argued more forcefully for the elevation than Master Torra, and it was his eloquence, many felt, that had spelled the difference.

*   *   *

Kerebos sat in the cold rain.

For hours he had watched the lines of *Aharoni* filing into the *syna.* Everyone in Kwan Aharon had turned out to pay their respects to the Grand Master, but none had knelt so long beside the coffin as he. He stared past those *Aharoni* who glared at him from the queue. He knew they blamed him for Dokein's death, which grieved him exceedingly. It distressed him more that they were right.

Dokein, he thought, *you would have shown me the way, but I killed you for your trouble.*

Kerebos focused as a dripping, bedraggled Antiphon approached. The new Grand Master's robes wore like dishrags. He stopped and regarded Kerebos with sad eyes.

"Did you see him off?" he asked.

Kerebos nodded.

"I wanted you to see him while he was alive, you know," Antiphon said sorrowfully. "Then, when he came around, we had other things to worry about."

"I believe you," Kerebos said hollowly. "It's best this way, though. At least I didn't contaminate his going."

"Many of his last words concerned you," Antiphon replied. "He asked me to save you."

Cold wind tore into them.

"You've tried your best," Kerebos said. "Waste your time somewhere else."

Antiphon leaned over the seated *ikar.*

"I want you to command the city's defenses," he said. "You know more of such things than any man."

Kerebos blinked in disbelief. "What?"

"You heard me."

"You ask me, Kerebos *Ikar,* to take up my sword again?" he rasped. "What would your Council say to that?"

Antiphon shrugged. "They said yes. We need you Kerebos. Save Kwan Aharon from Pontis' greed. We have a very great store of weapons at your disposal. Use them and our soldiers as you see fit."

"Why not just give it to him? He's going to take it anyway."

"Because Dokein didn't want that," Antiphon snapped.

Kerebos looked at the line of *Aharoni* mourners stretching into the misty distance. He did not love these people. He did not even care for them.

180

"How can I honor Dokein by killing for him?" Kerebos asked sardonically. "Is that what it comes to?"

"There are times to fight," Antiphon growled. "You have fought too long without God at your back. War on His side for a change."

Kerebos looked into the Grand Master's bloodshot eyes, reading their hope, fear and frustration. "I am sorry, Antiphon," he said. "But the answer is no."

Now there was revulsion in Antiphon's eyes, too. "Just when you're really needed, you surrender," he spat. "I expected as much." He turned and slipped into the crowd.

I'll leave this city, Kerebos thought. *It has its fate, and I'll find mine.*

That evening the rain stopped briefly. As Kerebos stood on the walls and looked toward the desert, he was joined by Selah. Never had he thought her so beautiful. Her unbound dark hair cascaded upon bare shoulders and her eyes were filled with desire and understanding. She stood directly before him.

"I'm leaving Kwan Aharon," she said. "Will you stay here and die?"

Kerebos shook his head.

"Come away with me," Selah proposed simply. "That way neither of us is empty-handed."

Kerebos rubbed his stubbly chin and looked over the nearest residential area. He saw warm light pouring from apartment windows and secretly imagined himself an average man living an average life. With Selah. He could forget his memories and start over. Perhaps he could finally honor his father by having, and caring for, a son of his own.

Is that how it shall end? he wondered. He nodded. "I think I'll go with you."

Selah threw herself into his arms and gave him a quick squeeze. "I'll let you know when I'm ready," she said. "Give me a day."

Kerebos nodded again, but said nothing. Selah stood on her toes and kissed his cheek.

"You won't regret it," she promised.

erebos sat on his bed and stared into a lamp. His longing for Selah was as a great hunger. His chest tightened when he thought of pushing her onto her back.
He felt voracious, anxious and more than a little ill. He remembered
her legs around him, her breath in his ear.

What would Dokein think? he wondered with a grimace.

Fast footsteps in the hallway. Yeshua burst into the room. It took
a moment for Kerebos to notice the wooden sword in the boy's hand.

"It's war!" Yeshua cried. "The Council has again refused Pontis,
and that means there's going to be a fight!"

Kerebos shook Selah from his mind. "Is that so? Does that please
you?" He remembered some of the things he had done to captured
children and suppressed an urge to vomit.

Yeshua plopped onto the floor and adjusted his sword's loose cross-
hilt. "Pontis will never win," he proclaimed. "Not with you here."

Why did he say that? Kerebos thought. "What if I'm not here?" he
asked softly.

Yeshua laughed off the notion. "Hey!" he suddenly exclaimed
and withdrew Mistaaka from beneath the bed. He hefted the
sheathed sword, his eyes aglow. "Wow!"

"Put that back!" Kerebos snapped.

"Is this the one you used?" Yeshua asked, awed.

Kerebos' face wrinkled in disgust. "Yes," he admitted.

"Juntha said *landesknectos* name their weapons." The boy looked
at Kerebos. "Is that true? Hey, what's wrong?"

Kerebos swallowed. "It is true, but it no longer matters. I'm not the man I was."

Yeshua stood and tried to heft the blade. "God, it's heavy! Did you use both hands?"

"Not usually," Kerebos murmured. He was repulsed by the jealously that anyone, even a child, handled the sword.

Yeshua gave Kerebos a look over. "Can you still wield it?"

Kerebos' mouth was dry. He wrestled an urge to snatch Mistaaka from Yeshua. Also, to his infinite disgust, there was the tiniest yearning to use it on the boy.

"Yeshua, put the sword back," Kerebos said mechanically.

"My father probably couldn't even lift it," the boy lamented.

"Your father is mightier than I," Kerebos found himself saying. "Didn't he bring me to Kwan Aharon as though bound by steel?"

Yeshua appeared unimpressed. "Oh, God did that," he replied. "My father priests because he isn't a fighting man like you."

"Your father is a great man," the *ikar* grumbled. "Always respect him." Kerebos felt a hypocrite. Here he berated a child for not supporting a man he himself planned to desert.

"Could you teach me how to use this?" Yeshua begged. "I want to be a swordsman, not a man like my father."

Kerebos found words difficult. His mind was a morass of past dreams, present hopes and an impossible future. "Yeshua," he said, "remember your scripture: 'whatever you take into your hand, you take into your heart'. Look at me," he concluded feebly. "I'm an animal."

The mighty sword hissed with pleasure as Yeshua slid it from the sheath. It glowed like black ice in the lamplight.

How many children I've killed with the thing! Kerebos thought. "'Shua," he whined. "Put it into the scabbard, *please!*"

The boy ignored him. "I wish you were my father," he said and offered the hilt to Kerebos. "Show me how to use it."

The hilt grew in Kerebos' eyes until he saw nothing else.

"Please," Yeshua entreated.

Kerebos reached for the sword with reluctant desperation, shaking like an addict as his hand wrapped around Mistaaka. Suddenly everything came into focus. He again saw his terrible purpose. Why had he even tried to forsake the sword?

Kerebos closed his eyes and rubbed the blade against his cheek. Mistaaka whispered to him and promised to set him free.

Kerebos was home.

Yes I'll kill for Antiphon and his God, he told himself. *If I can't earn salvation I'll sacrifice for those who can.* "Where's your father?" he asked.

"I think he's in the weapons room with the captain, no wait, he's in his chamber. Why?"

Kerebos studied the sword edge with a discriminating eye and said, "Tell him I'll be along."

Kerebos waited in the basilica's ancient, domed garden. He sat beside the fountain into which Antiphon had pushed Montanus, dragging a morose hand across the rippling surface.

What's the difference between water and blood? he mused. *Why does it wash away blood, but not the opposite?*

Kerebos was deep in thought when Antiphon disturbed him.

"The basis of life," the Grand Master said wearily.

"What?"

Antiphon pointed at the water. "That."

"Oh."

Antiphon sat next to the *ikar*. "I'm sorry I couldn't come immediately," he said. "It's not that I'm not thrilled with your offer, it's just that the Council asks one thing of you. So do I."

"Isn't my service enough?"

"Apparently not."

"I will die for Kwan Aharon," Kerebos complained without rancor. "What else do you people need of me?"

Antiphon cleared his throat. "We want you to live," he replied. He managed a smile. "You walked right into that one."

"Don't I breathe? Want to feel my pulse?"

"I want you to be an *Aharoni*," Antiphon said. "Since you can't, I want you to do the next best thing."

Kerebos turned a suspicious expression on the priest. "What's that?"

Antiphon nodded at the water. "I must baptize you."

"That will make me an *Aharoni*?" Kerebos ridiculed.

"No, but you will no longer be Kerebos *Ikar*," Antiphon explained. "The Council would feel better about entrusting our families to you."

Kerebos grinned maliciously, saying: "Then I'll be allowed to kill for the holy men?"

"Well, yes."

Kerebos stood, towering over Antiphon. "I'm sick of fighting you people!" he snarled.

Antiphon showed no fear. "Talking to yourself?"

Kerebos appeared ready to strike, but withdrew. He walked in a little circle, muttering: "Damn, damn, damn." Suddenly he tore off his robe and climbed into the fountain. He dropped to his knees, bowed his head and said: "Reborn me, priest. Be quick about it."

Antiphon was caught off guard but rallied. He stepped into the pool and laid a hand on Kerebos' thick neck. "Do you renounce your sins and the work of the Evil One?" he asked.

"What am I supposed to say?"

"Say yes."

"Yes."

"Do you acknowledge the life, death and resurrection of the Savior, the son of God?" Antiphon continued.

A brief pause.

"Yes."

"Do you believe in the forgiveness of sins?"

A long pause. Kerebos nodded faintly.

"I must immerse you," Antiphon warned. Kerebos nodded again and the priest completed the action. Kerebos came up sputtering, blowing cold water off his lips.

The Grand Master released the *landesknecta*. "You are reborn, Kerebos. Go and sin no more."

Kerebos wiped water from his eyes.

"How's that feel? Good?" Antiphon asked.

Kerebos smiled wanly. "Yes," he replied, "but I'm sure I'll get over it."

Antiphon aided the *ikar* to his feet. "I'm sure you will, too."

They stepped from the fountain. Antiphon turned away as Kerebos dressed.

"You want to address your troops now?" the Grand Master asked. "Or do you wish to wait until all of them have deserted?"

"Before we do anything, I want to see that wondrous armory from the dawn of time," Kerebos growled. "I hear the all-wise Juntha swears by its treasures."

185

"I must flog him, someday," Antiphon sighed.

Kerebos recalled Yeshua's last visit. "Get in line. Let's go."

As they walked along Antiphon shook his head. "Baptized Kerebos *Ikar*," he chuckled. "Who would've believed it?"

"Not I," Kerebos replied. "Two more miracles and you're a saint."

Antiphon and Kerebos walked down the brick lane between the sanctum and basilica; each bore an unlit torch. Artisans and townspeople bowed to the Grand Master or shot suspicious glances at the *ikar*.

"There aren't many folk around," Kerebos observed. "Have they departed?"

Antiphon nodded. "Many to the *Chaconni* lands, if you can believe it."

"Will *any* of them fight?" Kerebos asked.

"Some."

They stepped aside to let a donkey-cart pass; the wooden wheels rattled across uneven cobbles. Kerebos took a moment to observe the dilapidated, whitewashed apartments before him. Laundry dangled from the windows.

"To think that I've missed living like this," he mocked.

"This is an old part of town," Antiphon replied and stepped off the curb. "The newer buildings are in the outer ring."

"Strange how nice are the priests' quarters," Kerebos said.

"We're not landlords to these people," Antiphon answered with a scowl. "Kwan Aharon's citizens live as they like."

A group of laughing youths darted from between two buildings, and down an alley. Kerebos peered after them into a dank, gloomy backstreet.

This city's a giant rathole, he thought. *One elhar could stymie an army for weeks.*

The companions circumvented the crowd by a produce stand, and turned onto a wide, even boulevard. A steep hill loomed before them, atop it a lonely, massive structure. Kerebos instantly knew that the building was far older than anything else he had seen in Kwan Aharon.

Antiphon indicated the impressive construction, saying, "There she is."

The armory's granite walls were mottled gray. It boasted neither windows nor arrow slots, which only stressed its frowning bulk. The armory looked over-large for the knoll and Kerebos wondered that the hill had not flattened. The place appeared stout enough to survive any assault, or even the end of the world. Whoever designed the place had been serious about discouraging visitors.

"What's it doing all the way out here?" Kerebos asked.

Antiphon shrugged. "Many hundreds of years ago it was in the Sanctum, before the old basilica burned." he said. "The Order moved into its present location and just kind of stayed there. We had neither the resources nor inclination to rebuild our fortress after that. Certainly not to the old standards."

Kerebos gazed over the haphazard town. "Too bad for us."

They found some very steep stone steps and labored to the top. Antiphon was winded by journey's end and gasped, "Whew! I'm not going to be much good in a fight, I'm afraid."

"I'll find you a small sword," Kerebos replied and scrutinized the armory. He sensed the walls' vast thickness. "Where's the door?" he asked.

Antiphon had recovered his breath. "The other side," he said. "Come."

Kerebos followed the overgrown path, grunting as another hill came into view, a mere hundred paces away. Nothing but a few granite blocks crowned that incline's flattened head. "Another weapons room?" he asked.

Antiphon nodded. "Was. We needed the stone."

"I'll bet a tunnel runs between the two."

Antiphon turned and cocked an eyebrow. "It has long since been filled in. You know your cities, don't you?"

"I've had my share," Kerebos said softly.

"I shouldn't wonder. I've never heard of *landesknectos* being denied any place they'd set their hearts on."

"That's true. The thickest walls pale beside the determination of evil men." Kerebos replied.

Antiphon shivered. "Good thing Pontis isn't bringing your lads with him."

"Very good, indeed."

Antiphon approached a wide, gray door which was half again his height. The knobless portal, constructed of some strange metal, looked new beside the mossy stone.

"Who tends this place?" Kerebos asked.

"No one." Antiphon replied. "I can't remember the last time somebody entered this building." He handed Kerebos the torches and withdrew a keyring from beneath his robe. Each of the three large keys bore a number. "They say these only work in the hands of the righteous," he said skeptically.

"Then you'd better use them."

Antiphon placed one of the keys into the lock and twisted, but no luck. He tried the second, then last key, before the heard a click. He smiled feebly. "'The last is first and the first, last', that's how it goes," he said.

"It doesn't look open," Kerebos responded.

"No, it doesn't, because I've disarmed only the first of the defenses." Antiphon tried the first key and was rewarded by a grating sound; the door vibrated beneath his touch.

Kerebos guessed that some sort of heavy device was being retracted from the door and into the walls. The rumblings soon ceased.

Antiphon used the second key. The door cracked open with a wheeze and air escaped round its edges. "The ancients had some way of maintaining a constant climate," he intimated.

Kerebos was impressed. "Would save the weapons," he replied, stepping out of the door's path as it swung around. The door was at least a foot thick, completely solid and with no signs of mechanisms. The jamb was smooth as well.

"I suppose so," Antiphon agreed. "Tinder those torches, will you?"

Kerebos complied and handed one to the Grand Master. Antiphon went first into what turned out to be a surprisingly narrow walkway. Kerebos followed, perplexed by the freshness of the air. They had not gone a dozen paces when they found another door.

"Didn't we just do this?" Antiphon muttered and began the key ritual. Again they heard the curious groanings from within the door, then the hiss of escaping air. Antiphon lead Kerebos into the armory proper, which was blacker than darkest night.

"We're walking on wood," Kerebos said, his words echoing.

Their eyes adjusted quickly and this is what they saw:

They were standing on a small, stilted porch. Circular balconies, at least three levels, ran horizontally along the interior circumference. Retractable steps hugged the wall at regular intervals. The floor was a pit below them; metal glimmered faintly in the torchlight. Kerebos lay flat and thrust out his torch for a better view. The lowest level was crammed with armor. Shimmering chain mail rested on "T" stands. Full armor leaned against the stone wall, standing vigil like silent warriors. Crates of pikes and hauberks littered the floor.

Antiphon knelt beside the *ikar*. "That big cylindrical thing shoots metal balls through the air," he said. "Look, there's a ramp; let's go down!"

Kerebos hurried into the pit. He studied a suit of armor and whistled.

"What's that?" Antiphon asked from behind.

"Mine." Kerebos wiped dust from the metal's black surface. He wrestled a gauntlet off the stick-figure dummy and onto his own hand. He turned a contrite smile upon Antiphon and said merrily: "It has *spikes*!"

They worked their way around the room, which fanned out beneath the upper level. Kerebos realized that most of the "hill" was probably solid building. A closet dotted the wall every ten feet or so. Inside each of these was an awesome cache of swords and daggers.

Kerebos shoved the torch into a wall cup and snatched the nearest blade. He inspected the rune-encrusted scabbard.

"What have you there?" Antiphon asked.

"Swords."

"Are they still good?"

Kerebos backed out of the closet and slammed the weapon into the nearest patch of bare granite with all his might. There was a loud clang, his arm numbed, but inspection of the sword revealed not the slightest mark. His eyes glowed red in the firelight and he whistled again.

"By Desia, what a blade!"

"It's that good?" Antiphon squeaked.

"Mm-huh." Kerebos lifted the cross-hilt. "Can you read the scabbard?"

Antiphon took the weapon. "Let me see...ah! Magnannon!"

Kerebos leaned closer. "Who was he, some great king?"

Antiphon shook his head. "It's a metal, sort of."

"Whatever it is, it is wonderfully tough," Kerebos praised. "Your people must have been very learned, indeed."

Antiphon laughed. "It's more than just strong and light! Watch this!" He pulled the whining blade and a smell like flint filled the air. Smoke rose from the sheath before the sword was halfway free, and by the time it was clear, the edges had burst into flames. White flames. The small inferno brought the entire chamber into light.

"Magnannon will burn for hours!" Antiphon cried. "Dokein had once told me that, but I didn't believe him." He took a swipe at some racked spears, and sliced them as though they were straw, leaving them smoking along the points of intersection. He laughed. "What do you think, General?"

Kerebos stared at the white flames with dread.

*   *   *

Later Antiphon and the *ikar* toured the outer ring. Kerebos found this part of Kwan Aharon to be very impressive. Well-conceived streets, tidy shops and quaint residential districts combined as effectively as that of the newest *Chaconni* city. Magnificent fountains gurgled in every square and the palm trees seemed as numerous as people. Even the Foreign Quarter was well kept.

"What's that you're humming?" Kerebos asked.

Antiphon looked surprised. "Am I?"

"Yes."

"Probably something I've been working on. I don't sleep so well, so I write."

"Writing!" Kerebos harrumphed. "That's no way for a grown man to spend his time." He looked favorably upon the towering defensive wall. "I approve. It'll be hard for anyone to get over that; they'll have to try the gate."

"Is that good?"

Kerebos flapped an arm. "Might be. We can concentrate our forces, though their commander will try to spread us out." He nodded at a square building. "The projectile weapon and that dump would be make a nice couple. Or maybe I'll place it behind the gate."

"How much of the armory can you use?" Antiphon asked.

Kerebos rubbed his chin. "All of it," he replied. "Even those flaming swords and arrows."

"What's wrong with them?"

"Nothing."

Kerebos inspected the empty barracks and was dismayed by their slovenly appearance. Sloppy soldiers were bad soldiers, he felt, and found himself hoping for time to whip the mercenaries into proper shape.

"I had the men gather in the square so you could address them," Antiphon told the brooding *ikar*. "They're waiting for us."

As they approached the indicated square a large number of uniformed men turned apprehensive gazes upon Kerebos. "How many?" he asked.

"Three hundred, last tally," the priest replied. "Sorry it couldn't be more. Look how they stare at you."

Kerebos hung a grim face. "I'll take care of them."

"I'm depending on some civilian help, as I've told you," Antiphon said. "The Council is working on it right now."

"Great."

They walked the last fifty paces toward the meeting place. "Lots of *Aharoni*. Good," Kerebos grunted. "They won't run."

"And the foreigners?" Antiphon asked, concerned.

"If I can bribe them into staying until the *Chaconni* arrive, I'll have them," Kerebos confided with a subtle grin. "Because if I handle it right, Pontis' men won't let them leave."

"I hope you know what you're doing," Antiphon sighed. "This is no game."

"Didn't you beg for my services?"

"Just be careful," Antiphon cautioned.

"I've killed more men than your Order has saved," Kerebos stated flatly. "I'll off many more before this battle is through. If there is any man you should trust to run a war, it's me."

The soldiers did not even pretend to hide their interest in Kerebos, though the majority maintained an air of defiance. Truth be told, many of the more seasoned mercenaries had hung around for the sole purpose of clapping eyes on the dreaded warrior.

Silence fell over the square. A path parted for Kerebos and he

191

walked into the crowd. He smiled knowingly as they opened a patch of ground for him. Antiphon followed, fully aware that the mercenaries paid him not the slightest interest.

Antiphon lifted his arms and shouted, "Men, this is Kerebos *Ikar*! He shall lead you!"

Kerebos, half a head taller and far broader than the greatest of them, basked in hostile stares. "Grand Master, leave me alone with my brothers," he said.

"What are you doing?" Antiphon asked in a suspicious whisper. "This is no time for *landesknecta* braggadocio."

"No?" Kerebos scoffed, studying the faces. "That shows how much you know. That's exactly what these boys need. Rented swords crave two things," he elaborated. "Money, mostly, and a pinch of adventure. You supply the first, I'll furnish the latter."

Antiphon looked around. "All right," he said, "I'm going. Keep me informed."

"I'll be along. Do you have any swift boys I could use as runners?"

Antiphon frowned. "I'll see what I can do."

"Good," Kerebos replied. "But don't send Yeshua."

Antiphon began to smile but turned suddenly angry. "That's easy for you to say, *ikar*," he complained. "How do I ask my men to risk their sons but withhold mine?" He stormed off.

Kerebos watched until the Grand Master disappeared down a sidestreet, then fitted his most intimidating glance. "Gentlemen," he growled. "My name is Kerebos." He glared at them. "You've heard stories about me. Good. Maybe we can dispense with," he slowed, "...unnecessary problems."

No one chose to speak, though a nearby, grizzled archer viewed Kerebos as though he were a bullseye that needed feathering. Kerebos pointed at the man.

"Come here, you!" he said.

The *Aharoni* tried to look anonymous.

"Yes, you," Kerebos repeated in a kinder tone. "I'll try not to bite."

The archer adjusted his steel cap and stepped out from the crowd. Kerebos approached him and held out a hand, saying, "May I see your bow?"

The *Aharoni* looked shocked.

192

Kerebos laughed. "I know, *landesknectos* can't shoot. I admit, it's been a while." He took the bow and strung it, then purloined a scarlet-feathered arrow from the man's quiver. "But I haven't always been *ikar*." He aimed at a far pole. "My father used to say I had a special talent for the bow. How does it pull?"

"Low and to the right," the archer replied sullenly.

Kerebos loosed and missed the target by an embarrassing margin. "Damn," he said, squinting into the distance. "It's been twenty years. Give me another arrow."

The archer complied. Kerebos again bent the double-curved bow. "About two men high," he said, then shot.

The arrow whizzed into the pole as predicted. The archer nodded as thunder rumbled overhead.

"Another one!" Kerebos demanded. That one splintered the first.

The *ikar* returned the weapon. The archer stood shaking his head in disbelief. "A very fine shot," he admitted.

"What's your name?" Kerebos asked.

"Tohu."

"You've commanded before, I can tell."

"I have," Tohu confessed without enthusiasm.

"Very good. You're now lieutenant of archers."

Tohu nodded.

"Your first order is to get some lads over to the armory," Kerebos said. "Empty it."

"Did the oldtimers leave us anything of use?" Tohu asked.

"Yes, tell us!" someone shouted.

"You won't believe what they left you," Kerebos said in an awed tone. "We're definitely going to win. Oh, yes," he raised his voice. "The Grand Master has tripled your salaries, effective now."

A pleased murmur went around.

"So let's look lively, and I'll get you through in one piece," Kerebos promised. "Officers follow me to the staff room."

Six men fell in behind Kerebos. "Come on!" he snapped.

They walked toward the officers' quarters in silence. Soon they were seated in what was supposed to be a staff room, but smelled like a winery. Kerebos appraised the men and was greeted with cynical expressions.

193

A sad looking lot, he thought, remembering his *elhari.* "All right," he started, "I want reports on the state of your commands. Include your evaluations of the city's defenses and any suggestions on improving them. I want them within the hour." He smiled. "Remember that Pontis' army will be well informed of our city and disposition due to those less noble souls who have gone over."

If any of them can't whip up that report in an hour they're going to find themselves behind bars! Kerebos thought. "Dismissed. Meet me in the officer's mess with those reports. We'll have some food and get acquainted."

Half the officers looked heartened by the *ikar's* confidence, but the others appeared unchanged. Kerebos was pleased to note the two groups sat apart. The officers rose and saluted in *Aharoni* fashion, both hands on breast and bowed head, then filed from the room.

Kerebos was contemplating an "accident" for the three uninspired commanders when Tohu stepped into the room. There was a bounce in the archer's step; his new lieutenancy was obviously sitting well.

"I've sent for horses and wagons, lord," he said, stroking his beard. "I'm going to need them to clear those weapons."

"Good."

"Where do you want the stuff?"

"Here's as good a place as any to dole it out," Kerebos replied. "Did you find the suit I marked?"

"Aye."

"Have it sent to my room."

"In the basilica, lord?" Tohu asked.

"Yes, but I'll be back in an hour."

Kerebos felt a severe stab of regret. *How will I tell Selah?* he wondered, though in his heart he felt she already knew. *Can I do it?*

Tohu turned to leave but stopped. He favored Kerebos with a good-natured grin. "Going to tell the Grand Master about the generous raise he just gave us?" he asked.

Kerebos could not help but laugh. "I suppose I'll have to. Anyway, I've got to go back there. I forgot my sword." He looked appalled. "Can you believe that?"

194

Selah inched aside the woolen drapery and peeked down into the empty *Syna* at Kerebos, who sat slump-shouldered in the last pew. Only this hour had she learned of his intentions to leave the city.

What's he doing, praying? she wondered. *Of course! He feels guilty about betraying me!*

Kerebos began mumbling and Selah's heart fluttered. She leaned over the rail in an attempt to make out the words.

He must be talking about me.

Kerebos sighed audibly and stared up at the ceiling, where clouds of incense had gathered. Selah ran lightly to the next balcony; from the improved vantage she could see his profile.

"Please," he petitioned the vaulted ceiling.

Selah was stunned by the display of weakness, but the reaction soon passed into something like sympathy. He looked so mournful, she wanted to take him in her arms. He covered his eyes. All hostility drained from Selah.

"Kerebos!" she cried, before she could stop herself.

"Lord Kerebos!" Tohu called, barging into the *Syna*. Gray light streamed in from the open doors.

The *ikar* stirred and cleared his throat. "Yes?"

"I brought your armor," Tohu said. "Captain Remeth has sent a valet to assist." Tohu looked around the dark chamber. "Are you ready?"

Kerebos glanced up at the lofty balconies. Had someone called from there? He nodded, saying, "Let's go."

They marched from the building.

*   *   *

195

The perfumed valet adjusted the cuirass. "Still too tight, my lord?" he asked, fidgeting with the buckles.

"A bit," Kerebos replied gruffly, battling an urge to smack the fop.

"It won't let out any farther."

"Then it'll have to do. That will be all."

The floor trembled and Kerebos' helmet spilled from the bed and rattled across the floor.

"The fourth one today!" the squire squeaked.

"Yes. Get out."

Kerebos looked in the mirror. He was back in armor for the first time in months; it frightened him how much he liked the feeling. *Please, God*, he prayed, *don't let me slip back, don't abandon me to the darkness.* He caressed the excellent armor, and thought: *God help me, but I can't wait to kill.*

He smiled wanly at his reflection, saying, "You'll never make it."

Kerebos reached for his knuckle spikes and rolled them around his palm. *You enjoy these things too much*, he thought. For the first time he missed his conscience; he hated being all alone with morality. *But of course, you're not moral*, he reminded himself. *Rapist. Child killer. Father slayer.* Tears started in his eyes.

"Enough!" he shouted. Another tremor passed through the earth.

Kerebos screwed in the forefinger spike. "That's for meekness," he whispered.

Then the next. "That one for mercy."

Then the third. "For the pure of heart."

And the last. "For those I've persecuted for their righteousness' sake."

He looked again at his reflection. "It's the only thing you're good at."

Somebody knocked on the door.

"What?" Kerebos asked.

"It's me, Yeshua!"

Kerebos quickly brushed his eyes. "What is it 'Shua?"

"Father sent me!"

"Come in, then. But only for a moment."

Yeshua stepped inside. He bore a paper package.

"Why are you dressed like that?" Kerebos demanded.

"I'm going to be a runner!" Yeshua stated proudly. "Juntha is going to get me a knife, too."

Kerebos lamented asking the Grand Master for messengers. He

196

grabbed the boy's shoulder. "Promise me you'll stay away from the fighting."

"I'll be fine," Yeshua guaranteed.

Kerebos flicked the parcel. "What is it?"

"It's from father." Yeshua reliquished the gift. "It's one of his."

"Thank you," Kerebos replied. "Now go back to him."

Yeshua stopped at the door. "I'm stationed in the Outer Circle!" he cried smugly, then scampered from the room.

Kerebos shook his head while turning attention to the package, which he weighed in his big hands. It was light. He snapped the twine binding and the wrapping fell away, revealing a magnificent snow-white cape. Kerebos unfolded the plaited garment, wishing he could feel it through his gloves. A note fell from the cape and he scooped it off the floor.

Kerebos, it read. *Wear black no more. When you find yourself in the dark, remember the Master you could have been, and still might be. Antiphon al-Caliph.*

Kerebos was touched by the gesture. He wondered what kind of Grand Master another twenty years might have made of Antiphon as he slung the cloak over his shoulders and clasped it around his neck. It was light and just the right length for campaigning. Again he peered into the mirror. *I look different.*

Kerebos hitched Mistaaka to his belt and left the chamber. He lumbered down the hall; a damp breeze filtered through the shutters. *More rain*, he thought glumly and started down some steps.

"Kerebos!" Selah called.

The *ikar* stopped in his tracks and whirled to face the woman who, clad in snowy gown, was perched atop the stairway.

"Lady," Kerebos said. "I was just coming for you."

Selah's exquisite features were twisted in torment, her long hair in disarray. Her eyes were puffy. She had been crying. She placed a small hand on her breast and asked: "Have you forgotten me?"

A year earlier, Kerebos would have found it impossible to feel pity for another human but as it was, his heart felt cleft in two. "No, you're ever in my thoughts."

"You said you'd take me from this place," she whimpered. "I was yours. Why have you changed your mind?"

Kerebos felt dizzy; he wished himself dead. "I'm sorry, but that's impossible now," he droned. "Can't you see that?"

Her dark eyes blazed suddenly. "All I see is a man too weak to create his own destiny," she said with a sneer.

"So be it," he replied sadly and continued his descent.

"Oh, Kerebos!"

The *ikar* stopped.

"I love you!" Selah wailed as though the admission hurt. "I really do! Doesn't that matter? Don't you love me?"

"It's all the more reason to leave me alone," he answered miserably. "I'm sorry."

"*Please*," she begged, bursting into tears. She took two steps down the flight. "Let's leave Kwan Aharon and make our own choices!"

Kerebos wanted to hold her so badly it hurt. Why not run off with her and build a farm somewhere? He could throw Mistaaka into the deepest ocean, and ignore the world as it sank around them. Selah was his salvation, an earthly and corporeal reward for his many sufferings. Might it be just that easy?

Had she accosted him an hour earlier, Kerebos would have succumbed, but now he could not. He stared a long moment before replying, "Forgive me, lady, but such happiness is not meant for me."

Selah tiny hands clenched into fists of frustration. "Oh, how noble," she said so scornfully he felt stripped of skin. "Is this how you finish? Another gutless dupe bending to a silly Order and its foolish Grand Master?"

Kerebos turned and started down the steps.

"Do you hear me, Kerebos *Ikar*?" she shrieked. "You're not a God!" She laughed scathingly. "You're not even a man!"

Somehow he made it to the bottom without falling, though he felt as though laboring through knee-deep mud.

"Go ahead!" she sobbed. "I don't want you! Is death so much easier than thinking for yourself?"

Kerebos reached the door but was too weak to open it.

Selah smiled savagely. "I've read your pathetic scriptures," she scoffed. "I know what they say!" She pointed to the door. "Go and die!"

Kerebos closed his eyes and nodded. He pushed open the door and stumbled from the building.

Selah threw her hands to her face and sagged back into the wall. "Go out there and die," she wept.

erebos and his pruned officer corps studied a scouting report. After receiving incomplete and/or incompetent assessments from some of the officers, Kerebos had acted decisively. Two of the men were immediately thrown into the brig with the promise that they would be killed if they attempted to stir up trouble. When Kerebos arrived to arrest the third hack, a notorious alcoholic named Pewp, the man was found floating in his bath, wrists slashed. That suited Kerebos fine. He preferred to run lean on officers.

The shortage of troops was an entirely different and more serious matter, however. There was no way to defend the entire outer wall with the measly three hundred men afforded him, and Kerebos would not even try. He planned a nominal struggle for the gate before falling back into the Sanctum, where shorter lines would provide the Order's best chance. This did not mean he would grant the *Chaconni* their own way with the outer ring, though. He had hatched a few nasty surprises for the invaders, some real morale checks, including a flanking assault with some of the unearthed terror weapons. The battle for Kwan Aharon might prove short, but it would certainly be interesting.

Kerebos wore a sour expression as he sized up the map. He looked at Colonel Nuun, a willowly, middle-aged *Aharoni* and said: "Half a day's march, eh? Is this report reliable?"

A scowl settled on Nuun's sallow face. "Aybil al-Addam is the most faithful rider I have," he replied indignantly. "He'd have made officer long ago if I could spare him from the field."

This one's going to be trouble, Kerebos thought. *Doesn't much care for my orders. Oh, well, he's not the first.* "All right," he said, then turned to Captain Remeth. "Have anything to add?"

Remeth, the youngest of the lot, had a chiseled, handsome face—almost pretty—which might have been stone for all its emotion. Kerebos had yet to decide if the man was lost in thought, or none too bright.

"Not at this time," Remeth said blandly.

"Tohu?"

The archer rubbed his hands together in anticipation; his beady eyes danced with delight. "May I place half the strings above the gate and keep the others moving about?" he asked. "That'll keep Pontis honest. We'll hit them where they aren't."

"I was going to suggest that," Kerebos allowed. "Where will you be?"

Tohu grinned. "Wherever it's most dangerous, m' lord."

"Then you'll be at the gate with me."

"Fighting alongside the *ikar*," Tohu chuckled. "And mother said I'd never amount to anything."

Remeth ran a swarthy hand over the aged cannon. "I've read about this weapon," he said. "Mighty we *Aharoni* used to be."

"Can you operate it?" Kerebos grunted.

"Yes."

"Can we place it on the wall?"

"No, lord," Remeth answered as he inspected the breech.

Kerebos made a "why not" face.

"It recoils with the power of God's breath, hence its name— *Yaathra*," Remeth elaborated, peeking down the barrel. "I don't believe it's ever been used."

"Shouldn't we test it?"

Remeth's abrupt smile surprised Kerebos. "With your permission, I'd like to do just that."

"Take it outside the city," Kerebos replied. "Feed me the results as soon as possible. I've a few ideas for this thing."

Tohu puffed to the *ikar's* side. "General, these Magnannon arrows are fantastic. Fantastic!"

Kerebos eyed the proffered fletches. The shafts were black, the heads dull silver. "Oh?"

Tohu motioned to some men dragging a suit of armor. "Prop it against that wagon, boys!" he cried then winked at Kerebos, saying, "Watch this!"

Tohu struck an arrow against the flint alloy at his belt and the head burst into flame. He strung the arrow, pulled and loosed; a streak of white hissed through the air and slammed the armor, vanishing in a shower of sparks.

"It disappeared?" Kerebos asked warily.

"No, m' lord, come see," Tohu replied.

The arrow had sliced through armor and wagon and had burrowed into a brick wall. Inspection revealed the breastplate had liquified around the entrance hole. Kerebos nodded approval.

"Nice, huh?" Tohu asked.

Kerebos wiggled the arrow from the wall, finding it still aflame. "How does one extinguish it?" he wondered aloud.

"Burying them seems to do the trick, but don't douse them in water; they'll just heat up," Tohu replied. "Too bad we've so few of them."

"How long will it burn?"

"A goodly while, but they aren't accurate for very far. These metal shafts seem a tad heavy."

Kerebos studied the blaze, saying, "They'll fly far enough."

*   *   *

Someone shook Kerebos.

"Wake up, General!" a soldier cried. "The *Chaconni* have arrived with the dawn!"

Kerebos sat in the bunk and blinked. He was still in armor. "It's morning?" he asked groggily.

"Yes!"

Kerebos grabbed Mistaaka and stumbled from the building. Soldiers were hastily assuming their posts in the pale light. Kerebos found Remeth near the open gate. The captain was tallying mounted scouts as they rumbled into the city.

"What passes?" Kerebos demanded.

"My lord," Remeth nodded calmly. "Pontis' force is almost upon us. Scouts confirm that Count-General Pyrros leads the army."

"Pyrros, eh?" Kerebos snarled and adjusted his cloak.

"You know him?"

"Scraped swords with him once, years ago. He was lucky to escape alive." Kerebos withheld what he had done to prisoners he had taken.

Remeth replied: "Apparently their force is not as vast as was reported. Maybe they've split up. New estimates indicate less than ten thousands all told. Less than two thousand horse."

"So much for Nuun's 'faithful rider'," Kerebos said. He gazed at his distressingly few soldiers and the scores of citizen volunteers. "What I wouldn't give for an *elhar*," he muttered.

Remeth awaited orders with an impressive detachment. Kerebos was forced to reevaluate the man. Certainly Remeth was no *landesknecta*, but he had nerve and would probably prove stalwart.

"See how they deploy before you place your men," Kerebos ordered.

Remeth saluted and turned to a sergeant. Kerebos looked to the *Yaathra* and thought: *'God's breath', eh? We shall see…*

Colonel Nuun and a force of cavalry burst into the city and reined their horses. Nuun began barking orders to the gathered infantrymen. Kerebos made for the colonel.

Nuun gave a lazy salute. "I request permission to attack the enemy on the flat," he said, then pat his jittery horse.

Kerebos frowned. "Pyrros is unimaginative and clumsy, but even he will be able to demolish your small band," he said. "I want your archers on the walls. Forget brave strokes."

Nuun chewed his lip in silence.

Kerebos checked his ire. "The *Chaconni* have two thousand cavalry," he reasoned. "You have seventy. Be smart."

Nuun looked down his long nose. "The barbarians should have brought more to attack the Holy City!" he blustered. "May I not serve God the best way I know, or will you keep me caged like a rat? What good is cavalry behind walls?"

Kerebos disliked the arrogant colonel, and knew he would grow to detest him, but the man had spirit. "All right," the *ikar* grumbled.

"Pyrros will allow you to approach, hoping to catch you between pincers. Get close enough to fire a volley, to take out their commanders." Here the *ikar* raised his voice. "Engage them with arrows only. Hit them once, then desist. I need you on the walls. I'll tell you when to sally."

"A volley?" Nuun asked with disdain.

"And that's all," Kerebos warned. "And if you get 'tied up' on the plain, I'll shut the gates on you. I'm not risking the city so you can glory hound."

Nuun wheeled his mount and returned to his men. Kerebos stared after him a moment, then raced up a spiral staircase and onto the wall. "Hurry!" he exhorted slower men.

Tohu was already there, deploying his men.

Kerebos looked over the sparse plain toward Pyrros' force, which spread from the horizon like a widening pool of blood.

"General!" Tohu cried and saluted.

"Ready?" Kerebos asked.

"Indeed," Tohu replied. "My lads got their pay and are waiting for you to supply some excitement!"

Kerebos shook his head, disarmed by the lieutenant's sharp humor. He looked over the pride of archers who seemed ready enough. Some fingered their weapons in anticipation, others regarded the *ikar* with expectant eyes. He guessed their thoughts: *We'll see if this legionary is all he's cracked up to be.*

"They look it," Kerebos granted. "Make the enemy pay dearly for the gate, Tohu. Be ready for my signal to fall back. Save the Magnannon for closer quarters."

"Yes, Lord," Tohu replied and approached the legionary. "They've a new name for you," he confided with an odd grin.

Kerebos braced himself. "What?"

"It's Tattanos," Tohu whispered with a *Chaconni* accent.

Kerebos' eyes became as slits. "That means 'herald.'"

"I know. I served eleven years in the Old Kingdom before coming home."

"Why Tattanos?"

"You know why, m' lord. Some think you're the prophet from the Scriptures."

Kerebos turned slightly aside. "What do you say?" he asked softly.

"Don't know, m' lord. I'm not a religious man, myself. Two of my lads swear they've dreamed of this battle, though," Tohu divulged. "Since they were little boys."

Kerebos tried to control his shaking. He felt destiny throwing a saddle over him. "Do we win?"

"One says yes, the other no," Tohu replied.

A man might do both, Kerebos thought. He pulled himself from the funk and grated: "If they're not sure, then tell them to keep quiet."

"Yes, General," Tohu said and returned to his men.

An half hour later Kerebos pointed down into the city at a mounted man. "You!" he screamed. "Fetch your worthless Colonel! Now!"

The terrified horseman made off at a gallop but it was long minutes before Nuun arrived; he rode at a leisurely pace, entourage in tow. His expression was one of indecision.

"What is it?" he called up at the livid *ikar*.

Kerebos leaned so far over the wall he almost fell. "Get up here *now!*" A crowd of satisfied infantrymen snickered; they held little love for Nuun or his riders. "Are you deaf, dwarf? NOW!" Kerebos thundered.

"Oh, very well," Nuun replied as though he had a choice. He gave his men a nod of affirmation then dismounted. He proceeded to the wall with proud steps, but there was fear in his eyes.

Kerebos yanked him up the last three steps, crying, "What kind of fools do you have as scouts?" His face purpled with fury.

Nuun, who had bragged he would "endure no abuse from a barbarian murderer" wilted on the spot. Having only heard about Kerebos' fury, he was unmanned by the genuine article.

"I, I don't know what you mean!" he stammered.

Kerebos wrapped a hand around Nuun's neck and shook him with such force the man's helmet flew off. "Don't know what I mean?" he mocked, slamming him against a crenelation. "Look, idiot!" he cried, waving at the approaching army.

"What?" Nuun whined.

"*There are landesknectos!*" Kerebos bellowed so loudly the entire quarter heard.

Groans passed among Tohu's men then down the wall.

"My riders said nothing of legionaries!" Nuun protested, covering his face as Kerebos belted him onto his knees. "It can't be!"

"Yes it can! You think I don't know what an *elhar* looks like?"

Nuun tried crawling away. "No, no!" he sobbed. "They'd never march beneath Pontis. Why would they do that?"

Kerebos kicked him into the air. "To get me, fool," he replied. "Listen, you short yard of dog vomit! You're getting your wish about meeting Pyrros 'on the flat!'"

"Yes, lord!"

"Concentrate your archers on the *landesknectos*. Kill as many as possible!"

"Yes, lord!"

Kerebos turned to the blanching Tohu and said: "Get this piece of dung out of here before I kill him! And send a runner to tell Antiphon that there are going to be legionaries in the house."

Armies, like men, possess distinct personalities. Pyrros' divisions exuded arrogance and approached Kwan Aharon as though assured of success. Banners flapped bravely in the pre-storm breeze and brass horns blared constant challenge.

But none of the Old Kingdom's units marched with the legionaries' swagger. Even at a distance Kerebos could identify the *landesknecta* precision. He saw Triskeles' white-crested helmet and felt the *Boru* looking at him.

Yes, old comrade, he brooded. *We've unfinished business.*

It was with a curious pride that he marked the determination in the legionaries' steps. Whatever else might be said, he had trained the finest force in the world. He realized the grim irony that he was going to get that *elhar* for which he had earlier wished.

When the *Chaconni* were within a half mile, Kerebos ordered Nuun from the city with a promise of retaliation for poor performance. Kerebos watched the cavalry muster and had a sudden misgiving. *Should I stop them?* he wondered. *No, Pyrros must be deprived of Triskeles.*

The *Aharoni* knights, the pride of Kwan Aharon, displayed brash confidence. Burnished plate mail shined from beneath long robes; plumed helmets feathered the air. Every horseman's bow bragged some lady's token, a scarf or a bit of ribbon, and their steeds pranced proudly. Every head was high as they rode through the gate.

Kerebos found himself thinking of Selah and his heart sank. "I'm sorry," he sighed, unheard among the shufflings and shouts.

The *Aharoni* sallied forth.

Legionaries drew fortitude from their long history of invincibility, but the riders' valor sprang from another wellspring. *Faith?* Kerebos wondered.

Nuun was the last to leave. Kerebos noted his glazed expression and again reconsidered the attack order. Nuun spurred his horse and was gone.

Kerebos glanced at the infantrymen near the entrance. Unlike the horsemen, the taciturn mercenaries did not bear chivalry as part of their kit but valued survival above all else. *All men fight for different reasons*, he reflected. At the moment he could not think of an adequate reason to kill or die for Kwan Aharon, and the realization depressed him.

Nuun's small force fanned out as it approached the enemy. The *Aharoni* slowed up and tossed off a few volleys, but continued directly for Pyrros' host. It soon became evident the riders had no intention of stopping.

What's that fool doing? Kerebos thought, although he knew. He remembered the colonel's blank expression.

The horsemen gave, shrill, undulating battle cries and drew swords.

"Damn!" Kerebos cursed as the *Aharoni* reformed into a wedge and drove straight at the *landesknectos*.

Perhaps Nuun wanted to redeem his inaccurate dispatches, or maybe he wished to confirm his bravery, but whatever the reason, he charged the *elhar*, which had already assumed battle formation.

"Desia's rotting heart! The fool's gone mad!" Kerebos cried.

Two *alaes* of Pyrros' cavalry thundered forward to meet the *Aharoni*, but Nuun's greatly outnumbered force did not waver. A roar lifted from Pyrros' infantry and broke on Kwan Aharon like a wave.

Tohu muttered: "This won't take long."

"It's all for Nuun's pride," Kerebos groaned. "I should've known."

Nuun did not commit himself until the last instant then slashed left into one of the *alaes*. The *Aharoni* cut through the cavalry wing

206

like an axe through cheese; all Kwan Aharon shouted its admiration.

The sound of clashing steel and snapping lances floated back to the city as did the screams of beasts and men. Many *Chaconni* went down in the charge, but a bare half of Nuun's men were still mounted as the *Aharoni* exited the enemy flank. The two *alaes* ran a broad elipse and turned back toward their countrymen, trapping the *Aharoni*. Worse, Pyrros ordered forth another *ala* that had been hiding behind his main force.

Tohu noticed the fresh cavalry. "Oh, no!"

Pyrros' archers opened up and Nuun's men were caught in a rain of arrows. Red pools of blood appeared on white robes and many *Aharoni* dropped from the saddle, or shrieked as their crippled horses crashed onto the ground. The *Aharoni* were strafed mercilessly before the *alaes* finished with swords, to the deafening approbation of Pyrros' men.

"Would that I were out there!" Tohu growled. He turned to his men, bawling, "Prepare to feather those bastards!" The archers nodded in fierce agreement.

A handful of the *Aharoni* horsemen formed a ring to meet the enemy charge. One of the last to die, Nuun fought with considerable bravery, bleating frenzied commands until an arrow took him in the jaw. He fell onto the ground, spitting blood and broken teeth then righted himself and stumbled to his horse just in time to be pinned to the animal by a swarm of arrows. The steed bucked a short distance then rolled over on its master. The remaining *Aharoni* were dispatched quickly.

The *Chaconni* infantry marched over the fallen, stopping only long enough to dispatch the wounded.

"They'll get theirs, by God!" Tohu promised.

Kerebos was surprised by Tohu's passion, but unimpressed; he had heard too many unanswered oaths in his career.

Cavalry scouted Kwan Aharon's perimeter while infantry took position. Many incautions riders soon discovered just how powerful were the *Aharoni* bows before learning to keep a respectful distance. Tohu himself took out one of these, a beautiful shot of nearly three hundred paces.

"Nice," Kerebos praised, then looked behind for Remeth. "Have the *yaathra* placed behind the right gate!" he told the captain, who acknowledged with a salute.

Kerebos turned back toward the *Chaconni*. He saw siege equipment among the supply wagons and made out the Scriptus inscriptions on the larger machines.

God, I'd kill Nuun if he weren't already dead, he thought. *How could his men not see that?*

Two thousand soldiers marched toward the far side of Kwan Aharon, but at such a distance that none were shot. Kerebos sent some of Tohu's archers to shadow the force, assigning them two runners. Yeshua happened to be one of these.

Back on the gate, Tohu was a man transformed. He fumed and bellowed as he paced the wall, hunting for targets. "Here the hammer falls heaviest, so here I stay!" he told Kerebos.

Kerebos smiled inside, thinking, *Some men fight for vengeance, if nothing else.* "Find a bow for me," he commanded. "I'll help with your revenge."

Out on the plain, Pyrros' army was deploying. A full battalion of archers, the *landesknectos*, and most of the siege machines were heading for the gate. Other battalions flanked the main push, and another was reserved behind what was shaped up as a command post. A steady trickle of riders raced to and from the Count-General's center of operations.

Tohu muscled through a knot of archers and handed Kerebos a beautifully inlaid bow of bone. "From the armory, Lord Tattanos," he said with a smile. "Works fine, too. I just skewered a horseboy who came too close."

Kerebos took the weapon and eyed the *landesknectos*, who lifted their greatshields as they advanced. Triskeles was in the rear. "You see that pale one in the flank?" he asked.

"*Boru?*" Tohu squinted.

"That's Triskeles *Elhar*, my former second in command," Kerebos said. "Kill him if you get the chance."

Tohu nodded. Even in Kwan Aharon, he had heard of Triskeles. He ignited and notched a Magnannon arrow. "No better time than the present, m' lord."

Chapter 24

The flaming arrow fell short, angling into the dirt a dozen feet from Triskeles, who sneered at the missile and ordered his men forward. The legionaries approached at the quick step, shields overlapping.

"Sorry," Tohu mumbled and snatched his quiver. "Should've let you try. Probably won't get another clean shot."

"Down!" Kerebos bellowed, pulling the archer flat.

"What..." the *Aharoni* said as a cloud of arrows hissed over the wall.

Those who had not heard Kerebos screamed as shafts appeared in their bodies. One man took an arrow in the nose, which sprang from the base of his neck. He fell backward with a thunk.

Crouching, Tohu ordered his men into volley position. They hugged the facade, turning sweaty faces to their commander.

"On my mark!" Tohu cried.

Another swarm of arrows whistled overhead and arched into the city. Men screamed.

"Now!" Tohu barked.

The *Aharoni* leaped to their feet, aimed, loosed and ducked. Shrieks. Kerebos peeked over the wall. A *landesknecta*, pierced through shield and breastplate, was hopping about, clutching the magnannon shaft that burned in his chest. Steam whistled from his armor as though from a kettle.

Triskeles, safe in the rear, ordered a "tortoise shell" and his men interlocked their shields overhead. Arrows and rocks bounced off the shell, and even the magnannon had difficulty passing the layered defenses.

Kerebos ducked another *Chaconni* volley. "You got a few," he told

Tohu. "But they're bringing their gear to the gate. They must be stopped! Aim for their feet, whatever!"

Tohu relayed the order to his men, who pulled their special arrows. "Now!" he yelled. They leaped up and fired. More hair-raising screams. Tohu again knelt beside the *ikar*, a wicked grin on his face. "They didn't like that round, m'lord! I think we can handle two shields at this range. Smell the flesh burning? I like mine well done!" Another rain of arrows. "Again!" he cried.

The *Aharoni* stood and fired...then the second *Chaconni* volley hit. Most of Tohu's men crashed onto the stone, riddled with arrows. One man near Kerebos clutched the arrows in his forehead as he laid down in a pool of blood.

Tohu called for his men to sound off. "Staggered, you know better than that!" he berated himself. "Stupid!"

Kerebos slapped the archer in the arm. "They're dead," he grumbled. "Command those who still live."

Tohu nodded listlessly.

Kerebos motioned to a runner, who was hiding behind a barrel. "Hey, boy!"

The lad peeked around the wood. "Lord?"

"Tell Remeth to send all the bowmen he can scrounge, and to find what Pyrros is doing behind us! We should've heard something by now!"

The runner scurried for the steps, arrows sparking the stone near his feet.

Kerebos turned to Tohu and said: "We'll fake a discharge, then duck; we'll get some of them after they shoot."

"Yes, General."

"On three, then," Kerebos ordered.

Tohu informed his men of the ploy. As they waited for the right instant Kerebos realized that this was the first time in months he had been genuinely happy. *God forgive me*, he prayed, appalled.

Tohu looked nervous.

"Here we go," Kerebos said. "Three. Two. One. Now!" They sprang to their feet and discharged.

Captain Remeth received the message and acted immediately. In addition to archers, he sent some slingers, saying, "Tell Lord Kerebos

210

I'll soon know about the perimeter."

"Captain Remeth!" another courier shouted, slipping by some infantrymen.

A large stone flew over the wall and rattled down the cobblestones. Others followed in quick succession, smashing walls, roofs and people. A drizzle started. More rocks fell. One boulder squashed Remeth's aide, who curled around the stone like a dead spider.

"Boy!" Remeth called the runner, who was staring with horror at the aide.

"Yes, sir!" the messenger snapped to attention. "Ethanim sent me!"

"What news?"

"Another force from the desert! Looks big!"

Remeth slapped his scabbard in dejection. "Blood of the Savior," he cursed. "I'm truly a seventh son. How many?"

"Can't tell yet."

Remeth thought quickly. "Tell Ethanim to hold until further notice. We must not be cut off from the basilica. I'll confer with Lord Kerebos. Go."

The runner sprinted away.

Remeth reached the wall and raced up the enclosed steps, emerging just in time to dive beneath an angry press of arrows. He landed on a dead archer, whose bewildered eyes stared into the gray heavens, then rolled sideways and gazed around. Things looked bad. Bodies lay strewn across the stone. Here and there a man dragged himself through the sticky blood. Flies buzzed Remeth's ears.

Kerebos, Tohu and a few of archers were huddled against the facade. Remeth crawled over bodies to his commander, who appeared to have lost his helmet. "General!"

Kerebos looked annoyed. "Why've you left your post?"

"Another host from the desert!"

A loud boom echoed through the city, shaking the wall beneath them. The *landesknectos* had started on the gate with a battering ram. Sputtering fireballs fluttered through the sky and crashed onto a thatched building.

"Damn!" Kerebos said. "What strength?"

"I don't know."

Kerebos shook his head. "I hoped we'd seen his entire hand. Get an estimation, then report."

BOOM, went the ram. Kerebos' teeth rattled.

Remeth saluted. "Yes, Lord. Shouldn't take long."

"See that it doesn't. Go!"

Remeth crawled back over the bodies and slid down the stairs.

A *good man*, Kerebos thought, wiping sweat and drizzle from his eyes. More fireballs hit the city. *It'll all be burning soon*, he thought. *Almost time to retreat. Have to do something about the elhar, first.*

An engineer called from the steps. "General! The enemy's working the gate. Pour the oil!"

BOOM!

Kerebos shook his head. "Too late, they've already gone into their shell. Besides, we shouldn't soak the wood. They might burn it as a last resort."

Kerebos grabbed Tohu.

The archer's brown eyes shone beneath a bleeding brow. "M' lord?"

"Hold this position until you've exhausted your arrows. Then make your way to the Sanctum. I'll see you on the holy walls."

BOOM!

Tohu grinned without mirth. "You think Almighty God'll save the basilica?"

"He helps those who help themselves," Kerebos replied.

Tohu nodded toward the *landesknectos.* "They help themselves."

Kerebos gave a cynical chuckle and made for the stairs. Moving nimbly for a big man in armor, he leaped some bodies and took the narrow steps three at a time; he exited into a cloud of acrid smoke and began coughing. A cursory glance revealed chaos and devastation. Fires raged unchecked, devouring entire builings. Men ran hither and yon, shouting. Bodies lay pinned to the ground by arrows. And the heat!

BOOM!

Good thing the Sanctum's all stone, Kerebos thought, licking salt from his lips. He ran to the gate and stopped beside the *yaathra.*

"Is it loaded?" he asked the gunners, a middle-aged sergeant and two others who looked too young to shave.

"Yes, lord!" the sergeant shouted, eyeing the buckling gate.

"Remeth put strange things in there. Uh, lord, hadn't we better clear out?"

BOOM!

The valves splintered and crackled. A hinge whined as it tore from the wall. Kerebos had flattened enough cities to know the gate was finished. Soldiers pressed around him. Someone suggested retreat.

"We'll be all right, boys," Kerebos said calmly. "You think I didn't prepare for this?"

BOOM!

Part of the gate gave with a shower of splinters as a huge, iron wolf's head screeched into view. The head, ears pinned back in fury, leered hungrily at them for an instant before it withdrew.

"Lord help us!" a soldier cried.

BOOM!

"Calm down!" Kerebos snapped, squinting against smoke. "Open the gate!"

The soldiers looked as though he had asked them to dance. Kerebos pulled Mistaaka and growled: "Open it, I say. We'll be fine." No one moved to comply so he laid Mistaaka against the sergeant's chest. "O-pen-the-gate," he said slowly. "We're going to shoot them. What do you think the *yaathra*'s for?"

The soldiers reluctantly obeyed.

"Not both doors!" Kerebos scolded. "Just the right one. Quickly!" He looked at the gunners. "You know how to use this thing?"

"Yes, lord!"

The gate was cracked just enough to provide the *yaathra* a clear shot. Kerebos relished the open-mouthed expressions as the legionaries stared into the cannon, their hands still on the ram. He pointed Mistaaka at them and cried: "Fire!"

The *yaathra* spoke with a mighty roar and a tongue of blinding flame. Rocks, nails, knives and chains ripped into the enemy. *Landesknectos* exploded in showers of blood and bone; armor became shrapnel and leveled many others. Kerebos gazed down the slick trail of viscera, weapons and severed feet.

"Close the gate!" he commanded.

The *Aharoni* slammed it shut but, unfortunately, the *yaathra* had mauled much of the latch.

213

"Wedge it with swords!" Kerebos directed.

Still no activity outside the gate as the *landesknectos* struggled to comprehend the sudden loss of half their force.

A bloodsmeared archer tugged Kerebos' elbow. "My lord, we can't hold anymore! They're bringing up some ladders!"

"Is Tohu still alive?" Kerebos asked.

"Yes, yes, but we're out of magnannon!"

The *landesknectos* resumed the attack, howling through the compromised gate. The *Aharoni* were thrown into a near panic as the frenzied legionaries began widening the holes.

Kerebos thought a brief moment, gazing over the burning city. "Well fought, then," he told the archer. "Send Tohu to the basilica. We'll need him there."

"Aye, lord!"

Remeth and a trio of swordsmen lumbered up. "Lord, I suggest we pull back," Remeth said as his companions looked balefully upon the gate.

"Give the order," Kerebos replied.

Remeth passed the word. A cornu horn blared the retreat.

"I'll see you men in the Sanctum," Remeth told his comrades. "Get moving."

"You don't take too long, Cap'n!"

Kerebos eyed Remeth, then the gate. "Let's try another *yaathra* bolt."

"We'll never get it open with those swords wedged there," Remeth replied.

"Do we need to?" The *Aharoni* were now in full retreat around them; the *ikar* grinned suddenly, saying, "Guess we load it ourselves."

Remeth nodded.

They shoved whatever they could down the barrel. Rocks, weapons, arrows, horseshoes, armor, boots and bones went in before and after a double charge of powder. Last of all Kerebos plugged the hole with a hefty stone.

The *landesknectos* bayed promises of torture at Kerebos, who ignored them. "Let's push it to the gate!" he yelled.

Remeth cut the *yaathra* from its mooring and Kerebos laid into the carriage until veins bulged from his neck. Slowly, the twenty-foot piece began to roll.

"Keep coming," Remeth directed, pulling from up front.

"Kerebos!" the *landesknectos* cried as the *ikar* nestled the cannon against the gate. One of the *yaathra's* wheels snapped off and the gun lurched sideways. Remeth grabbed a piece of flaming wood from the ground.

The legionaries were almost through! Even now one was wiggling through a hole.

Remeth's handsome face paled as he looked at Kerebos. "There's no fuse," he said.

"What? We need one?"

Remeth nodded stoically. "Unless we'd like to kill ourselves."

Kerebos snarled, saying, "Well, I don't have any in my pocket. Let's get out of here!"

Remeth waved toward the steps. "Grab that bow," he suggested. "We'll use the string."

Kerebos frowned. "Right."

"Kerebos!"

"What?"

Remeth smiled. "Thank you."

Kerebos had taken twenty strides when Remeth detonated the charge. The *ikar* was hurled headlong by the concussion and landed face down near the wall. He felt dazed, sick. His ears rang. He struggled to his knees and weaved around toward the gate which, for the most part, was gone. Part of the *yaathra's* smoking breech was all that remained of Remeth and the gun. Outside the wall was a fresh paste of *landesknecta* remains.

God go with you, Remeth, Kerebos thought and staggered down the rubbled street. The city was farther gone than he had anticipated. Every building, it seemed, was burning and some had spilled into the avenue. The heat and smoke nearly overwhelmed him. *At least the flames aren't white,* he thought.

The basilica's bells tolled dimly above the sputtering flames. Kerebos took his best guess of their direction and cut down a smoky alley, convinced he would never see the Sanctum.

Antiphon watched in dismay as citizens and soldiers crowded through the gate beneath him. *God, what a mess I've made of it.* he thought, sick at heart. *I wish Dokein were here. He'd know what to do.*

Antiphon sweat inside his armor. The linked mail weighed upon his shoulders and gave him a headache. He hated how the baldric inhibited breathing, too. He looked past the burning quarter toward the distant east wall and stiffened. Were those men clambering over the wall? They were! Pyrros' soldiers were in the city!

"Hurry!" Antiphon shouted down to the gate. A mother with a wailing infant caught his eye and he felt suddenly lanced in the stomach. *How could I have sent my son out into this?* A lightning bolt touched down in the outer ring and the drizzle intensified. Black clouds rolled over the city. *Misery and destruction*, he pondered, bowing with grief. *I've lost my Master, my city, my Order, my woman and*, he could hardly think it, *my son!*

Antiphon composed himself as Torra waddled to his side. The old man looked out of place and supremely uncomfortable in a breastplate.

"Master, we must shut the gate," Torra said gravely. His son, too, was one of Kerebos' runners.

"A few minutes," Antiphon said, turning away to hide his tears.

"As you wish."

"Where's Kerebos?" Antiphon grumbled.

"None have seen him."

A platoon of archers reached the wall and appropriated the spot above the gate. One of them, a peach-fuzzed youth with a bandaged forehead, dropped a quiver near Antiphon's feet and notched an arrow.

"Excuse me, Grand Master," he said.

Antiphon meandered down the wall. *Yeshua, Yeshua. Oh, to see my boy again!*

Kerebos was lost. He leaned against an apartment building and gathered his senses, trying to reconstruct his path. *Left, left, two blocks, right*, he thought. *I must be heading in the right direction.*

A detachment of Marines, unmistakable in their gaudy lacquered armor, emerged from a far crossway. Kerebos withdrew into the alley and flattened against the wall, counting the Marines as they rumbled past. *A battalion at least. Probably headed to the Sanctum*, he reasoned. *They'd be getting orders from someone in a good observation spot.*

Having gathered his breath, Kerebos jogged down the alley.

Though the fire had spared this area, clouds of smoke made it difficult to determine his position. He found himself wishing he had gotten to know Kwan Aharon as he hurdled a capsized donkey-cart, turned a corner and reached a dead end. He kicked in a door, ploughed through some shoddy living quarters and exited onto another dingy backstreet.

Kerebos took another time out and debated the wisdom of trying for the Sanctum. It was probably surrounded by now. Why not lie low until darkness then steal into the desert? He forced the appealing thought from his mind.

I will die in this city. I will run no more, he thought. *I owe Dokein that much.*

He rounded a bend and ducked beneath the remains of a shattered fence, emerging into the brief yard of a whitewashed manor. He thought he heard more *Chaconni*, crouched against the house a moment, then slipped onto a narrow street. Porches and laundry hung overhead.

Kerebos' heart jumped into his throat. In the distance, like a light at the end of a tunnel, loomed the basilica's white walls. He started forward as smoke rolled across the lane.

Someone emerged from a shop and slipped warily toward Kerebos. The individual, dressed in a shabby cassock, bore a burden over his shoulder which looked like a child wrapped in a blanket. Slinking nervously forward like a rat in search of a hole, he did not notice Kerebos until almost upon him.

"Hello, Montanus," Kerebos said, icily. "What've you there?"

Montanus gasped; his ghastly, scarred face went ashen; he dropped the child. Yeshua half rolled from the blanket.

As he looked at the unconscious boy, Kerebos felt mingled pity an fury. Yeshua was bound and gagged, and had obviously been beaten. New bruises covered his face and dried blood trailed from his nose. Rage filled Kerebos. He said thickly, "Step away from my boy."

Montanus glanced frantically about, trying to decide which way to run. He leaned left and Kerebos prepared to pounce. Montanus drew a dagger. "Stay away!" he cried, voice cracking.

"Why did you come back?" Kerebos ground out. "Trying to ensure my capture?"

217

"Let me go," Montanus sniveled, drawing a stained purse from his cassock. "I have gold!"

Kerebos swatted the wallet and coins clinked down the cobblestones. Montanus yelped as Kerebos grabbed his wrist and shook the dagger onto the ground. "Why do you have the boy?" Kerebos demanded. "A gift for Pyrros?"

Chaconni voices sounded the next block over.

"Oh, no, no!" Montanus replied. "A trade, that's all! Him for Selah!"

Kerebos eyes widened. "Selah? You shouldn't have said that, Montanus. You really shouldn't have."

Montanus tried backing from the *landesknecta's* grip. "You brought Pyrros here, didn't you?" Kerebos grilled, squeezing harder. "To find me?"

Montanus doubled over and whimpered: "No! No, I swear it!"

Kerebos released the arm but stomped hard on Montanus' foot, snapping the arch. Montanus howled.

"Careful," Kerebos warned. "You'll alert your friends." He let the priest curl into a ball. "Why not run to Pyrros now?" he taunted.

Montanus slid to the wall and gazed up at Kerebos. "They're going to kill me!" he blubbered.

Kerebos smiled as he pushed his cloak aside and drew Mistaaka. "No they won't."

"Help! Help!" Montanus screamed.

"There are many reasons to kill you," Kerebos announced. "I'm obeying them all. It would be a sin to let you live."

Montanus looked up at the black sword and cackled: "What about your state of grace?"

"I never had one."

Kerebos served Montanus a vicious slash across the throat and the priest's jugular exploded with a crimson burst, hosing the *ikar's* legs. Blood bubbled between twiglike fingers as Montanus grasped his throat and crumpled onto the street.

Kerebos sheathed Mistaaka and knelt beside Yeshua, who looked even worse up close. He unstrung his cloak and gently wrapped the lad then, with a final glare at Montanus, gathered the boy in his arms. He started toward the basilica. *Please, let me get him safely inside first*, he pleaded. *Then do as you will.*

Kerebos' heart was pounding as he reached the end of the lane. Every second he expected some assailant to block his path. He passed through some smoke and found himself in the field before the basilica.

The gates were still open.

Antiphon saw the first Royal Marines and knew the time had come. He did not even try to hide his tears as he told Torra: "Lock it up."

Antiphon moaned as the gate creaked closed.

"Hold it!" an archer yelled.

Antiphon looked and saw Kerebos racing across the sward that separated Kwan Aharon and the Sanctum. Marines were hot on the *ikar's* trail; Yeshua dangled from his immense arms.

"'Shua!" Antiphon cried. He watched for a few seconds then went down to the gate. "With me!" he commanded some archers as he tore out to the *ikar*. *Aharoni* cheered from the walls.

Kerebos was rolling along at a tremendous pace, despite his burden. He smiled at the Grand Master an instant before taking a crossbow bolt in the shoulder. The blow sent him sprawling.

At first Kerebos did not know what had happened, then he felt blood oozing down his back. A cold pain spread through his torso. He tried to breathe, but had lost his wind. He forced himself to his knees and reached for the boy. Antiphon and the other *Aharoni* were beseeching him to rise, but he barely heard them. It seemed his ears were clogged.

Archers shot at the closing Marines as Kerebos straightened his senses. *Hurry!* he exhorted himself, but even that sounded muddy. *Get up before they slip a dirk into your back!*

"Quickly!" Antiphon said and crouched beside Yeshua, feeling for a pulse. A knot of archers flanked the Grand Master, strings drawn. Antiphon lifted his son and handed him to a soldier. "Run!"

The archer darted for the basilica even as Yeshua groaned for his father. Antiphon grabbed Kerebos, saying, "Thanks. Can you run?"

Bowstrings twanged as Kerebos labored to his feet. "I'd better," he grunted.

The archers held the rear until out of missiles, then started for the gate, passing Antiphon and the wobbly Kerebos.

"Leave me, I'll be fine," Kerebos told the Grand Master.

"Be quiet!"

"Run, Grand Master!" Torra shouted from the wall.

Bolts fell around their feet and whizzed by their heads. Kerebos redoubled his efforts, ignoring the pain. Tohu emerged from the Sanctum and aimed a flaming barb.

"Hurry, m' lord!" he called.

Now it was Antiphon who slowed; he was almost spent. "How do you run in this stuff?" he complained.

"*Landesknectos!*" Tohu cried.

"Oh!" Antiphon coughed and slipped.

Kerebos dug his heels and turned for his friend. The field was littered with casualties, but many others were streaming from the city. Kerebos easily identified some *landesknecta* greatshields. He bent and grabbed Antiphon by the shoulders. "Up you go. That's no place for the Grand Master. Damn!"

There was a bolt in Antiphon's back. Kerebos eased Antiphon back down.

"Through my spine," the Grand Master gagged, convulsing. "S-sorry. D-dead."

Kerebos throat constricted. "Antiphon?" Nothing. "Antiphon!" He stared at the corpse in disbelief before turning a bleak expression upon Tohu. A collective wail rose from the walls.

"Shut the gate," Kerebos rasped.

The *Aharoni* archers redoubled their efforts. "There's still hope, Lord!" Tohu protested.

"Do it!" Kerebos replied. "They want me, and they wanted him, they'll get neither!"

Tohu prepared to argue, then turned and dashed into the Sanctum. An instant before the gate slammed home Kerebos spied Selah, arms outstretched. He stared at the closed gate in agony.

"Run, general!" Tohu shouted from the wall. "Get out of here!"

Kerebos pulled Mistaaka as he faced the incoming enemy. He knew the *landesknectos* had orders to kill him at all costs and that Pontis had laid a huge ransom on his head. He had no choice but to lead them all away from the Sanctum. That alone would give Selah and Yeshua a chance. He started for the city, slowly at first, but picked up speed. Thankfully, his shoulder had gone numb.

Kerebos angled toward an unoccupied quarter and, to a man, the enemy repaired course to intercept. He ran with all possible speed. If he could reach the city, he would lead them on a merry chase. He grinned slightly, recalling how he had abused the Royal Guards in the forest. Each step brought him closer to the enemy. *Do they have the angle on me?* he wondered calmly. Another dozen steps brought him to the imagined point of intersection; he beat the legionaries by a heartbeat. *Guess not.*

The *landesknectos*, disgusted at being outpaced, cast away their greatshields. The gap began to narrow. Arrows whizzed at the *ikar* from all sides as he aimed for some burning buildings. *Almost there!* he thought.

Kerebos realized too late that the structures were tighter than he had suspected. Greedy red flames left only the slightest path. He doubted he could make it through. *But they'd be crazy to follow.*

"Kerebos!" a *landesknecta* cried.

Triskeles survived the gate, Kerebos realized. Ten steps from the fire and the heat was already unbearable. *I must be crazy!* He covered his face and plunged between the walls of fire.

The pain was worse than anything he imagined. He could not see, could not breathe and his head swam so violently he was unsure he was still on his feet. All he heard was crackling flames and, he fancied, skin roasting from his body. Just when he felt he could go no farther, he stumbled into freedom.

Only then did Kerebos hear his own screams. He crashed onto the ground, huffing and squirming. The first legionaries to make it through had lost interest in everything except tossing their scorching helmets and rolling on the ground. Subsequent arrivals were literally burning as they screamed from the flames.

Kerebos gained his feet and reeled blindly down the road. It was a short time before he could see through his tears. He debated where to run and decided anything was better than again braving the fire. Then an idea struck him—the armory. He could hole up there until he starved. Pyrros and Triskeles would waste days trying to get him, which would buy the *Aharoni* precious time to fortify the Sanctum.

Kerebos ran on.

erebos had been pinned down by some marauding *Chaconni* but had finally escaped via a drainage ditch. Word reached Pyrros about his whereabouts, however, and soon the entire southeast district was flooded with soldiers. It was the remaining *landesknectos*, though, who picked up Kerebos' trail.

A *sestari* was scouring the buildings on the lane leading to the armory when it stumbled upon the *ikar*. Kerebos had been hiding behind a stone fence between two houses. One instant he was alone in the cold rain, and the next two legionaries came crashing through a window at him. The first, a *Boru*, landed in the brief yard, rolled and was on his feet before the glass settled. The second, a topknotted *sestar* bearing a flaming magnannon sword, was close behind.

"*Ikar!*" The *Boru* cried as he closed.

Kerebos struggled to his feet but slipped in mud. He slid hard into the fence and the bolt snapped in his back. Kerebos screamed and went dizzy from the pain, which charged through his body like an electric shock. Blood seeped down his back and pooled in his boot.

"*Ikar!*" the *Boru* repeated and lunged.

Somehow Kerebos diverted the thrust with Mistaaka, but the *Boru* adjusted and stabbed recklessly downward with the pommel spike. Kerebos leaned forward in the nick of time and the blow fell harmlessly over his shoulder; he kicked the *Boru*'s feet out and rolled aside as the man's face struck the stone fence.

Kerebos was on his feet.

The *sestar* dashed in but made the mistake of leading with his naked shield arm. Kerebos severed the wrist with a blinding stroke. The *landesknecta* dropped the flaming sword and grabbed his spurting stump as he slumped glassy-eyed to the ground.

"Idiot," Kerebos criticized, then stopped cold. Mistaaka had snapped halfway up the blade. "Goddamn," Kerebos whispered, feeling as though he had lost an arm. He sheathed the sword's remains then finished off both men with the magnannon weapon.

A sound like metallic thunder charged the heavens and numerous bolts of blue tickled the city. The rain was coming down in torrents as Kerebos slipped across the street toward the armory. Legionaries whooped from either end of lane and rushed him.

"Kerebos!" Triskeles bawled as he took up the chase; his gaunt face was dirty and his helmet crest singed to the nub. A *razai* of *Chaconni* followed in his wake.

Kerebos hit the armory's grassy hill full speed and clawed his way to the top even as Triskeles reached the base.

"Spread out!" the *elhar* commanded.

Though he had keys, Kerebos knew he lacked time to coax the armory's elaborate defenses. He would have to kill the legionaries as they came up the hill. He peeked down at the thirteen rabid *landesknectos* then beyond toward the two *razai* of approaching *Chaconne*. Kerebos knew he would never leave the incline alive.

The thought troubled him mightily.

To some men death inevitable brings solace, but to Kerebos it heralded only dread. The *ikar* felt physically sick as he imagined standing before the *Aharoni* God's judgement.

So this is how it shall end? he asked himself, swallowing the lump in his throat. *All your games and a little repentance couldn't save you, huh?*

Kerebos was seized with a desire to curse God, Dokein and anyone else who had poisoned him with the impossible notion of redemption. Looking into Triskeles eyes, he was convinced that some men were created simply as vessels fit for wrath.

Laboring up the knoll, Triskeles gave Kerebos a hungry smile. Kerebos pointed the magnannon sword at the *elhar*.

I might be damned. he thought. *But I can still kill. He's my vessel of wrath!*

Triskeles barked an order and the legionaries fanned out so they could attack Kerebos from many directions. Running toward one of the men, the *ikar* slashed down the slope with the burning blade. The *landesknecta* stopped out of reach, grinning as the other legionaries continued up the hill.

"Cowardly bastard!" Kerebos snarled at the man.

"Kerebos!" Triskeles cried from the *ikar's* right flank. Kerebos raced over toward the *Boru*.

"I'm waiting, Triskeles!" Kerebos taunted, brandishing the flaming sword. "Let us see how you like the flames!"

Triskeles stopped on the slope and leaned back on his haunches. He snatched a dagger from a thigh belt and flung the knife at the *ikar*. Kerebos sliced the flying weapon in half, sending shards past either side of his head.

Triskeles appeared momentarily unsure.

"That's how I'll cut your neck, three legs!" Kerebos laughed. Large hailstones began to pelt the ground; eery, rhythmic thunderclaps haunted the gloomy skies.

Two *landesknectos* gained the hilltop and charged Kerebos' left flank. He ran to greet them. The forward legionary, bearing his weapon in a vertical defensive position, screamed as the *ikar's* blazing sword clove through his wide blade and into his solar plexus. The magnannon burned furiously once inside the man. Steam and boiling blood spewed from the gashed cuirass, hosing down Kerebos.

Kerebos kicked the dead legionary off the blade with his foot.

"You!" he smiled fiendishly at the other *landesknecta*, whom he recognized as a former bodyguard.

The second man almost tackled Kerebos before he could deliver a strike. Almost.

Kerebos shortened the legionary's battle cry with a side slash to the neck; the headless body, neck stump steaming, stumbled past the *ikar* and crashed down the slope.

The *razai* of arriving *Chaconni* archers began to position themselves at the hill's foot. Their frantic commander urged them to quickly arrange themselves. *Chaconni* infantry raced up the street to join the bowmen.

Kerebos whirled to greet the remaining *landesknectos*. He hoisted the magnannon blade into the air with both hands. Screaming for vengeance, the legionaries closed with him.

"Fire!" the *razai* commander ordered his men.

The *Chaconni* loosed their shafts…and not only at Kerebos.

Arrows whistled up the hill.

Kerebos was shot through the left arm and hand. He dropped his sword as an arrow passed through his palm. The other fletch pierced his manica and pinned his arm to his side.

Kerebos yowled, stumbling toward the armory and out of the archers' sight.

If Kerebos bellowed in pain, Triskeles shrieked in betrayal. Behind the *elhar*, all but one of his men were mortally stricken.

"You traitorous bastards!" Triskeles cried, flinging himself flat. "I'll kill you all!" He grabbed the arrow which jutted from his leg and broke it off. He threw the shaft toward his betrayers. "Tell Pyrros he's a dead man!"

Behind the *Boru*, dying men tried unsuccessfully to crawl or stagger after Kerebos.

Down on the street, the *razai* commander scolded his men for not adjusting their aim to compensate for the knoll's sharp incline.

"You should have killed them all!" he bellowed. "Now we can't see them!"

When the archers' officer suggested to the infantry captain that the footsoldiers clamp up and finish the *landesknectos*, the infantryman flatly refused. He pointed out they had no idea how many of the dreaded *landesknectos* had perished in the volley, if any.

"Get them long range." he suggested.

Up on the flat, Triskeles gained his feet and lumbered toward Kerebos.

"I'll have you, at least," he told the *ikar*. He chuckled grimly. "You thought you'd escape me?"

Kerebos snatched the magnannon sword off the ground and made a slow, staggering retreat toward the armory. He was careful to remain out of the *Chaconni* sights.

"I'm here, Triskeles!" he grated, fighting pain and nausea. "I should have killed you long ago."

The two men circled each other, each of them well aware of the other's fighting style.

"I will win." the *Boru* said confidently. "You were unfaithful to my trust and," here he slowed, "…sacred admiration. It is just that you pay with your black heart."

Kerebos empathized with the *elhar*.

It is right. he thought.

The arrow in his leg seemed to barely affect Triskeles. The pale-skinned *Boru* smiled malevolently; his eyes danced with evil delight.

"With your black heart!" he repeated. He lunged at the *ikar's* chest with his sword's point.

When Kerebos sought to cut the attacking blade with his own he realized, too late, that Triskeles had outmaneuvered him. As the *ikar*, dizzy from blood loss, committed himself to the parry, Triskeles sprang left and drove his sword into Kerebos' right side with all his great strength. Armor screeched. Triskeles' slippery blade sprang a full foot from Kerebos' back. Kerebos dropped the magnannon sword.

Triskeles leaned close and looked into Kerebos' eyes.

"I told you!" he beamed. He grabbed the arrow in Kerebos' arm and pushed it deeper. "Now nothing else matters." the *Boru* finished.

Growling, Kerebos slammed his forehead into Triskeles' face, breaking the *Boru's* nose and front teeth. As the bleeding *elhar* fell backwards, Kerebos punched him in the face with his gauntlet spikes, goring the left cheek and blinding the pale, blue eye. Triskeles fell onto his posterior.

"From the 'black heart' to you!" Kerebos gave a weary, low laugh. Grabbing the hilt that stuck from his stomach, he exerted all the power of his mighty thews and withdrew the blade. The sword sighed in satisfaction as it slid from the armor.

Dragging his right leg, Kerebos managed toward the groaning Triskeles. He stabbed the *elhar* in the stomach.

"And so is that," he said.

Triskeles roared as his own sword pierced his body, and writhed in the mud like a wounded snake.

Kerebos limped back to reclaim the flaming sword, then made his slow way to the armory. He reached the door and, drawing a key from his belt, inserted it into the lock.

The first of the timid *Chaconni* made their way to the hilltop.

Triskeles pointed at Kerebos; blood gushed from the *Boru's* ruined eye and mutilated cheek. "Shoot him, you bastards! Kill him!"

he insisted, dragging after the *ikar*.

Kerebos smiled as the armory door yawned open. He looked into the darkness.

My tomb. he thought. Breaking the key off in the lock, he stepped inside.

"Kill him!" Triskeles commanded as though he were their captain. The archers shot.

Half a dozen steel-tipped arrows sailed through the door. All missed Kerebos.

Reaching the door, Triskeles leaned against it and pushed it shut, locking the *ikar* inside.

"Got him!" he gave a congratulatory sigh. "How will you escape this prison, Kerebos?" he raised his voice.

The next round of arrows feathered Triskeles; he slid to the ground and lay still.

Inside the round building, Kerebos smiled as he heard the door lock behind him. *How shall you get me, Triskeles?* he taunted the *elhar's* ghost. *Now that your "allies" have failed you?* Kerebos felt life ebbing from him. His fingertips and other extremities were beginning to tingle.

I guess I'll die in peace, after all. he shook his head. Guiding himself with the light from the sword, Kerebos hobbled down the narrow hall. "Some herald of God you are," he mocked himself.

Then he noticed the thin, glowing blue streak on the pitch black, domed ceiling. An arrow, missing him by inches, had flown into the hold and scratched the magnannon lined wall. The ancients had lined the inside of the building with the non-corrosive metal.

That's strange. Kerebos squinted at the smouldering blue streak.

Then the blue line burst into flame. White flame.

"My God!" he gasped, too petrified to do anything but watch the flames. "I knew it!" he said miserably.

The blaze spread with a purpose. In no time Kerebos was choking on bitter smoke. Sparks dropped all around, igniting the pit below and chewing into the porch and its supports. The *landesknecta* stomped his feet in an attempt to wake himself.

"No!" he screeched.

The *Chaconni* outside, now many hundreds strong, laughed in response. "Hot enough for you?" they asked.

The heat and miasma overcame Kerebos and he fell to his knees. Dejected and dazed, he thrust the sword into the timbers and laid his head onto the wood. The sword was a florescent blur in the thick smoke.

"Awake! Awake!" he told himself.

The porch supports snapped and the structure tilted to one side. Kerebos saved himself by grabbing the cross-hilt. He hung over the flames, screaming. He tried to swing himself up but his injured arm refused the task.

"No!" he coughed, mucous seeping from his nose. Icy hot flames tickled his feet. All around him the fire burned blindingly bright. The sound was as a gale in his ears. "Noooo!"

The loft shifted beneath his weight.

Through slitted eyes, Kerebos saw a robed Antiphon walking towards him. The Grand Master moved slowly, oblivious to the flames. He stood over the *ikar*, his expression stern yet kindly.

"Antiphon!" Kerebos sobbed, weak with pain. He glanced over his shoulder at the burning pit. "Help me!"

The priest addressed him with an expectant stare. "Repent," he said.

"I can't!" Kerebos protested, shaking his head.

Kerebos' legs were burning. He smelled his flesh. "Unworthy," he replied. His hand began to slip from the hilt.

Antiphon glared at him.

"I can't!" Kerebos wailed. "Help me!" He hung on until the flames began to eat his fingers then nodded slowly in defeat. "Save me," he said. "Save me, please." He reached for Antiphon but his burning fingers closed on air.

Kerebos slid into the pit of white fire.

Chapter 26

The final battle for Kwan Aharon never came.

Coinciding with Kerebos' death, the weather became so violent that hostilities were temporarily postponed then, after a series of devastating earthquakes, suspended altogether. An uneasy truce was established between both parties, with Count-General Pyrros as nominal master of the city, but this state of affairs was shortlived. The *Chaconni* were abruptly recalled to Korenthis to help quell civil unrest, and those few who managed to reach the capitol were immediately thrown into battle against the *Boru*.

A brief respite was granted Pangaea, in which time the planet returned somewhat to normal; then the dam burst. Quakes and tidal waves lashed the continent non-stop, decimating the population. Old scores were soon forgotten as people concentrated upon staying alive. It seemed the world tottered on the brink, maybe even stepped back a little during this brotherhood of exhaustion, when things took a catastrophic turn for the worse.

Some suggested a volcanic eruption, others blamed a meteor, but none knew what blackened the sky. The heavens slowly clouded over, as though a curtain had been drawn, and thus it stayed. Neither sun, moon nor twinkling stars showed their light. Rain did not fall.

It grew colder and colder and colder.

Food quickly ran out, then fuel for fire. Men fed upon men, hunting each other in the perpetual night. Great cities and tiny hamlets alike burned. Smoke rose from a million blazes, but it grew colder still. Men prayed for mercy, but found it only in death.

The land froze first, surrendering to a thick layer of ice, then the oceans. Pangaea swelled and cracked.

Seeking refuge from the cold, some few *Aharoni* finally tunneled into Kwan Aharon's remaining building, the armory. The magnannon interior had been scoured by fire so hot that even the smoke had burned. Nothing remained.

Except Kerebos.

Most of the *ikar's* body was charred beyond recognition, but his torso was hardly touched, and his handsome face wholly unscathed. More curious still, his head was ringed by a small circle of shiny, unconsumed Magnannon. Script had been etched into the metal by an unknown hand: "Sleep yet another age, until the Word releases thee."

The *Aharoni* were too far gone to draw wisdom from the marvel and hardly considered the mystery before devouring the remains, but the *ikar* had evidently met some great good upon death.

Kerebos had died with a smile on his face.

APPENDICES

Tactical Organization

Even in Desia's era the legion as a tactical unit had become something of an anachronism. Most of Pangaea's civilized states were in the process of adopting the Chaconni "division" which had abandoned the legion's rotating line in favor of a thin, flexible shield wall. Adherents to the division touted its adaptability, but in reality the Chaconni had moved away from the legion for expediency's sake. It simply required too great an investment to properly train the rotating lines.

Unlike other armies, the landesknecta legion always entered battle at full strength (1555 men). The smallest unit, a sestar, was comprised of six legionaries and the commander, or sestari. The sestar drilled as a separate squad, as well as a fully integrated arm of the larger whole, which accounts for the fluidity of the legion.

Six sestari (legionaries and officer) comprised a cohar. Six cohari and a commander made an elhar of 259, and the elhari plus the ikar fill the complement. All officers except the ikar have a rotation in the line. If an officer is killed or disabled in battle, he is immediately supplanted by his "first". An elhar has a First Cohar, a cohar his First Sestar, and so forth. A breveted command does not necessarily become permanent. A superior, for any number of reasons, may not wish to elevate a "first".

A few hundred "branded" recruits are invariably on hand. These men have survived the rigors of indoctrination and the branding of the Scriptus, but have not yet been assimilated into the legion proper. Until a death or disability opens a hole in the line a recruit can look forward to months as cooks, squires, armorers or messengers.

A recruit killed in training or battle is buried as a legionary, but without full honors. If killed in his first official action, his sword is not recycled but is destroyed. A legionary killed by a superior on Winnowing Day is technically guilty of insurrection and is posthumously fed to the sharks.

233

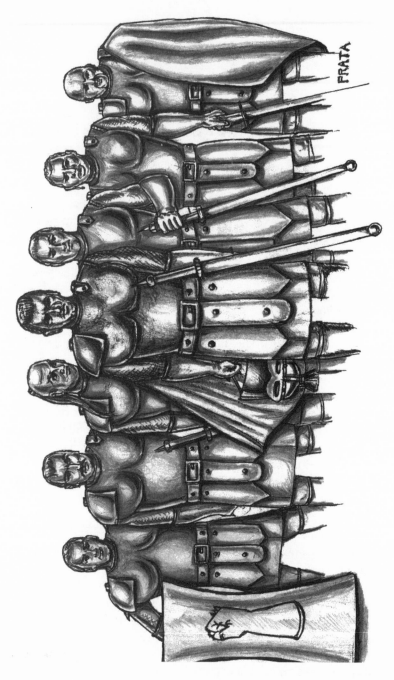

Kerebos and his Elhari

Landesknecta Arms and Armor

The legionary of Desia's day was equipped with a sword of his choosing, a dagger and a round shield. A thrusting spear was soon added to help combat cavalry. Armor was mainly chainmail, Chaconni fashion. Spired steel caps were also worn. Curiously the landesknectos' trademark black was initially rejected by Desia, who favored elhari of varying colors, but was revived after a few generations.

By the time of the Third Republic the legion had largely settled their kit and there was virtually no change until Kerebos' day. Sword lengths were standardized, the thrusting spear exchanged for a throwing pilum (later two) and the divergent elhari colors supplanted by black—although colored helmet crests were utilized for communicative purposes.

The armor of Kerebos' legion was well crafted, but plain. A knee-length chainmail shirt covered by a steel breastplate and woolen kilt were stock. Tall leather boots, encased in steel plates, and scaled gauntlets protected the limbs. A gorget and crested helmet, with flat neck guard and adjustable eye slits, enclosed the head. With his four foot, rectangular greatshield before him a landesknecta was virtually invulnerable. Legionaries have been run over by cavalry and survived unscathed.

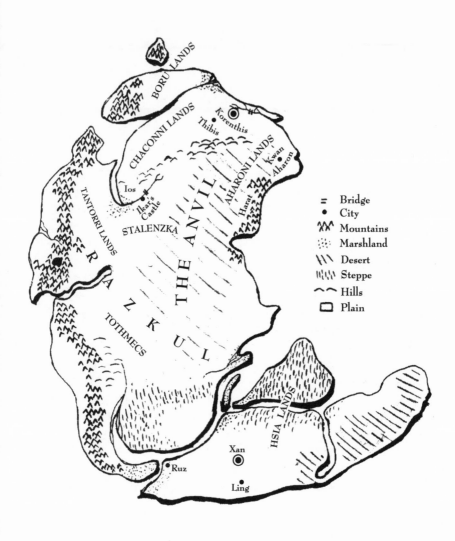

Legend:
- ＝ Bridge
- • City
- ᴧᴧᴧ Mountains
- ⋮⋮⋮ Marshland
- ⫼⫼⫼ Desert
- ⫼⫼⫼ Steppe
- ⌒⌒ Hills
- ▢ Plain

BORU LANDS

CHACONNI LANDS

Thibis

Korenthis

Ios

AHARONI LANDS

Harat

Kwan

Aharon

Ikar's
Castle

STALENZKA

TANTORRI LANDS

R
A
Z
K
U
L

THE ANVIL

TOTHMECS

HSIA LANDS

Xan

Ruz

Ling

Pangaea

History of the Landesknectos

The discord of the Ducal Wars reduced many of the Chaconni states to shambles. The endless siphoning of seasoned border garrisons to provide men for Korenthis left much of the kingdom susceptible to Boru and Razkuli raids, but the crown could ill afford to assign loyal troops to those rural areas most affected by the barbarians. Only when the Boru began settling in the western province of Ios (Kerebos Ikar's birthplace, incidentally) did King Phaetis grant that something had to be done.

The call went out for the raising of local auxiliary legions, and the borderlands tried their best to fill the levy. Most of these units were understaffed, undertrained, poorly lead and miserably equipped. The Tenth Auxilary was such a one when young Viscount-General Lex Desia took command.

Desia, fresh from the intrigue of Korenthis and viewed as something of a maverick by his peers, was sent west with no regular troops, little money and a nearly impossible task. Speculation that he had been chosen because of his questionable devotion to the crown gained credence when Phaetis seized all Desian holdings, but the general let this action pass without comment. Furthermore, the following year he amicably renounced all claims to his familial seat and, in a detailed letter to the General of the Army, Filangiris Kloz, disavowed politics in total and the Chaconni nobles in particular. Because of this highly publicized action the king reaffirmed support for Desia—though in fact he had nearly recalled the general for execution!—and raided his modest treasury to obtain a handsome stipend for the Tenth Auxiliary. Desia put this biannual allotment of gold to good use.

The summons went far and wide that the general sought swordsmen at all cost; he soon found himself swamped by deserters from the underpaid regular army and the ducal camps. Desia, as military governor of Ios, had the applicants' names legally changed, complete with supporting documenta-

237

tion. When charged that he had accepted traitors to the crown into his ranks, Desia was more than happy to supply the roll to Korenthis (the chiampuglia was born) and as Phaetis had recently sent the Tenth a shipment of gold, and the ducal camps had suffered the bulk of attrition, the matter was dropped.

To the core of professional soldiers Desia added felons, highwaymen and even those Boru and Razkul invaders he had been sent to eliminate. After a few seasons he could afford to be selective and only the most able men were retained. Exacting size, strength and endurance requirements were added a few years later.

After Phaetis' assassination Desia abandoned even the pretense of homage to Korenthis. Ios provided all the general's necessities and he made it very clear that any foray into the province was an act of war. The Senate of the Second Republic had too many pressing issues to spare time or money on the errant Tenth. Anyway, the barbarian invasions had been halted and that was why the auxiliary had been raised to begin with. Besides, Desia was the most able administrator Ios had known and the population was very attached to him.

Had the Tenth stayed its early course Chaconni history, indeed all Pangaea's, might have traveled a vastly more beneficient path, but in the last decade of his life Desia became engrossed with spiritualism. It was his First Elhar, a man named Orvus, who introduced him to the evil religion of the Tothmecs. Orvus, a Razkul and by all accounts a true believer, created a monster in his master. Armed with his newfound philosophy (and considering the makeup of his recruits) it is small wonder that the Tenth swiftly remade itself into perfect oppressors.

The Black Legion was born.

Lex Desia

Of his early life there is little to indicate that the first ikar was destined to become a villain. The second son of devoted parents, he was raised in White River Palace just outside Korenthis. Except for a severe fever during his infancy Lex Desia was a happy and healthy child who excelled in his studies and athletics.

One interesting tale regarding his youth (never substantiated) may offer an insight into Desia's mind. Engaged in a debate concerning "the divine right of kings" with his tutor, Desia stated that since he denied any higher power the notion made little sense. "What is to prevent an earthly man from disobeying his lords?" Desia expounded, to which the tutor replied: "Only this," and produced a walking stick.

"And if one fears not the rod?" Desia inquired.

"Then one has not tasted it."

The next day the teacher resigned his post, stating that his student had threatened to kill him.

Young Viscount Desia was reputedly quite charming and was a favorite with the ladies, who admired his rugged good looks and impeccable dress. He possessed universal taste in women and drew little distinction between maidens and the married. Subsequently, Desia was forced to defend himself in a number of duels, but the other houses soon learned not to challenge him. It was a well kept secret, however, that he favored only prostitutes by the time of his first commission in the King's Guards.

Tall, strong and well connected, Desia rose quickly in the Guards. He was an excellent rider and jumper and served briefly as instructor for his unit. His military record was solid, except for a black mark from one of his commanders (later removed) and proved very popular with his subordinates and peers. He is reputed to have killed six men in his first engagement.

Two curiosities were noted by one of his superiors, Albeitas Kloz, who thought them important enough to commit to paper:

"I fear the viscount's utter disregard for money, except that amount needed to support his whores, has a detrimental effect upon his men, who look to him for constancy and example. Also, it has been suggested that he lacks proper respect for his noble station."

Kerebos and Lasctakos

Of the many tales surrounding Kerebos' early years, the first meeting between he and his future benefactor, Lasctakos, is the most revealing. Even at an early age, Kerebos was plainly marked for some great doom.

Lasctakos Cohar was gambling with his remaining sestari, and though a skilled card player, had already lost his favorite dagger and a large sum of kraal. Vexaras, the First Sestar, clapped loudly as he won again. He swept coins off the table and into a woolen purse.

A knock on the door. Lasctakos shushed his underlings.

"What?" he demanded, still smarting over the last hand.

"We've brought the recruit, sir," came the muffled reply.

The men looked at each other. "Boros' killer," Vexaras said.

"Enter," Lasctakos commanded.

The heavy wooden door swung open and two landesknectos pushed in a chained youth. The youngster, huge and beefy, wore nothing but his bonds and a loincloth. His stomach was discolored by burns, and oozed fluid from cracked skin; his Scriptus branding had yet to scab over. Black hair hung over eyes which were dark and suspicious.

"So that's the murderer?" Lasctakos asked. "Leave him and go."

The legionaries released the captive and departed, securing the door behind them. Lasctakos studied the boy. *Big, but young*, he thought. *Not even eighteen, I'd wager.*

"He has pretty curls," Vexaras said. "Gotta give 'im a proper haircut."

"Hard to believe he killed Boros," another chimed in.

Lasctakos locked gazes with the prisoner. "Actually, not too hard to believe at all," he said. "Boros was a fool. Vexaras, unbind him."

Vexaras obeyed but did not return to his seat.

Lasctakos sat on the table a few feet before the youth, who remained impressively undaunted. "Death's the penalty for killing your commander before Winnowing Day," he began. "Did you know that?"

The boy shook his curly head.

"Answer!" Vexaras growled and slapped the prisoner's posterior.

"I did not know," the boy said.

"Then you're stupid as well as rash," Lasctakos replied. He pointed to the Scriptus burn. "You're wearing the laws right over your bowels."

"I can't read."

"Another farm boy," Vexaras chuckled.

Lasctakos nodded his shaved head. "Why'd you kill Boros?" he asked.

"He asked me to."

"Oh?"

"Said I should kill him if I didn't like the name he gave me. Smacked me in the face, too."

Lasctakos turned to his sestari.

"Boros did call him out, sir," one admitted. "It was one of those 'fight or get killed' situations."

Lasctakos eyed the boy. "So you didn't like your chiampuglia? What did he dub you?"

The boy's shoulders dropped a half inch.

"Stand at attention!" Vexaras snarled and served the lad a vicious backhand across the cheek.

The boy was still glaring at the sestar when he replied: "Patricides."

Lasctakos looked thoughtful. "'Father killer,' was it? You offed your sire?"

The boy sighed deeply. For the first time he looked vulnerable. "I didn't mean to, lord."

"So it's run away and join the Black Brotherhood, then, cover up your sins?" Lasctakos' blue eyes narrowed. "How old are you?"

The boy hesitated but managed to reply before Vexaras struck again. "Fourteen," he said.

"Fourteen?" Lasctakos echoed, astounded. He looked at Vexaras. "Fourteen? That goddamned Boros! He's lucky he's dead or I'd kill him myself."

"It's a sickening thing," Vexaras agreed.

Lasctakos tried but could not swallow a chuckle. "Guess the ikar's raiding cradles, now. So you don't like your name, Patricides?" he asked.

"I do not," the boy replied quietly.

"You want to kill me for calling you that?"

Silence. Vexaras struck again. "Answer! I'm not going to tell you again!"

The boy ignored the blow and stared full into the cohar's eyes. "Yes," he said.

Lasctakos burst into laughter. "Gotta score him high on honesty," he told the others. "Vexaras?"

"Sir?"

"Think I could wriggle around the Winnowing Day thing? Sounds to me like the lad stumbled into a trap."

Vexaras shrugged. "The ikar's a forgiving man."

Lasctakos returned to his seat. "I think so, too. Administrative punishment, then. A night with the sharks ought to do the trick. If he survives, he's got what it takes, if not, we didn't want him anyway."

The First Sestar looked dubious. "As you say, sir."

Lasctakos nodded at the boy. "Survive the night and you're my new Sixth Sestar. Dismissed."

Patricides saluted and turned for the door.

"Boy," Lasctakos called.

"Yes, lord."

"Let's pick you another name. What grabs you?"

Vexaras snorted. "Shouldn't we wait till morning to see if that's necessary?"

Lasctakos said: "No, I've got a feeling about this one. Either he's going to be ikar one day, or holds the keys to hell in his pocket. What will it be, boy?"

The youth thought back to his brief education and came up with something appropriate. "Call me Kerebos," he replied.

Vexaras grabbed him by the scruff of the neck and thrust him toward the door. "Yeah, we'll call you that if you're still breathing when the sun comes up, pretty boy. Out!"

Kerebos gave him a long look before turning to Lasctakos and saluting. "By your leave."

"Right. Get out of here," the cohar answered good naturedly.

After Kerebos was gone and they were all seated Lasctakos cautioned: "I wouldn't irk that cub, Vex. One day he'll kill you."

Vexaras flapped his lips and grabbed his kraal. "Oh, please! Who's deal?"

Glossary

Aharoni   "people of Aharon" A mostly nomadic, desert dwelling folk. Their cultural and historical hub is Kwan Aharon.

ala/alaes   A Chaconni designation for a column of cavalry. Size varies, depending on adjacent infantry.

Boru   A fierce, warlike race from the inhospitable northwestern region of Pangaea. The last people to cling to feudalism.

Chaconni   The most populous and industrious of Pangaea's people. Once fully half the globe paid homage to their crown.

chiampuglia   "battle name" The nom de guerre given a landesknecta recruit after his "branding" and before final assimilation into a unit.

cohar   A junior officer among the landeskectos, equivalent to a Chaconni lieutenant.

Ducal Wars   A period of internecine warfare and internal strife for the Chaconne. Many noble families were permanently dispossessed (or killed) before a democratic protectorate was established in what became the "Second Republic".

elhar   A senior landeskecta officer who reports directly to the ikar, equivalent to a Chaconni colonel.

Harat   A barren, sparsely populated Aharoni land famous for banditry and inpassable mountain ranges.

Heretos Ikaros	Kraal in its most potent form. This claylike drug is manufactured for the ikar alone.
Hsia	A numerous folk from the south of Pangaea, easily distinguishable by their narrow eyes and copper skin tone.
Imperial Rangers	A collection of small, mounted squadrons charged with keeping the extensive Chaconni highway system free of thieves, while collecting tolls and regulating trade.
irbarzi	A dangerous wolf-like creature of the steppe. This bony, striped animal is capable of great speed, its legs being over three feet long.
ikar	The supreme commander of the landesknectos. The ikar holds life and death decisions over his men and, in theory, is their spiritual leader.
King's Guards	"Scarlet Guards" "Royal Guards" This elite division recruits exclusively from the Royal Marines and remains under the direct command of the crown. They serve as bodyguard, maritime soldiers, cavalrymen and, in rare cases, shock troops. Only a fullblooded Chaconne could hope to rise in their ranks.
kraal	A strong, leafy narcotic favored by the landesknectos and culled for them by their subjects, the Tantorri.
Korenthis	The Chaconni capitol. By all accounts a majestic and beautiful place. Notable for its many public works, including baths, sewer systems and running water.
landesknecta	A common legionary.
magnannon	A wonderfully strong and durable metal smelted by the Aharoni during their cultural apex. When properly struck, magnannon burns brilliantly, making it an ideal terror weapon.
Pangaea	The world. A single continent surrounded by rough oceans.
Power Guard	A landesknecta unit charged with a specific task of short duration. Consists of two cohari.

245

razai   A squad of archers.

Razkuli   A collection of uncivilized plains dwellers. One of the
                      few groups on Pangaea to openly practice cannibalism
                      and human sacrifice. What laws they possess are dictat-
                      ed by their chief tribe, the Tothmecs.

Royal Marines   A branch of the Chaconni military with a reputation of
                      effectiveness and élan. One of the first units to discon-
                      tinue usage of the tactical legion in favor of inter-
                      changable divisions.

sestar   The most junior commander in the Black Legion,
                      equivalent to a Chaconni sergeant. Commands six
                      legionaries and is responsible for the development and
                      assimilation of recruits. A sestar maintains power of
                      corporal punishment over his charges.

Second Republic   A transitional period for the Chaconni people wherein
                      the Senate and popular elections were revived. Ended
                      with the restoration of the Grasmilios line.

Stalenzka   Relatives of the Chaconni. This tribe is noted for its
                      skill as artisans and in the working of all metals. Its
                      peerless armor sells at fantastic prices.

Syna   Church.

Tantorri   "the horsemasters" This folk once ranged far and wide
                      through the interior of Pangaea but for decades had
                      lived under shadow of the ikar's "protection". They are
                      charged with maintaining the legion's lands and sup-
                      plying slaves. Tantorri horses are greatly desired by all
                      and turn great profit in all corners of the world.

Thibis   The ancient capitol of the Chaconne. Once nearly
                      destroyed by counterrevolutionaries, it is the perma-
                      nent seat of the powerful Vasilex clan.

Tothmecs   "the enlightened ones" This class of Razkul is generally
                      feared and despised as both bloodthirsty and cruel.
                      There is reason to believe their philosophy influenced
                      Desia during his first years as ikar.

The Alphabets of Pangaea

	A	B	C	D	E	F	G	H	I	J	K	L	M	N	O	P	Q	R	S	T	U	V	W	X	Y	Z
Aharoni																										
Chaconni																										
Boru																										

247